HOPE & DESPAIR
1st Edition

About the Author:

Roman Payne was born in Seattle in 1977.

He left America in 1999 and currently lives in Paris.

For more information about the author, please visit:

www.romanpayne.com

Acknowledgments & Legal Statement:

This book is a work of fiction. Names, characters, places, and incidents either are products of the author's imagination or are used fictitiously. Any resemblance to actual events or locales or persons, living or dead, is entirely coincidental. This book is published by ModeRoom Press.

ISBN 978-0-6151-8650-4

© 2007, 2008 - Roman Payne / ModeRoom Press

Cover Design: ModeRoom Press

Cover Art: "In the Garden of Hope and Despair," by Roman Payne; oil on canvas, 33x24 cm, 2007.

Hope & Despair

by Roman Payne

BOOK I

Tales from the Terrace

BOOK II

Songs from the Cellar

BOOK III

Fables from the Fields

BOOK I

Tales from the Terrace

CHAPTER I

We had then those nights upon the terrace with the colonnades that overlooked the walled gardens below. Our lips were for each other and our eyes were full of dreams. We knew nothing of travel and we knew nothing of loss. Then, on those mornings when we awoke entwined, we would leave the bed and house together and walk down to the waterfront. There, we drank sweet coffee on the banks of the canals, while the early boats took passengers on through the city. And while the sun rose up over the building tops, the world passed by and around us. We believed in places far away but they didn't concern us. Ours was a world of eternal spring, until the summer came.

She was still practically a girl then, on those first days of early May when the two began to meet. In the garden, they were together and wore nothing. They wove words for each other like clothing, only to cast aside. At one moment in the day, while lying in the grass, she left him to go pick fruit for the two of them to eat. By the far garden walls where the apricot trees and figs grew, she knelt down and filled her hands with tender fruit. Then, while standing up to return to where he was waiting, she heard our voices walking in the garden in the cool of the day, and she was afraid because she was naked; and so she hid herself amongst the trees. The fruit she had picked, she dropped, and it scattered across the grass.

Once we were gone and she was certain she was alone, she ran back to her lover and told him to take her inside. "I am cold," she said. He covered her with the blanket and then he covered himself and the two hurried in the house.

They spent their mornings together in the sun-washed markets of the Lower Quarter of the city. At midday, they would eat lunch on one of the quiet bridges spanning the canals; and afterwards they'd make their way up the hill to the house where she lived. The house belonged to her father. He lived and worked abroad in the West Islands and it was almost always empty, so she lived there alone. And whenever she was alone that spring, she asked him to come. And when she asked, he came.

Like us, they were new lovers, and like all vernal lovers, they never once realized or cared or even gave it any thought that there might exist others like them, that others loved as they loved. For them, there were but they and the warmth of the sun.

Walking past the lattice in the warm tincture of spring, through days that were long and becoming, the two strolled together through the arboretum hand-in-hand, among the new flowers abloom with peach petals like folds of skin. Overhead, the green lacquered leaves in the tree bows rattled in the soft breeze. Here the two would stop a moment, to linger on each other's eyes, upon each other's parting lips. They would walk then on, leaving prints with their feet in the soft grass wherever they stepped. Once, she picked a leaf from a rhododendron bush and pushed it deep into the palm of her lover's hand...

"Palm, palm! . . . What a funny word!" Her voice was full of happiness. She turned to him and asked him, "Nishka?"

"Yes?"

"Why do they call you that?"

"Palm?"

"No, not palm! . . . Not, why do they call you palm! Why do they call you Nishka?!"

"But only you call me Nishka," he answered, softly caressing the leaf with the tip of his finger.

"Well, why do they call you Nikolai, then?"

"But you know," he smiled coyly, "I didn't have a name at all until I was twenty. Then one day, someone called me Nikolai and hung it around my neck with a string and there it stayed."

She looked at him without speaking. Her eyes grew wide and bright. She wondered if what he was saying were true. He slipped his hand back into hers and asked, "Why do they call you Nadja?"

"But I told you a million times, Nishka! What are we going to eat tonight?" She was always hungry it seemed.

From the arboretum, there was a little tree-lined road that wound up the hill and ended at the walls of the gardens that surrounded her house, and that surrounded the other houses in the city's Upper Quarter. Often the two lovers sat in those gardens late into the day until that hour came – that sad hour of spring when, in the early evening, the sun hid itself; and there wasn't yet that hotness of summer that made up for it so the air became cool and covered in shadows; and it would have been altogether a sad moment, if it wasn't that these lovers had each other and didn't care either way. Usually, at this time, they would go inside and Nikolai would begin making dinner in the kitchen. Nadja would sit on the sofa and watch him cook, or else she'd flip through one of his many books he had lying around her house. The evenings were an idle and happy time for them.

In the still privacy of night, they would eat together and talk endlessly and lie with candles on the terrace. Nikolai would've cooked spiced cheeses, breads with peppers, hot vinegars with vegetables. There was always plenty of cool wine to drink.

Once they had eaten, she would ask him to read to her a tale from one of his books. She loved the sound of his voice when he read and she would lie near him listening with gentle attention. All through the night, she would lie for him. She would lie for him like a bow, softly drawn; and when he would finish reading, he would set his book aside and his hands would go to her. They would pass slowly over her waiting body – softly spread – her hands would come to meet his and she would touch them for just a moment. Then she would cast them aside and merely lie for him. She would stretch beneath those hands, those strangely shaped and heavy gentle hands that coursed her warm skin, the soft slope of her waist. His hands passed now and then beneath the bands of elastic stretched taught over the bones of her hips – stretched taught like the lathe of the bow where she received him well. Kneeling above her, he would rub sweet oils on her skin. And she would stir softly.

Tired, the two lovers lay together outstretched with thick blankets soaked in sweat and wrapped around their skin, cooling quickly – it was still only May, and the air was mild at night.

"Do you feel that?" she asked him in a whisper.

"The drops on the skin?"

"Yes, the drops."

"Yes. What is it?"

"Nothing," she breathed, turning over.

"Nadja?"

"Mm hmm?"

"Why were you so alarmed this afternoon in the garden?"

Nadja leaned up towards Nikolai. She took her hand from the blanket and touched his face; she stroked his sandy chin with her smooth finger and looked long into his eyes, saying nothing.

"But why were you so alarmed this afternoon?"

She was silent another moment and then suddenly, in a single gasp of bewilderment, that enthusiastic delight peculiar to her, she cried… "But Nishka! Do you mean when I went to go pick fruit?"

"Yes, then."

"Oh, Nishko! If only you had been there with me. I tell you Nishka, I could paint what I saw. Someday I will."

"What did you see?"

"Well... the leaves were shimmering like coins in the sunlight. The leaves that fell, they crunched like wafers under the man's foot, and under the woman's too. They crunched under their feet as they walked in the garden near where I was picking fruit. And they spoke too. I heard them coming and since I was naked, I was afraid and I ran back to the blanket to get you. That's why I wanted to go back inside."

"Like wafers?" he asked, "How will you paint the wafers?"

"But stop, Nishka!" She pressed her hands on his knee as her eyes grew wide, "It was like that! They were walking in the garden and their feet crunched the leaves like wafers. And when they spoke..."

"They spoke? What did they say?"

"But, Nishko!" she puffed, turning her mouth down in a pouting face a little deflated. "Maybe they didn't speak. Maybe after all I imagined the whole thing. Yes, maybe there were no people walking in the garden at all."

"But of course there were, Nadja. If you heard them."

"Yes, there were. There were people."

Then the sound of fanning branches swept over the terrace and the birds dropped one by one into silence.

CHAPTER II

It was an evening the two came back late from town and a warm rain started coming down, at first gently, it then turned into a heavy downpour. The lovers came running across the garden beneath the bows of the plane trees towards Nadja's house. Nikolai stopped in the path to pick Nadja up to carry her inside, and she flung herself over his shoulder and clung tightly to his back; and during all this her sandal fell off her foot and it landed on the gravel in the midst of the path. In the beginning, she was scared but then she laughed and let him carry her off. She thought for a moment that her feet would never again touch the ground. He ran with her upstairs and brought her to her bedroom and laid her down on the bed. Her shoulders soaked the linen. Outside, the rain was landing heavily on the stone surface of the terrace, flinging drops wildly against the railing; the sound came loudly through the open glass doors. Nadja jerked under his grasp. She wanted to change first out of her wet clothes, and tried to reach for a brush on the nightstand to brush the water out of her hair. She tried to get up but Nikolai clasped her on her shoulders and laid her back down and pushed her back firmly into the bed, and began pulling off her wet clothing. The rain in her hair soaked the pillow beneath her head. She moved no more, but just looked at him, and he at her. The two stared steadily at each other. Then

Nikolai slowed down. He gently undid the clasp of the damp dress that was fastened loosely around Nadja's tender throat, and slid her soaked cotton sleeve down off her shoulder. From her soft arm, he removed the wet lace. He took her gold bracelets off and set them aside. He set his hands beneath her bare breasts and slid her dress from her belly down to her knees. She stirred and made a soft sound. He passed his hands over her skin beaded with rainwater and came up to offer her the wetness of his lips. She took them to hers while drawing her hand through his own wet hair to let the water fall down upon them both. So much wetness and so much warmth. She shivered with pleasure each time she felt a drop of water fall from his hair onto her skin. She felt him upon her, lingered long; and when she finally wanted to rest, to turn him over like a worn animal and lie upon his body to rest awhile, she did so. She pressed his hands tightly and then looked bright into his eyes for what he'd done to her.

Nadja lay quietly for many moments, eyes closed, her belly rising and falling in measured breathes, the sound of rain fading to the background. Then, as if caught by a ringing in the ears, she opened her eyes wide and held them fast to Nikolai and clearly called out to him...

"Nishka!" ...as if she were falling upon an idea that had emerged suddenly with great importance and had to be said right then and not a moment later.

Nikolai looked back at her.

"Yes, my Nadiushka?"

"Oh, nothing."

"Nadja . . . tell me!"

"You know, Nishka, for a time when you were carrying me through the garden, I really felt my feet would never again touch the earth."

"Were you scared?"

"Yes, I was. A little, Nishka, I was. But I wanted it." She paused. "You know, Nishka? I wanted to go even higher. I wanted my feet to never again touch the ground."

15

"Never to touch this mortal earth?"

"Yes, this mortal earth! . . . I wanted you to take me all the way up, and there I would bear beautiful things for you." In saying this, she was recalling a myth he had read to her a few days before.

"And there you would bear beautiful things for me?" He kissed her throat and told her, "Sweet girl, whoever you are . . . you, holiest of perfection…" And while his hands fell down, his words lifted, "…up until I saw you, love, I knew only mortal toil," as if it were just a myth he were reciting, though he'd forgotten all but she, the woman, who lay before him now, "…though I don't know which goddess you are, I will construct an alter for you. Yes, I will make you an alter on the highest peek in a far-away place, and there I will make sacrifices for you in all the seasons." And sullen his words grew as he said yet, "Only, I implore of you, dear goddess, let me live long and happily. Let me know the light of the sun. Let me be always happy and live to the threshold of old age. Let me be a man prosperous among the people…" and he finished there and pulled Nadja in towards him.

"Oh, Nishka," Nadja cried to him while pushing his shoulders back so she could look at his face, "Nishka, you can have whatever you want!"

Thus went that night as the swarms of unpossessed rains timbered on. Upon the surface of the broad bed, those lovers slept. Their lips were for each other and their eyes were full of dreams.

CHAPTER III

The next morning was clear and brought sunny scents of acacias up from the garden to flood the terrace. Nikolai came out with wide bowls of coffee and sweet cream and set them on the table. Nadja was busy spreading her clothes out over the railing, hoping they would sometime dry. Nikolai left the terrace and went downstairs and out into the garden. He returned sometime after, holding Nadja's little sandal in his hand that she had dropped the night before. She smiled at him and reclined on the dry lounge that they'd brought out for the day. Nikolai sat beside her and drank the coffee. Nadja didn't drink any coffee, but preferred instead to lie quietly and keep her eyes closed. She kept her head in Nikolai's lap. Once he finished his coffee and hers, he curled around her on the lounge and the two fell asleep again. Later, when they awoke, Nadja's face was on his and the sun fell across her cheek. She inhaled and turned her mouth inwards to kiss him.

"I dreamt," she whispered into his ear.

Nikolai opened his eyes.

"I dreamt," she whispered again.

"What of?"

This response had a strange effect. Nadja suddenly jerked away as if now it was crucial to tell all and tell it quickly. She looked at Nikolai with big eyes and began as if to narrate her dream…

"Oh, it was strange, Nishka, it was really strange!" Then she frowned, "But now I don't remember."

"Do you want to go into town, Nadja?"

"I want to lie here with you."

"Me too."

The tree limbs dipping over the terrace railing shook off the last drops of the previous night's rain from their mild leaves on the patio stones. The sun, meanwhile, made its warm ascent through white wisps of clouds. Nadja fell asleep once more against Nikolai and breathed deeply. Nikolai kept awake and stroked the soft mound of her hair flung about here and there on her forehead and cheeks. He listened to her as she slept. He worshiped her every breath. And those times she would sigh or give a start, he knew she was experiencing another strange dream.

That afternoon, the two decided to go down to the Lower Quarter and rent a boat and row out through the canals. They packed a lunch and walked down to the waterfront and Nikolai chose a boat and got the oars, and the two rowed out to a little island in the delta where the canal emptied into the harbor. There on the island, they roped up the boat beneath the shade of the cypress trees that hung over the shore of sand and stones, and spread out a blanket and the two sat in the shade and ate a great meal of bread and cheese. They drank sweet wine and kissed for a while. Once Nadja was back in the boat, seated with her face obscured so only her pouting lips showed beneath the brim of her broad spring hat, Nikolai untied the ropes and got in the boat and pushed off. The canals were calm that afternoon and the two rowed a long while.

By mid-afternoon, Nadja was hungry again and Nikolai too was tired from rowing; so they decided not to row anymore, neither to wander around the markets, nor to stay in town any longer, but rather to go back up to the house and cook dinner. Nadja asked Nikolai if he wouldn't read her a story from one of his books after they'd eaten. The two walked slowly through the arboretum. They walked through the lingering warmth of the day; and when they came to her house and entered into the garden, Nadja stopped suddenly and wouldn't move...

"What is it?" Nikolai asked.

"Why that sound?"

"What sound?" Nikolai looked around the garden. He surveyed the lawns and the trees of fruit and the walls of rock.

"Oh, it's nothing after all." Then she paused. "Nikolai?"

"Yes, Nadiushka?"

She didn't answer right away. She seemed upset and when he asked her why, she began to explain to him that she wanted to be the one to make dinner on this evening since he made dinner every night.

"But why do you cook everyday, and not me?"

"I like to cook."

"I want to cook you something today!"

"Okay, Nadja, what do you want..." he began to ask, but she was gone before he could finish. She had flown off to run about the garden and was wildly picking the fruit that was ripe and had fallen from the trees and was scattered in the grass.

"I going to make us a salad!" she yelled back to him. All the while she gathered plums, apricots and figs, "A great big salad!"

Nadja was busy for a long time in the kitchen after that; and when she finally came out to the terrace, she had a sprig of parsley in her mouth and held a giant bowl in her hands. Nikolai was lounging with a novel that he quickly tossed aside.

The two ate the salad and Nadja was very proud of it and it was very good . . . with brightly-colored fruit, savage honey, minced leaves of mint, golden thyme and tender walnuts. Afterwards, she brought a wooden board with grilled bread baked with cloves of purple garlic.

After dinner, Nikolai cleared away the plates. Nadja asked if it wasn't time for the story yet.

"If you want," he told her, "Which story should I read?"

Nadja liked the old tales the best, the myths and fables. Nikolai went inside the house and returned with a small cloth-bound book. "It's called, 'The Tale of False Dmitry.'" He gave the setting: Russia, some centuries ago. "Have you heard this one before?"

"Of course I have not!" she frowned. Then she smiled and kissed her lover's elbow and settled back on the cushions to listen.

He began to read:

The Tale of False Dmitry

Across the frozen tundra of Siberia, the great Tsar Dmitry was riding with his entourage of five armed men. They were traveling to pay respects to a famous holy man who was said to be on his death bed in a little hut somewhere in the T– Province. After riding for many weeks, they arrived at the hut off the side of a road, alongside a river in a clearing of snowy birch trees.

The six men dismounted their horses and the guards waited outside while the Tsar crossed the yard and entered the hut. Inside, true to rumor, there was the holy man lying on his back, breathing his final breaths. He was gaunt and pale as a flake of bone and lay motionless beneath a thin blanket of animal skin.

The Tsar knelt down beside the cot to pay his respects. He closed his eyes and crossed the holy man with three fingers and began to utter a prayer for the sacred man in the name of Russia; yet while he was doing so, he saw a vision: Before his eyes, the holy man turned into a serpent and lashed out at the Tsar. The Tsar leapt backwards. The serpent recoiled then and his form returned to that of a human. From the cot where he lay, the holy man looked into the eyes of the Tsar and told him in a feeble but steady voice that the Tsar must not interrupt the holy man's private journey to death, and that he is to leave the hut immediately. Furthermore, the holy man added that whoever so much tries to enter the hut of the dying man, while he is busy dying, shall suffer a painful death. After this, he fell again silent, save for a rattling in his throat. Hereupon, the Tsar panicked. He leapt up quickly from the side of the cot, and as he did so, his crown toppled from his head and landed on the floor. The Tsar ran out of the hut in great alarm.

The bareheaded Tsar approached his entourage where they were smoking up by the road. "We must leave here immediately and return to Moscow!"

"But Lord Tsar Dmitry!" cried one of the guards, "You've lost your crown!"

"True, it seems to have toppled off my head," the Tsar responded. "It is back in the hut." This-upon, he sent the weakest of the five men to fetch it.

"Semyon! Go in and fetch my crown." Semyon obeyed and went off towards the hut. When he reached the doorway, however, he halted and began to scream. The Tsar peered through the trees to the hut and observed Semyon standing by the door, clutching his throat and yelping in agony. All the while, large black boils amassed on his face and neck and blood frothed on his lips. Blood then began to drip from every orifice of his body, including his eyes, and he spewed blood from his mouth. Semyon then collapsed and died.

The Tsar decided he would need to send his strongest guard in to get the crown. This guard obeyed and trudged his mighty self off to the hut where he met the same fate as Semyon. At the doorway he stopped and began to scream while clutching his throat. Meanwhile blood issued forth from his body until the moment he collapsed and died. The Tsar observed this scene with an eyebrow raised while his three guards stood behind him in a clump, trembling with fear.

The Tsar turned then to his last three men and ordered them all to go together to fetch the crown. Although the guards affirmed they would always obey the orders of the Tsar, they first raised fearful objections…

"But Lord Dmitry," one said, "we will do as you command, but if you wish us to all go in and fetch the crown, we will all surely die. And then you will have no entourage to guard you on your way back to the capital and you will be robbed and killed by brigands!"

"Yet my faithful guards," responded the Tsar, "if I've no crown to wear on my way back to the capital, no one will know that I am Tsar and I

will not surely die!"

"Yet your steed is a fine one, Lord Tsar. They will want to rob you if for your steed alone."

"As my steed is a fine one," the Tsar said cleverly, "it shall surely outrun the brigands!"

"But Tsar! Shouldn't you try to fetch your crown yourself? After all, you shall not die at the door of the hut, for you are Tsar and therefore you are God himself and are immortal!"

"My faithful guards," replied the Tsar, "as I learned the last time I had the flu, I am weak as any mortal man and therefore am not immortal like God himself!"

"Yet Tsar…!"

…After some more attempts to convince the Tsar in this manner, the Tsar finally became tired of arguing and acquiesced. He agreed to leave his crown in the hut with the holy man. And so off he rode, with aid of his three armed men, towards the capital.

Some time later, when the snow was thawing in the T– Province and the icy floes were breaking up on the river that coursed through the birch wood forest, a tall and swarthy brigand, traveling alone, arrived at the hut where the holy man had been on his deathbed some time ago. The brigand stopped at the road, dismounted his horse, drew his sword and entered the hut to see what he could find to steal. In the hut, he found the corpse of the dead holy man rotting on a hay-stuffed cot. Worms were busy gnawing at the cadaver and it stank a wretched stench. The brigand plugged his nose and searched around the hut for spoils. There, on the earthen floor near the bedside, he found a golden crown encrusted with jewels. He immediately recognized it as being the crown that belongs to the Tsar himself, for many stories circulate about such a crown. The brigand quickly snatched the crown and put it on his head. A perfect fit! Then, raising his sword, he left the hut and immediately rode off for the capital.

The brigand arrived at nightfall at the Tsar's palace at the old Tsarskoe Selo and demanded at the gates to be let in. The gatekeepers mistook the rider with his crown to be Tsar himself, and let the imposter in. When the brigand entered the palace, he found the real Tsar Dmitry, *crownless, seated at his desk eating haring and looking over some papers. This false Dmitry approached the desk and swiftly raised his sword and slew the real Dmitry.*

After this, 'False Dmitry' – as he came to be known – stormed the palace and rounded up all of the Tsar's men. He demanded to know why they had let a crownless imposter into the palace in his place. Those who objected to the sovereignty of this False Dmitry the brigand – among them of course were the three guards who had been present when Dmitry had lost his crown in the holy man's hut – were swiftly executed. Those who took the imposter's side and bowed to kiss his hands and feet, were spared their lives. The wife and the mistresses of the Tsar now were all disgusted by the fact that they had been deceived into sharing a bed with a Tsar who was really an imposter for so many months – though in fact it had been the real Tsar. And so off they went, one by one, to clean themselves in the bath and then spend some happy moments in the room that would become the new bedroom of False Dmitry the brigand.

The wife and the mistresses of the new Tsar bore him a total of five sons and he ruled for twenty years. Then, one summer when the mountain ash trees in the garden were in bloom and the air was hot and fragrant, False Dmitry's five sons rose up and slew him.

Nikolai closed the book and set it down.

"That's it?!" Nadja asked.

"Yes. His five sons slew him. That's the end of the story."

"But, Nishko! That's a horrible story!"

"Why horrible? It's my favorite."

"Your favorite? But it can't go like that! The real Tsar, the good Tsar, he died when he shouldn't have. And this false brigand character won."

"But in the end he didn't win. And besides, it's a true story, it's real history, and so it must go like this."

"I guess if it must," Nadja sighed with displeasure, turning over on her back, "but I don't like it. It's really grim, Nishko. I want a story next time with good hero."

"A good hero? Alright, my Nadiushka, next time I'll read you, 'The Myth of the Seven Sisters.' It has a good hero."

"What does it speak of?"

"Constellations in the sky."

"No, Nishko!"

"Why no?"

"I want a story that takes place on earth!" Nadja paused and bit her lower-lip. "Yes, a story of the earth." Nikolai rubbed his thumb lightly on Nadja's teeth. She dropped her head down low and then raised it again, "You know, Nishka . . . back when I was hiding in the trees?"

"No, when was that?"

"But you know, Nishko! Back when I was picking fruit and I heard that man and woman walking in the garden."

"Yes, yes, I remember you telling me…"

"Well, Nishka! Listen! When I was hiding behind the trees waiting to go back to you, I kept thinking that I wished the tops of those trees would grow over so much that there would be no sky at all. No sky or constellations or any of that, so that all we would see if we looked up would be leaves of the trees.

"Rafters of leaves…" Nikolai considered this with a knitted brow. "Then there would be no blue sky, Nadja. There would be no sun, either."

"Yes, but it was because I wanted only you and me and the earth to exist. I don't want the heavens and the sky and all of that. I just want only the earth. You and me, the earth and our terrace…"

Nikolai pulled Nadja in close to him. "Okay, my lovely. No stories of constellations. Next time I'm going to read you, 'The Myth of Helonius.' It has a good hero and it speaks of the earth. I have the book back at my room in town. Next time I go there I will bring it. It has an honest hero. It's not my favorite story, but you might like it."

"The myth of whom?" she asked.

"Helonius."

"Helonius." Nadja considered this a moment, "Is he a white knight, this Helonius?"

"Somewhat."

"Okay, Nishka. I will wait for you to bring this book."

CHAPTER IV

The gardens were vibrant in the coming days with the scarlet tanagers singing in the trees and the fragrant hyacinths and sweet alyssums leaking pollen in the spring air. We came at once through the archway to the neighboring yard and found a place on the grass spotted with sun and yellow flowers. She sat beside me, full of desire, flashing those lynx-like eyes. It was strange the way she used to thank me then. And the way her smooth hips cradled my hands. This body of a young woman was new to her, and she offered me praise for its place in the world, among the flowers and trees of spring. She offered me praise in the way morning's light praises budding eyes. The way she tried her body then, testing its movements as one slowly eases into a lake to feel the temperature and the calm fluidity of its waters. I touched her thigh and she fastened her small hand on top of mine to keep it there. In those eyes, that appreciative look of youth; in those eyes, smooth as puddles of glass, the desires stirred between us. I sat with her in the garden, beside her in the shoots of grass, watching her as she cherished the discovery of her calves and knees – those healthy thighs which took their form and life beneath my carver's hands. I passed over those thighs, smooth as a sculptor passes hands through warm milky clay. She arched her back to offer me her waist and discovered the way her breasts sat firm on her ribs.

Glory that the flesh is warmed not just by the sun, but by the blood beneath the skin. Glory that the blood of life is known to us, we who are now alive. We, who are living, are now free. She brought her chin down to her collarbone and looked into my eyes. She sought my hand to return it to her waist. She thanked me again for those hips that seemed eternal then. And for those lips which learned of passion then. So now, anew and at last, our mouths fell together beneath the vast unfolding of day.

Between embraces, she would ask me things. She would wonder of the place where we were, of its history, of its future . . . "They are insomuch as the same thing," said I, wound around the undying moment, "all wound around." And with these, my words, she fell silent. A few more things I said; and then little by little, my voice drowned itself out.

A rumbling sound came from the sky.

"Will you tell me of that sky?"

To tell of that swirling sky . . . I leaned my head back to look at the sky . . . that great concaved firmament of blue. If only to tell of that singular sky. One would say an immense wooden bowl was overturned, spilling out fresh milk and wild blueberries. Beneath that sky, my eyelids fluttered and I summoned calmness to fall upon me.

Over the slopes of grass, a soft wind blew and the leaves of the carob trees flapped against the thin flakey bark on the limbs taking sun. I could hear people talking nearby and looked to the far off house where someone was sitting. There was blue-eyed Nikolai on the steps, he was waiting for Nadja. Now she had come from behind the trees and was walking over to him smiling. She wore her famous white cotton dress and her broad spring hat and met him and leaned up and kissed his mouth tenderly and laughed and the two clasped hands.

"It's a nice day today."

"Yes, it is." While he brushed a leaf off the top of her hat, she explained to him that the hat had lost its flower and she would need to find another.

"There are plenty in the garden."

Oh, there were plenty... Plenty of tender petals with glassy stems; plenty of flowering buds with lacquered leaves. In that garden, the sun came like bulb flashes as you looked up through the limbs of the white cherry trees. And as it burst in your eyes, you would sift your fingers through the sweet ribbons of grass beneath where you lay. Plenty of clover in that grass, plenty of leaves, plenty of rustling sounds and gentle little cries of pain. Cries of pain and little gasps of . . . What?! Has she gone and pricked herself with a thorn?!

I laughed then and looked to the far off part of the garden. There, I saw Nadja standing by the rose bushes. She was reaching over to pick a yellow orchid growing in the middle of them to put in her hat. She had been having trouble getting the flower and had pricked herself with a thorn. She gasped a light feminine cry and pulled her hand away and sucked at her little finger, all the while looking around herself.

I was tempted then to call her over to me, to summon her as had that yellow flower. While she continued looking around innocently at the rose bushes, thinking of an easier way to get past them to pick her orchid, I played with the idea of revealing myself to her... Over here upon the grass! Look, Nadja! Finally, however, I gave up the idea. I smiled and waved myself silent. At last, Nadja triumphantly stretched over the roses without pricking herself again or ruining her dress. She picked the single orchid, put it in the rim of her hat, laughed sweetly aloud, and ran back towards the house to find Nikolai. He was back on the steps, polishing the dust off his shoe with a leaf. He stood and admired her flower, kissed her on the mouth, and the two headed off to the gate which led to the road that went into town.

Down past the arboretum, a little road joined with the rose garden. At the end of the garden's long stone path, a paved hill lined with plane trees led down to the Lower Quarter of the city. The Lower Quarter began in the Canal District where a collection of waterways all ran off in separate directions, either south to the harbor, east to the Peninsula, or north to the sea. The tall narrow houses in this district all had yellow-tiled roofs. Some had their foundations above ground and were sturdy, while others sat deep in canals where they crumbled like sandcastles in tide pools. With the changes in seasons, the canals swelled and their waters rose up to nearly touch the first floor windows of many of the houses; and here you would see those who lived inside coming to poke their heads out and shake them at the flooding waters. Occasionally, an old aproned woman would reach her arms out of her window with a hefty bucket, so as to collect water to feed the potted plants on her windowsills. There were once many people in this quarter of the city.

On this day, the girl and I had taken a morning walk along the canals. It was at the soft hour of morning before the early boats had begun their travels through the city. I remember how, standing on a footbridge, she compared the pristine waters of those saltwater canals to liquid metal... "Lighted drops of mercury," she told me, "sliding down long silver mirrors dipped into the silver sea."

"And over there," said I, pointing to one of the freshwater canals that went not south to the harbor, but wound to the east through the industrial Shipyard District; its waters swished viscid and black as an early crayfish boat came trolling across it, "...over there, one would say a giant earthworm is stretched out on baked earth, panting in the sun." She looked at me strangely then, and the two of us walked on.

Now, was midday and the Lower Quarter, was bustling with people. To tell now of that Lower Quarter: with its spicy strangeness, its hagglers and costermongers wheeling carts. To tell of its quaintness, of the white linen spreads on the decks of houseboats where people would picnic, eating abundant meals. In old familiar squares, heroic bronze horsemen reflected the sun from glazed pedestals. All the while, city-peasants wandered in and out, carrying their wares through stooping doorways.

On this day, Nadja and Nikolai didn't pass through the rose garden to go into town as they usually did. Nadja wanted to show Nikolai her favorite hidden place in the city, and so she led him away from the stone path with his hand around her slender pinky.

She took him down a little lane that led to a steep descent of quartz-colored stairs cached beneath the bowers of tall leafy trees. It was a place of her childhood: those sunny years spent in the gardens of the Upper Quarter and in the house with the terrace and the orchards of fruit. Her father would often take her this way down to the harbor. He would hold her hand tight and lead her along. These stairs filled Nadja with joy, then as now. "Come Nikolai," she said after revealing her secret, urging that the couple keep along.

Just then a burst of sun fell through the leafy bowers overhead and washed Nikolai's face. "I want nothing more than to be," he said aloud and said no more but thought, 'at this singular moment,' walking along, 'with my Nadja on her private steps. I look around myself. I take in the sunshine…' and he felt the palm of Nadja's hand, her skin on his. All the while he made sure to memorize this moment so he could go back and relive it often; so he could replay it over and again for his entire life. He needed to make sure never to lose this memory.

When the couple reached the base of the stairs, Nikolai saw they had come to Krasota. The clean waters of the Krasota Canal flowed up against the embankment, lapping against the stones, leaving a green rind on the white marble like the patinae that coats copper. Nadja and Nikolai climbed up the embankment and over the wooden bridge that spanned the canal and soon the two came to the ancient clock-tower of the Bastion.

Unlike the nearby Canal District, here in Krasota, there were no crumbling piers or old fishing boats roped up along the canals. Here was a place of painted bridges and colorful, flower-lined walkways. Along the harbor, teams of swift flying sailboats passed magnificently by with great, bleached white sails filled with wind. Stately hotels lined the beach and little boutiques and houses lined the tiny roads that wound up to sunny vistas where leafy-terraced restaurants lay stacked in hills. Krasota was a neighborhood that knew of no grief and no sorrow. If a plague ever fell on the Minor City's Lower Quarter, one imagined this neighborhood alone would be spared.

Nadja had led Nikolai down the steps to the harbor so the two could spend the afternoon in Krasota and take a drink together at the Anchises Hotel. She had taken him to this hotel several times already, but this was the first time they'd come by way of her secret stairs, and this was the first time she wore a yellow orchid in her hat. Always, in the past, they came by way of the marketplace. Often they stopped there to buy herbs, to smell the spice-filled air and observe the vibrant market scenery.

In the Anchises Hotel, there was an atrium where the patio restaurant was. The tables here were laid and dressed in silk; artificial streams ran up and down, spanned by bridges woven of long-traveled woods. Hibiscus flowers dropped their golden pollen in the water and the trickling sounds of these streams met the flaps of the wings of tropical birds where they perched and sang, reigning like feathered kings over the luxurious restaurant, over the emerald ponds where gilded carp went their ways in their scaly armor. It was here that the best of society ate, drank and sighed to itself while heavy flourishes of imported banyan trees leaned as if in yawn.

Vladimir, owner of this, the city's finest hotel, was a close friend of Nadja's family; so when Nadja visited the hotel, the concierge and restaurant staff bowed with great respect before her. She had a favorite table beside a pair of ruby-colored parrots who perched on palm branches near a rockery fountain. While the bubbling water flowed down the shelf of rocks, the birds would nest their beaks in their feathers and squawk, their shoulders shimmering like mica.

A waiter brought the couple the wine list. Nikolai sat across from Nadja, and Nadja reached across the table and clasped his hand and asked him what they were going to drink.

"Blackberry wine?"

"That would be nice."

Looking around himself, Nikolai had that strange sensation again: that strong and sudden desire to need to experience and hold the moment for as long as possible. Looking across at Nadja, Nikolai thought, 'I must memorize every part of her face, every aspect of her form. I fear one day I shall have her no more. If she were to go…' With this, a chill passed through him. Nikolai's pleasant leafy bower turned at once into a cold stone cellar. The chill came and then was gone; and his cold cellar became once again a beautiful fortress of stone . . . a throne to the present moment, growing like the parrots' ruffled feathers, leading neither towards the future nor away from the past, but encircling itself like the mineral waters rolling on glass, or still yet remaining still like the wholly unchanging waters of the patio fountains that flowed down the stones to the pool to flow up and return again until one stopped and wondered... "How lucky I am!

"...If it isn't my favorite beauty in the city!"

Nikolai and Nadja turned their heads around to greet the happy voice of Vladimir who was approaching the couple.

"How are you, my dear Nadja?"

Seeing Vladimir, Nadja smiled her famous smile and her eyes lit up. She stood to let Vladimir kiss her cheeks and Nikolai promptly stood to shake the hotel owner's hand.

"What a handsome couple! It is good to see you both. And you," Vladimir smiled at Nikolai, "you're becoming a regular here at the Anchises."

Nikolai couldn't think what to respond at first, he turned to Nadja who bit her lip while looking back at her lover expectantly.

"Well..." Vladimir shrugged it off and turned to Nadja..."What will you two be having?"

"Blackberry wine."

"Blackberry wine it is," Vladimir nodded. Then he turned to Nikolai and swung his hand up in the air as a way of asking the young man's approval. All was decided. Vladimir smiled at the couple at went to place the order with the bartender.

Vladimir was a striking man of exceptional height, a distinguished man with a dark widow's peak, a structured chin, snowy grey temples, and impeccable manners. He was one of the most well-liked figures in upper-class Minor City society and had been a friend of Nadja's father for many years. For all his position, he was also well above snobbery and so happily he took over the waiter's job at times; or at least at the times when his dear Nadja came around. For her, he served the wine himself, a white towel draped over his arm. Nadja was one of the most precious people in Vladimir's life and this was all too clear when she came around; he lit up in her presence and became bright in spirits.

When the wine was served, the two drank, and it was very good wine with a light rinse that tingled sweetly on the tongue after the tartness of the initial blackberry taste made its impression. The first swallow went straight to Nadja's head and she felt a little dizzy and started to smile with a silly pout of her lips. Nikolai knew he too would start to smile in such a way once he'd had four or five good swallows and so he took them. Vladimir stayed and stood by the table and chatted a moment until he was called to business.

"Vladimir was born in Moscow," Nadja informed Nikolai when the two were alone.

"I like him very much," Nikolai replied.

"You should talk to him about Moscow."

They drank some more wine and began to feel very happy. A waiter brought a bowl of Chinese plums and they ate some. Nadja thought the plums were strange with their blanched white skins covered in little red spots, and she began peeling off the skins and leaving them on the table cloth and eating the juicy yellow flesh of the fruit beneath the skins, washing it down with little sips of wine which made her ever more gay and charming. Nikolai ate the plums with the skins and he also washed them down with the blackberry wine and wondered why there were no pits in the plums, though after a while he stopped wondering this and started feeling very light from the wine as well. When Vladimir came over later to talk to the couple, the two laughed and smiled and Nadja told Vladimir how much she loved seeing him and Vladimir smiled and his great thick eyebrows raised, and Nikolai smiled and probably would have told him too that he loved seeing him though he suddenly became shy.

"You see my skins," Nadja said to Vladimir, pointing to the pile of plum skins she'd amassed on the table cloth. Vladimir smiled and shook his head.

"I just don't trust them because their white with red spots," Nadja said, "They're like blushing people. They're like you, these plums,

Vladimir . . . except you don't blush. Maybe they're more like Nikolai. Are they like you?" She looked across the table at her lover and laughed and stroked his hand affectionately. "Why do they blush, these China plums? Hmm, Vladimir? Do China plums even exist? And how come *you* don't blush?"

Vladimir told Nadja he didn't know why he didn't blush; and he added charmingly that if he ever did blush, it would be she that would make it happen. Nadja seemed pleased by this remark. Vladimir then shook Nikolai's hand warmly and said he would have to leave the couple to get back to some paperwork in his office.

"Vladimir?" Nadja asked him at last as he was turning to take leave of the two. As she said his name, she hiccupped lightly and covered her mouth in surprise.

"Yes, Nadja?"

"Oh…I was just wondering, if by any chance you eat herring when you do your paperwork?"

Vladimir's smile turned into a great sincere grin. "So precious you are, sweet Nadja," he told her, "Enjoy your youth while it is here!" And with this he pressed her hand to his face and then let go and turned again and walked off towards his office.

CHAPTER V

From the hotel, the two lovers strolled through the Lower Quarter until they reached Fishmongers' Row. Nadja didn't like the smell of this street, but she liked its vibrancy. She liked the loose cobblestones, its narrowness, the old apartment houses that all leaned to the side. She liked the bustle of the merchant seamen wheeling carts of shellfish and packing them in cakes of ice . . . and the ordinary shoppers gathered around with cloth bags paying for goods. Here on Fishmongers' Row, Nikolai had his room. It was a dark little basement room down the side stairs in an alley off the street. Nadja knew which alley it was but that was all. Nikolai never once asked Nadja to visit his room and she knew he was embarrassed about his poverty in comparison to her affluence and so she never insisted on visiting it, though she wanted to see where he lived.

  On the corner of the passage where Nikolai lived on Fishmongers' Row, there was an old flower shop with rotten walls where Calico the flower seller worked. He was a tiny half-witted man with decaying teeth and a foolish smile and he spent most of the day dying his flowers out on the curb and soaping the dye out of the gutters with pails of water. When people came for a bouquet, he would run behind the counter in the flimsy wooden shop and sell them one; though it didn't seem like he sold too many flowers. Still he always seemed happy and he seemed to have enough to eat.

At times when the two weren't together, when Nikolai was in his room and Nadja wanted to see him, she would come to the flower shop and give Calico a message to give to him and Calico would scrawl it on a note and hobble back through the passage and down the stairs to deliver it to Nikolai. Nadja always had to read the note before it was delivered because half-minded Calico, though well-meaning, often didn't understand what she was saying and got the message wrong. Calico improved with time, however, and eventually Nadja would simply have to pass by the shop, admire the flowers Calico was dying or trimming or spraying with cheap scent, and say... "Write this Calico . . . Are you listening? Good!" and recite, "...My dear Nikolai, I will be at the Anchises Hotel [or in the gardens, or wherever] . . . please come as soon as possible. I miss you. [signed] Your Nadja." ...whereupon Calico would scrawl the note in big jagged lettering and hold it out for her to see while giggling his wide half-toothless, otherwise-rotten grin. He would then nod until Nadja would say "Good, good!" whereupon, he'd hobble off to deliver the note.

After this exercise, a knock would come at the door of the dark cellar room occupied by Nikolai, whereupon the inhabitant would leap up and shout "Calico!" knowing the happy reason for the visit. Nikolai would open the door, stretch his hand out to receive the note and ask by way of a joke, "Whoever is it from?" . . . whereupon Calico would grin and sputter out, while jumping up and down, "Beautiful girl! Beautiful girl!"

Nikolai would then slap Calico's shoulder amiably and take the note and Calico would hobble back up the steps to resume work, trimming and dying, trimming and dying. Sometimes Nadja tried to write the notes herself to give to Calico but these always got lost and were never delivered. It seemed Calico preferred his own penmanship.

On this day the two finished their drinks at the Anchises and ordered another bottle of blackberry wine to be wrapped up and some sandwiches to be prepared. Outside on the pavement, Nadja had to pick up her yellow orchid several times as it kept falling from her hat on to the ground.

"How come you didn't talk to Vladimir about Moscow, Nishka? You've read everything about Moscow!" Nadja asked Nikolai all kinds of questions while the two walked up from Krasota. When they passed Calico's flower shop, they saw the door was closed and papered up, and the windows were dark and Nadja wondered why although she knew it was because Calico was making his rounds at the cafés to try to sell flowers to their patrons. Still she didn't know why the door was covered in paper. From the bustle of Fishmongers' Row through the market-streets where the costermongers had their stalls on the bricks covered in loose hay, to the quieter old stone streets of the Canal District, on up through the rose garden, the two walked along feeling the sun, quietly feeling each other. When they reached the arboretum they stopped to sit and eat their picnic. The blackberry wine was well-iced and the sandwiches were sweet with honeyed bread and soft white cheese and the sun came consistently, cutting through the papery leaves of the great trees to light the lawns of the arboretum around the gazebo. "I remember this dream I was having," Nikolai started to say. Nadja asked when he had had the dream but he couldn't remember. "I'm not sure it was a dream so much as a struggle...."

"I'm not sure I understand, Nishka. What do you want to say?"

Confusion.

It was then that I came walking myself through the arboretum, strolling swiftly, as was my custom. I was walking in the cool of the day up from the rose garden. The nest of a starling fell from a tree and landed before me on my path; its carefully woven twigs crunched underfoot. Nadja heard the disturbance and looked up. She noticed me immediately and stared at me with unflinching eyes. 'Why not lead her away?' I asked myself. 'Shepherd her off.' I kept on my path. '...Or at least unsettle the garden with a little storm of dim, a rustling of cold shade!' I smiled at my inventions, though they were long from my desires. Affairs of the heart burned warm in my own chest and softly so;

thus I carelessly walked on my own, blithely wishing joy for all. I walked though an eternity of sunspots that lit the path in the garden and made the grass soundless underfoot. All the while, meek and simple-faced Nikolai sat innocently unaware beside Nadja in the gazebo, eating his sandwich with his head drooped low. With a breath of air I turned away from the couple and disappeared into the grove. All being gone, Nadja's breast heaved. She turned to Nikolai and blurted out loud and sudden laughter…

"Ah! Ha-ha!"

Nikolai looked up from his sandwich and wasn't sure why Nadja was laughing, but she continued to do so. Finally she quieted down and lay her head on his shoulder. He asked her a few questions but she didn't respond.

Coming back to her home in the early evening, Nadja was in unusually fervent spirits. Passing beneath the archway into the garden, she broke from Nikolai's hand and ran ahead and dove through the limbs of the trees in the orchard shaking out their fruit. The ripe fleshy seeds fell and scattered in the grass.

"I'm getting the fruit down!" Nadja shouted back to Nikolai in great delight… "I'm getting the fruit down!"

The sun cast long shadows over the rock walls of the garden, over the trees, and over the ripe fruit scattered on the ground.

"And what will you do this time with the fruit?" he asked her.

"I'm going to leave it in the grass!"

So saying, she ran back to him and grabbed his hand and held it in hers, and his hand was clean though hers was perfectly dirty from playing in the trees. The two walked on towards the house in order to be alone together. There they would lie upon the terrace and wait and let evening fold over them.

Nikolai asked his lover what she wanted.

"For you to touch me," she responded, "I want to look up at the sky and imagine we are up there together. Somewhere between here and that silvery moon."

"But we *are* up there together."

"Good. And you will hold me tight tonight when we sleep?"

"Yes, of course, my Nadja."

"And we will sleep beneath the sky here on the terrace? The weather is warming fast and we don't even need blankets."

"No. We don't need blankets."

And so that was the beginning of spring on the terrace. In the day, there was the garden below, the shadows of trees and the fruit on the grass. And in the night, there was sky, plenty of dark milky sky and more and more stars.

CHAPTER VI

"The End of Spring"

By June she was definitely a woman, her eyes had even changed a shade. No longer did she play in the budding trees like a child. Now that the trees were plentiful of blooms, she walked languidly beneath them. A coat of satin and silk. Soft, swollen lips, and gently swaying hips. She took her lover's arm on their promenades, always walking with her head high and proud. She was now a woman on the edge of the world.

    Nadja had known Nikolai for the entirety of a season. She now knew all the games to play, and how to taunt him. Still, she remained soft for him. Still she laid herself out for him, the nights they spent together when the June branches of the fig trees swept the terrace railing like brooms sweeping across patio stones. On that terrace they began to sleep more and more, with fewer or no blankets, now that the heat had come and lasted through till dawn when the sun arose.

    It was before daybreak and the larks in the trees were beginning their songs. The two were stretched out upon each other, wasted from making love. She on his breast, he upon her womb, they lay beaten in tired heaps of wet flesh like two victorious warriors, breathless from the battle, panting. Their lips were for their breathing, their eyes were for .

each other; and their thoughts were for the passage of time to remain with them here, now, and neither to pass them by nor to slip too far ahead in the thoughtlessness of passion and joy; but to remain with them in that place they shared of earthly things, of passion and mortal human love.

Now in June, the tone had changed. Lost were the kisses as fleeting and as numerous and hard to pin down as a nest of bees. Now the kisses were fewer. They were longer and deeper; and in each kiss there was for Nadja, as for Nikolai, some knowledge of the future, though what that meant was certainly confused, if not for her, than at least for him. As the season was waning fast, they thought of moments gone at last. He pulled her in tight, his lips were for her breath; while her eyes were for the heavens, and her lips were full of dreams.

With Nadja asleep, Nikolai lay thinking about how at the end of May, she had said she wished the two were up together in the sky . . . 'Between here and that silvery moon,' she had said. Now why did she want the heavens, he wondered, not understanding. When, back in the garden in early May, she had wanted the canopies of trees to cover and obscure the heavens and keep the heavens from the two lovers so that only they and their earthly home would exist. Now why did she want the heavens suddenly? 'What has changed?' he asked himself, 'Simply time has changed. . . overleaped itself.'

Nikolai pulled sleeping Nadja in close to him. Her breath deepened and he felt a salty tear of his own reflect off her cheek when he pressed his face to hers. He felt her and lay quietly listening, trying to memorize anew her sleeping breath for as long as she would be lying beside him.

CHAPTER VII

Vladimir had a birthday coming up that week. He insisted that Nadja bring Nikolai along with her to the celebration that would be held in his honor at the Anchises Hotel that coming Friday night, the sixteenth of June. It was to be an intimate gathering. Vladimir expressed regret that Nadja's father couldn't attend, but he knew that her father was doing business in the West Islands and wouldn't return to the Minor City until fall. Vladimir didn't extend the invitation to Nikolai personally, but asked Nadja to, and when Nadja told Nikolai about it, he flushed with happy anticipation for the event to come. Vladimir was obviously becoming fond of Nikolai. He spoke well of him to Nadja in their private discussions; and during those rare moments when he found himself alone with Nikolai, he chatted warmly and sincerely, never inciting an awkward silence. Vladimir had also, only recently, begun a habit of insisting to Nikolai that Vladimir was, as he put it, 'a man of discretion,' and that Nadja's relationships were her own concern and that he wasn't one to 'whisper while doors were closed,' so to speak. Nikolai always moved away from that subject when it came up, and would take on an embarrassed note as if he didn't understand what Vladimir was talking about, or why he insisted on this, although he did in fact know quite well the reasons for it.

Nadja spent the three days before the party painting a canvas that she would give as a gift to Vladimir. She suggested to Nikolai that he offer a certain kind of cigar that Vladimir would much appreciate, but finally Nikolai bought another box of cigars of his own choosing. While they were in town, Nadja bought some red ochre and when they returned to the house she set up her easel downstairs by a window looking out into the yard. Nikolai remained upstairs and read his books. At times he came down to see the progress of her painting. It was a warm scene of a street in the Lower Quarter with cobbled steps and old buildings. Nikolai wondered why she didn't go down to the Lower Quarter to look at her subject while she painted, but instead worked at the window where there were trees and flower beds, but no cobbled steps or old buildings. She explained to him that she couldn't paint something by looking at it. She was only capable of painting what she imagined or what was in her memory. Nikolai also wondered how she was able to paint so well, but she explained that she had had lessons and that anyone can paint well after taking lessons; and then she added, "Well it's not so good, perhaps," though they both new it was going to be an impressive canvas once it was finished.

The evening of the party, Nadja spent a long time putting ringlets in her hair. It was nearing eight o'clock and Nikolai worried they would arrive too late. He had quickly bathed and shaved and was dressed in a dark suit waiting downstairs on the sofa by the coffee table. He heard water running upstairs and knew Nadja had gotten back in the bath. She again had to dry and curl her hair and with the makeup in addition to that it was nearing nine o'clock and Nikolai knew they would be too late and was very worried and a little upset. When Nadja was ready, dressed in cream silk and tall heels, the two walked down the road towards the quartz stairs that led to Krasota.

The party was elaborate, and, for an intimate affair, there were quite a few people – all handsomely dressed and bright with smiles and lively talk. The extent of Vladimir's popularity in society was apparent with the turnout; and all bestowed lavish gifts. Vladimir thanked Nikolai warmly for the cigars. The canvas Nadja painted was his obvious favorite, and he extolled the gift to all present. Even the servants were made to set down there serving trays to comment on the piece. Nadja explained to Vladimir that he mustn't touch the painting or rub it against anything as the paint was still wet . . . although she knew that the paint was perfectly dry.

Nadja drank four glasses of champagne and was full of laughter. She danced with Nikolai all of the dances except the first, which she gave to Vladimir, and the third as well, which she also gave to Vladimir. Vladimir also had drunk quite a bit of champagne with all the toasts that had been made and Nadja at one point turned to him...

"You are blushing," she said.

Was Vladimir blushing?

"Oh, now I see that you're not."

Nadja thought Vladimir had been blushing but then she saw that he wasn't after all.

By midnight, the guests had all arrived and had given their gifts. Vladimir made a final tour with his new oil painting, gift from Nadja. Many of the guests asked Nadja if they could commission her for their own painting, and she laughed. There was a debate on where in the hotel the painting should be hung, but Vladimir was quick to inform his guests that this was a private gift and would be hung in his private home.

Behind the restaurant patio was another patio, very secluded; and after Nadja had snuck another little glass of champagne, she led Nikolai out there with the desire to kiss him.

"Do you want to dance more?" Nikolai asked.

"Oh no! Let's walk home. I want to be with you alone."

"You don't want to stay? I like these people."

"No, Nishko!" Nadja frowned, "We will go now."

The couple said a warm goodbye to Vladimir, whom upon their return they found standing near a stream in the restaurant explaining to some guests where a certain species of fish had come from. "Already leaving?" He kissed his sweet Nadja on the cheek and shook Nikolai's hand and told the couple to come by the hotel soon and he would leave off work to take a drink with them. Nadja sneezed about this and said it was because of the champagne and everyone laughed. She took Nikolai's arm and the two headed home.

The road was dark and the couple walked happily together, although at times Nadja fell far behind.

"Come, my little one!" Nikolai looked back and saw Nadja swerving a little as she walked. She stepped in her heels like a seagull, not seeing the ground; but the road was pitch black after all. "It's these shoes!" she called up to Nikolai as she stumbled along.

"What's wrong with your shoes?" Nikolai called back to her.

"You know, Nishka!"

"No, I don't, Nadja, what's wrong with your shoes?"

"Maybe they've been drinking a little bit, Nishka!"

"They've been drinking, your shoes?" Nikolai laughed at this, retrieving Nadja's arm to place it around his.

"A little, yes! . . . but Nishko!"

Nikolai smiled a great smile at her and she pouted her lips.

"My shoes have been drinking, Nishko. But I'll try to walk as good as you." She took his arm and the two kissed and they were very happy as they walked the rest of the way to the house, although Nadja did have more trouble walking. And well before they reached her house she expressed regret that they didn't have any champagne of their own to drink and she wondered where they could buy a bottle, but Nikolai informed her that there was in fact a bottle of champagne at the house and this cheered her up immensely and her happiness cheered him up and the two walked a little faster and were both in good spirits; and when they reached the walls of the garden, they stopped to kiss for a long time and talked about what a good night it had been.

CHAPTER VIII

Nadja wanted to drink some coffee.

"But we were going to drink champagne," Nikolai said, touching her chin as the two were settling out on the terrace. The sky was unusually dark. The moon was new and the stars were silent.

"But maybe I want coffee, Nishka. Not champagne."

"Are you sure?" Nikolai knew that whenever Nadja drank coffee in the night, or even after dinner, she tended to stay up all night and not be able to sleep. She would get loquacious and start all kinds of projects. Still, she insisted on coffee and Nikolai went to make some for her.

"Where is it from?" she asked later to her lover who was lying outstretched on the bedding on the terrace.

"Where is what from?"

"The coffee."

"Afric's shore," he said listlessly, eyes closing. He was drifting in and out of visions and playful losses of memory and consciousness. Nadja sat beside him, ankles crossed. Her legs, like fresh-split ivory, were pressed against her chest. She funneled her mouth to blow the steam away from the cup in her hands. Suddenly, she turned to Nikolai and shouted at him… "Nishka!"

"Yes, Nadiushka?"

"Do you think when I am gone, the wind will still blow on the harbor."

He stroked her calf with his limp fingers. "It didn't blow before you were here, so why would it blow when you are gone?"

"How do you know it didn't blow before I was here?"

"I'm older than you."

"But Nishka!" Nadja blurted. She looked at him, trying to see if he were telling the truth or not.

"Yes, Nadiushka, twenty-four years ago you were not alive, and I was more than alive; and I'll tell you then, the wind didn't blow on the harbor. Do you know when it started blowing?"

"No Nishka, tell me."

"It started blowing twenty three years ago…." His voice began to trail off as sleep overtook him again and again. Nadja sat always near him, mostly unmoving, though occasionally bringing the cup of coffee to her mouth in the darkness.

"Do you think it will be strange when I am not here?" she asked after a minute.

"But where would you go?"

"But you know…" and this time she called him by his full first name… "You know, Nikolai . . . as soon as it's summer I'm going to the West Islands to see my father." And here it was again. "I will miss you though, Nishka. I'll be back in the fall. But then it will be different because my father will be here at the house and we will no longer have our terrace, just you and me. We will have to meet quietly in town."

It was beginning again. This talk of Nadja's brought Nikolai back fully into consciousness. "What is the date?" he asked her. He felt himself coming into a sad wakefulness, thinking now fully these thoughts he had been pushing away since the time of their first meeting. Or perhaps he never believed them. Is it already summer? He saw before him a long strip of golden sunny shore and believed it when he saw it, and believed that it was now summer and Nadja was in the West Islands and nowhere near the Minor City. And here was this strip of sandy golden shore amid a land of iron ore. But his body was in the darkness, almost asleep on the terrace, and when he realized again that Nadja was still near him and that it was still only late spring, he grew happy and revived of all hope. But then his tired mind played another trick and now he saw himself walking in a garden, crunching crisp leaves underfoot. It was early spring and trees were drenched in sunlight, sweet as clover honey, and Nadja was fresh and devotedly beside him and the two were alive and in love and all of eternity lay before them. And then Nadja – not Nadja of yore in the ample garden, but Nadja of now drinking coffee in the darkness – touched his shoulder and he came away from sleep far enough to gather his senses and he recalled now that it was no longer early spring, and they had no longer that eternity before them, but that it was almost summer and she would soon be going away for true and real; and even if he could change this in dreams, it would change nothing of the fact that she would soon be going away and that would be that, and so she said, "The sixteenth," when he asked her what the date was. He opened his eyes and saw that Nadja had finished her coffee and was trembling lightly and he felt sad, no longer like sleeping. He sat up and pushed the bedding away from his chest and slipped his hand through the strap of her bra clinging to her shoulder, absent-mindedly. He asked her if she would want to stay there longer. Did she like it there? "Where?" she responded, in a voice so far away that he almost had to ask if she were talking to him or to someone else, though they were the only two on the terrace.

"In the West Islands," he said, "Would you want to stay there?"

"Oh," she said, sitting up straight, and then she leaned on his bare chest, and then sat up again. "I don't know."

"You don't know?"

"Nishko, why do you ask me this? I go there every summer. I have since I was little."

Then she paused.

"Do you want to know?"

"Yes, I want to know your life away from me," he said.

"Well, in the city there are old Roman ruins. And around there it smells. It smells worse than it smells here by our markets. But we don't go much down there. Our house is up by the embassies. You've never been to the West Islands? I'm sure you have!"

"You know I haven't. I've never left the Minor City in my life, except for some trips out to the forest nearby."

"Well, it's strange there. But maybe I do like it, Nishka. There is water to swim, and we have lots of maids and a nice cook. I used to like the other people my age but I don't anymore. I went to school with all of them. Some are nice. They are all very rich and they talk about their parents' jobs. I just mostly like to be alone and do lazy things."

Pause.

"You know, Nishka!" she squeezed his arm, growing excited, "There are the salt springs there. When I'm there, I like to float in the salt springs all day in the sun. The water is nice on the skin and it is very salty and the sun keeps it very warm and you just float all day . . . and everywhere there are palm trees!"

"And these rich friends of yours," Nikolai started in, growing more alert to the conversation. He was now sitting up and looking at the tiny specks of light in Nadja's eyes – practically all the light on the terrace was settled in her eyes, like two lighthouses lost in the oil-dark sea. "These friends," he asked her, "you never thought you should be better off being with one of them? I mean with one of the men?"

"No, Nishka! They are empty people. The men are just boys and they all dress in beige and they just talk about their fathers! You've never even told me about your father! . . . Well, we don't need to know those things…

"…My father is so serious," she continued after a moment, "Every time I think of him, I can't help thinking of how serious he is! I'll tell you, Nishka, two years ago it was August and my father wanted me to marry the son of some ambassador. He wanted me to because it would be very proper for me to do that. I laughed. 'Ha!' I said, 'Father, don't call me *marriageable!* . . . I'm going back to the house in the Minor City. Give me the keys!' Father said I already had the keys and I knew I did, and you know, but of course I didn't leave, but no Nishko. I'd rather . . . I'd much rather spend this summer with you in our little basement underneath the flower shop on Fishmongers' Row. That could be our new house. But you know I would!" Here Nadja kissed him.

"*Our* basement?" he asked her gloomily, "but you wouldn't want *that* basement! You wouldn't want anything to do with me if you saw the dreadful cellar I live in, little Nadja."

"Yes I would. Tell me about it. Please, for once, Nishka."

"No. Tell me more about the salt springs." He had never heard of such a thing.

"Oh they are . . . but you know all about them! Why do you play games with me?"

"No, I don't know of them. I've never been to the West Islands…"

Nadja readied her voice to speak. Her eyes began to water with the story she was about to tell… "Well, Nishka!…" and then she stopped.

"Tell me."

"You know, I just lie in the salt springs there and sleep. I sleep all day. You know, Nishka, perhaps your Nadiushka is a bit lazy. Yes, perhaps I am lazy. I sleep most of the day in those springs and I come back black from the sun. Oh, so black!"

"I can't imagine such a life," Nikolai said ruefully, "Last year I worked all summer giving lessons in an room with no ventilation. And the year before that I worked all summer repairing beams on the Otchajanie Bridge . . . but nevermind."

"You worked on the Otchajanie Bridge?" Nadja lit up at this. Her face shone with rapture.

"Yes, I did . . . adding plates to beams that were broken with rust."

"Oh!" she exclaimed and kissed him, "So that means that part of you is in that bridge! You know, Nishka, I love that bridge. I hate it, but also I love it."

"It's a filthy bridge . . . stained with the sweat of toilers, stained with the smoke of cargo ships that pass underneath."

"Sometimes I don't understand your poetry, Nishko."

"I don't know, Nadja," he said sullenly, "with you came a hope yet unknown. You know, Nadja…" Yet, Nadja seemed not to be paying attention. She was chasing a moth with her hand and started rambling about how one would go about building that great bridge that spanned their harbor. When she came back to him she admitted that she wished she'd had worked on that bridge with Nikolai instead of floating in salt all day."

"I envy your salt."

"Why my salt?"

What did he say? He wanted to say something else but couldn't find the words. And she kept drifting farther and farther away and he could feel it and he felt a profound drop into grief that rose back slowly until it was fully relieved by a soft return of a joy that coincided with her return to him. She told him, "Nikolai, just think… You worked all summer long to add yourself to the great Otchajanie Bridge, and all I did was add a little sun to my skin so it would be brown. I think your life is better than mine."

"No, Nadja. Before you it wasn't a great life. I slaved. I ate cheap scraps. I wandered around without anyone worth talking to. I kept to myself. When I was in a lucky mood, I was able to lose myself in books – in pages of false joy. Those were at the best times. The worst were those of wandering the streets of the Shipyard District or around Nesretan, looking for that little . . . well, nothing. Moreover I worked and worked the time away. I worked while everything wilted and died around me." He then rose up, "And you Nadiushka, you came along as a great hope. The purest hope."

"But now we are the same. We have the same things."

"Do you think so?"

"I don't know. We'll lose ourselves in books. I wonder how long that bridge is…" Nadja was sprightly now, ever-so distracted… "I want part of myself put into that bridge!" while she was blurting this, she jumped up and down on her knees… "Yes, I want part of me put into the Otchajanie Bridge. And you know, Nishkaloo, I want part of you put into me!"

"You . . . me . . . and the bridge," Nikolai said sullenly as Nadja's voice trailed upwards toward the swirl of the black sky; all the while his own trailed down to the dark terrace stone floor where it started seeping in, while he himself began draining from tiredness.

There was a pause in which a thousand remnants of unfinished dreams asserted themselves. Before Nikolai's eyes flashed a scene of men with spears seated at a table of empty plates . . . "Okay, Nishka!" came a voice, "You can put you in me instead of the sun. You will fall on me like drops, my Nishkalushka. I will have the sun first to be brown. Then, you will fall on me and make me white!

"…Do you hear me?" she cried, tugging on him, "This is my idea!" While she laughed, she kissed him and the sweet taste of her lips woke him up anew; and when it left, he yearned for it again, and so he leaned towards her to initiate another kiss; and she kissed him back but looked away and he felt this distraction in her kiss and it made him sad and gave him a hollow sorrow that could be felt in the gut.

"Nishka…"

"Yes?"

"I have to admit something to you."

"What is it, Nadja?"

"Perhaps I shouldn't have drunk that coffee after all."

With that she remained seated on her knees beside her lover curled to sleep. And although he was almost gone, his thoughts seemed clear and awake and he thought mournfully about this and many things.

He thought about how she would be leaving for the summer. He soon wouldn't see her for a long time, not before autumn. And as green as were the sturdy leaves upon the trees, so was their season a stranger to fall. He thought of this while she lay down beside him and wrapped herself in his arms. Yet with her soft body, the mournful thoughts continued. But he tried to not think of them. He tried to just think of her body; and he felt then as he drifted to sleep that she too was on the verge of sleep, though mistaken he was. He felt her heart with his limp hand. It was beating quite fast.

CHAPTER IX

The next morning, Nadja was missing. Nikolai woke up alone and looked around himself. The terrace was empty but for a stroke of sun wiping down the stones. He felt a strange clammy chill, as one experiences when recovering from a sudden faint. It reminded him of that time he had had an attack of vertigo and fell in the middle of the street in Herelzaberg one winter. The feeling of gathering his senses while sitting on a step in the doorway of a clothing boutique, sweating and feeling cold. The salesgirl at the boutique called a doctor to come for him...

...What is this? He had never been to any place called Herelzaberg! Was that in a dream or a book he had read? He pulled the blankets from his body and peered out to the garden; all the while trying to untie the remnants of dreams from his wakeful state. 'Where has she gone?' he asked himself, looking around for Nadja. Why, he wondered, had she not kissed him when she awoke? Perhaps she never even slept, he hadn't remembered her body beside him during the night. He hadn't seen so much as a star the night before overhead. In his dreams there were stretches of white sandy deserts. No, there had been no deserts.

While Nikolai sifted through his memory, Nadja slipped out

onto the terrace, slinking along in a night silk slip. She carried a large piece of paper and a box of Icelandic pastels.

"Oh!" she exclaimed. He had noticed her tiptoeing and turned to her. She didn't like it that she'd been noticed.

"Where were you, Nadja?"

"I wanted to draw you naked while you were sleeping, so I went to get my pastels."

"I mean where were you in the night?"

"Well, Nishka! You know about all that coffee I drank!"

Nikolai tried to pull the blanket back over him but Nadja tugged at it and insisted that it remain off. She then perched on a stool by the railing and scratched at her paper with her outlining pencil in attempt to draw him. Nikolai listened to the scratches on the rough paper until it stopped. He looked over and saw Nadja scowling.

"Why are you scowling?"

"I'm afraid I can't draw you as well as the world drew you." She dropped her pencil on the floor and went downstairs. "I'll come back."

Much time passed on the terrace. The birds lit up with song in the trees. Nikolai waited for Nadja to return for a long time until finally he got up, slipped on his underwear, and passed through the bedroom to go downstairs to find her.

She was perched by the window in the living room, looking out at the trees in the garden. Her mouth was open wide as she threw streaks of color with her pastels on the paper she clutched with fervent hands. It was a fantastical portrait of the acacia tree near the window. Her eyes were wide as her hand cut rapidly across the page, throwing vibrant streaks in all directions.

"Nadja!" Nikolai said in annoyance, "I was waiting for you upstairs!"

Nadja didn't answer him. She was too excited about the tree she was drawing.

"Nadja!"

"Nishka, quiet! I am drawing this tree! I was planning to come back to bed when it was finished."

"But you could be at this all day!"

Again Nadja didn't answer, but kept perched over her drawing paper.

"Okay, Nadja, I'm leaving. I'm going back to my room in town for a while."

"But Nishka!" She turned to him. A gleam of wet shone on her lips. "Tell me, Nishka, do you think these spots of pink look like the flowers on the tree?"

"Yes, just like them, but I'm going home." Nikolai walked up the stairs to the bedroom and found his shoes. He carried them down and set them next to the front door near where Nadja was seated with her sketching. Her nose was practically touching the window as she drew fragrant lines of color.

"Why are your shoes there?" Nadja demanded.

"I told you I'm going back to my room in town to organize things."

"But you didn't tell me that! And you don't need to organize things! Besides, your room is here…"

"Nadja, you're busy drawing. I don't want to wait for you to stop. I'd better go take care of some things."

"Nishko!" she growled.

"Nadja!" he growled back as he turned and started up the stairs to find his clothes. After he was dressed, he returned downstairs to put his shoes on to leave.

Nadja was silent, still immersed in her tree, and Nikolai stood studying his shoes that were propped by the door. Something was different. Now, one of his shoes was missing its lace.

"Where is my shoelace, Nadja?"

No answer.

56

"Nadja!"

"But I don't want you to go, Nishko!"

He looked closely at Nadja and saw that around her left wrist, the missing shoelace was tied in a bow. As if unaware of her new bracelet, Nadja continued to draw.

Nikolai smiled at her charm and walked up and kissed on the side of the ear. "That's amazing," he said, "You were able to tie a shoelace in a bow around your wrist with one hand!"

"No, Nishka, it's not amazing. Women know tricks like that."

After this scene, Nikolai gave up on the idea of returning to his room in town. He instead stretched out on the sofa next to where Nadja was propped as she worked and coiled around her and watched her draw, watched her happy face, felt her happy body, soft and naked, save for her silk slip and the leather lace tied around her slender wrist. The portrait of that acacia tree came out nice and the colors were very bright and wild and it became one of Nikolai's favorite pictures.

CHAPTER X

That evening, a heavy wind came across the harbor, pushing the clouds inland, bringing forth a moonless night. The path was dark and the winds blew and tree branches fell across the path as the couple made their way through the darkness into the rose garden.

When they reached the Anchises Hotel, they were surprised to find the restaurant empty, with Vladimir away on business and very few guests for the break between seasons. A new concierge brought a bucket of ice and a bottle of good Dalmatian wine. Nikolai noticed an abrasion on Nadja's wrist where his shoelace had been tied. Such a small wrist she had, such long arms, like her legs and slender neck. The two drank wine and Nadja got tipsy and began her loquacious talk...

"Nishka, you are pretty."

"Yes."

"You know, Nishka!"

"Yes, Nadja?"

"You know the part about *heading towards the bridge?*"

"What *heading towards the bridge?*"

"But Nishko! Why do I have to repeat myself always two times with you? Or are you playing with me?"

Nikolai looked at her and sipped his wine.

"That bit about: *from now on, you will be heading towards the Otchajanie Bridge.*"

Now Nikolai realized she was quoting from a story he'd begun to tell her once; he'd heard it or read it though he couldn't remember when or where.

"Who wrote that?" she asked.

"I can't remember."

"It's absurd anyway, Nishka . . . because if someone is always heading *towards* the bridge, *from now on*, he is never going to reach it and therefore he isn't heading *towards* the bridge at all, even if he *is* 'going in that direction' . . . isn't that what we decided?"

"Yes, that's right, but I don't know who wrote it, Nadja. I mean I think it's anonymous. Or no one wrote it."

"Or *you* wrote it, since you were saying it in your sleep the other night. You were saying it to me all night. Yes . . . I think *you* wrote it actually, Nishka."

"No, I think I heard it somewhere, actually. But I'm sure it's anonymous."

"What is the rest of the story?"

"There is no rest of the story, it's all about *heading towards the bridge*."

"So there's no heroine?"

"No."

"And no hero either?"

"No."

"So it's just a bunch of tangled up ideas!" she said with disappointment in her voice. "Well, I'm glad no one wrote it."

"Why are you glad?"

"Will you write me a story, Nishka? Then you won't have to read other people's all the time."

"I don't think I *can* write a story. I'm not a writer. Why are you glad no one wrote the story about heading towards the bridge?"

"No, I'm not glad about *that*," she told him, "I'm just glad that it has no heroine or hero."

"Why?"

"Because one can't fall in love with a writer of a story unless he's written a story with a heroine or a hero. Who can fall in love with someone who just writes a bunch of tangled ideas?"

Nikolai searched in Nadja's eyes. "If you like heroes better than ideas, why are you glad the story has no hero?"

"Because *no one* wrote it!" Nadja said with fury. Each moment she seemed to be getting more and more upset. "Anyway, you *can* write stories, Nishka. You've told me about some of them. I want one of the stories you read me to be something you've written yourself."

"But I don't have any stories!" Nikolai tried to think but he couldn't imagine himself having a story of his own.

"Yes you do! You told me that one you were writing in your notebook . . . about the henchman who stole the moon while his master wasn't looking."

Nikolai laughed and rubbed his finger on the rim of his wine glass.

"Remember? They all believed that he *did* steal the moon because there was no moon in the sky; but when they caught the henchman and searched his pockets, they just found a big round silver coin . . . and so they locked him up!"

"Yes, but that's just one little scene," Nikolai told her, "I have lots of those fragments. The difficult thing is stringing them together. You would have to string them together to have a good story. Maybe someday in the future."

"In the future?"

"I'm still almost young, you realize! Most great things are written by people of middle age. Someday, though, I will write you a story, my Nadiushka."

"Someday?!" Nadja exclaimed, "Someday is nothing!" She appeared to be growing sincerely angry now, and Nikolai wasn't quite sure why. She finished the puddle of rose-colored wine in the bottom of her glass and looked at Nikolai. Nikolai felt a sudden chill of cold sweat. Nadja apparently noticed this, because she started to rub his forehead with the smooth backs of her fingernails. She leaned forward to kiss him. Nikolai looked at her sternly and didn't take the kiss with appreciation.

"Oh, don't make your eyebrows like that," she told him.

"Like what?"

"You think I'm just a silly young girl maybe, because I like heroes more than ideas."

"No, you're not silly. One just wonders..." ...and he wondered why.

"Do you like having a young girlfriend?" she interrupted, changing the subject.

"I like having you."

"Maybe I'm too young for you, and too silly. And maybe I dream too much."

"I don't know if one *can* dream too much. Maybe one can. I don't know."

"It's so quiet here tonight." Nadja looked around the empty restaurant and then added, "What other kinds of story fragments do you have?"

"Just some random pieces I hope to make whole stories someday. If I can just string them together."

"String them," she repeated, considering the sound of the phrase.

"Yes, and then I will read them to you. And I promise, Nadiushenka, no ideas. Just stories."

"Tell me about one."

"Well, I have one about a baker's helper who lives in an attic and sweeps up flour all day. His job is to sweep up the flour used in the bottoms of the pans where the bread is cooked for the idle class to feed the birds in the park. He daydreams of greatness, and at night he drinks whiskey and smokes with his landlord. They talk about the future. And they plan for his greatness."

"Does he become great?"

"I'm not sure yet, maybe not. Maybe he just dreams that he will be great someday – and that is his greatness, that he lives it all in his head. In the meantime he sweeps flour. I haven't decided."

Nadja sat quietly listening.

Nikolai went on... "There will also be a story of a painter who eats rats. He doesn't have any money to buy food, and the rats are easy to catch."

"Nishka..." Nadja began in a low tone of voice, "Tell me one thing... when you see my paintings, do you think they are the types painted by someone who eats rats?"

"But no, Nadiushka! I think they are painted by a queen. A queen who lives in a happy garden on the moon and who eats ambrosia flowers and dusts the nape of her neck with their pollen."

"That's pretty. Why don't you write that?"

"No, I think my stories would have more things like old city streets burnt to the ground. In a shabby neighborhood called 'The Forgotten Quarter,' there would be a wooden house where a bald man would work fixing watches. His wife would spend her evenings shaking the ticks out of pillows. Upstairs a thirty year-old student would be studying by a feeble candle of cheap tallow. The rest of the rooms would be empty . . . Wait!" Nikolai sipped his wine and rolled his eyes around the restaurant to fuel his visions. The ideas were flowing upon him, "...No, not all the rooms upstairs would be empty. Some of them would be empty but the others would be let to strangers. A prostitute would rent one of the rooms. Her landlord, the bald watchmaker, doesn't know she's a prostitute. If he did, he wouldn't rent her a room in his house – you see he once turned away a tenant because he smoked raspberry tobacco – and so a prostitute would be out of the question. And so the landlord never notices the girl's clients coming up the backstairs. And she doesn't look a thing like a prostitute – in fact, she looks like a nice girl who might be in her first year at the university, but instead she's a young fallen woman and depends on prostitution to pay her food and rent and clothing. The other room, next door, belongs to the thirty-year old student. He is ashamed and afraid because his family has stopped sending him money and he doesn't know how he's going to pay the rent the next month, and the old bitter wife of the watchmaker doesn't like him to begin with, so she'll be happy to get rid of him; though her husband thinks he's an upright young man, though a little strange. But the landlord's expecting to get his rent, nonetheless, and doesn't know he won't get it. Moreover, it is almost Christmas time and that's not the time of year to be put out on the street. Especially when one hasn't any prospects."

"Nikolai," said Nadja, "Let's go home now."

The road back was dark after the two passed the lighted streets of Krasota. Nadja kept walking ahead, and then trailing behind. She said she wanted Nikolai to go the other way, to get that heroic book he'd promised he would bring to read to her from his room in the Lower Quarter. He agreed and tried to lead Nadja through the marketplace towards Fishmongers' Row, so the two could walk together and she could wait upstairs while he went down to get the book from his room; though she said she would rather walk back to her house alone and have him come after.

"Later," she insisted, "once you've found the book." She said that she didn't want to go near Fishmongers' Row on this night. She didn't want to be in that part of town. Not at this late hour of night. Nikolai reasonably took offense, insisting that surely no harm could come to her if she were in his company. But of course he could protect her!

"Of course," she admitted, "It's just that..." ...It was just that she didn't want to walk through this part of town on this particular night because of the uncleanliness around the market stalls. She wasn't in the mood for the smells of the streets there, the odors of the drunks and their yelling, as well as the stench of the grime that pervaded this neighborhood at night. She wanted rather to walk alone, by herself, through the milky dark and fragrant rose garden. There, surely no harm would come to her, even if she were by herself at that late hour. And Nadja was certainly one to explore alone and wander anywhere; anyway, Nikolai could hardly object to her wishes and said he would go by himself to his room in the Lower Quarter to get the book and would hurry with it, back to her house. She received his kiss on the corner of her mouth where the two stood on the far side of the Krasota Bridge. There, the two parted ways.

The street where Nikolai walked alone was quiet save for a solitary mendicant who crooned in a puddle of filth, and the rattling noises of some tin garbage can lids outside the butcher shop where some stray cats were fighting for discarded tendons. At the corner of Nikolai's passage, the mildewed shutters of Calico's shop were closed and tied with rope. Nikolai disappeared through the passage and hurried down the steps. He turned the key and went inside the room.

Inside, the air was dusty and stale. There was an unusual quiet, only the steady dripping of rusty water droplets from the faucet into the iron basin of the sink could be heard. Nikolai lit a lamp and hurried to his bookshelf. When his eyes passed from the wood to the bindings of books, an image of Nadja's lips entered his mind. He pictured the shape of her mouth. Then, a loud knocking sound came from outside in the alley, the passage from his door to Fishmonger's Row.

Startled by the noise, Nikolai ran quickly out into the passage but saw it was no one . . . just the wind slamming a shutter closed on one of the windows across the way. While inspecting the dark passageway, he caught sight of the dirty little mound of soil against the steel fence separating the walkway from the yard next door. There were some weeds growing in the mound of dirt and Nikolai noticed a clump of bright parsley growing too. He reached down and pulled the parsley from the roots. Dirt caked around the base of the little green plant. He smelled it: odors pungent and abundant. This would make a nice gift for Nadja, he decided. She had acted strangely on this night. He needed to be with her again. It was not pleasant being without her in the dismal passage, this fated cellar room.

Back inside, he searched on the shelf until he found the book. "The Myth of Helonius," the title read. It was in a thin volume bound in calfskin. He flipped through the pages, looked back at the parsley plant he'd set by the sink. He would need a little cup to plant the parsley in to keep it alive. Only one cup did he have in his possession and that was chipped. Better find something else. He remembered then an empty pill jar stashed beneath his bed. He had bought the pills at the apothecary a long time ago and now it was empty. It was an amber glass bottle. He retrieved it from beneath his bed and put the parsley in the bottle and admired the green of the plant against the amber of the bottle, just like copper coated in patinae. But now this was absurd, he realized . . . 'To present a lady like Nadja with a common herb planted in a chemist's drug bottle! What was I thinking?' Casting aside the vessel, he tossed the plant on the sink near the dripping faucet.

"The Myth of Helonius," was the fable she wanted. 'A white knight.' Was there no gift he could bring her? The book would be a gift. Yes, but she was expecting that! He imagined her then walking alone by herself through the rose garden, through the arboretum – alone in the dark on a moonless night. He pictured again her soft, full lips – the way her lower-lip folded down in that perfect curve as it did for so few women. The smoothness of her face, the roundness of her breasts – and how taught they had looked in the thin sweater she had been wearing on this night. And those sweetly rounded hips, small but fortunate, feminine and good. Nikolai stood in his cellar room and clutched his book and thought of what else to bring her. Nothing else. He quickly left his room and went back out through the passage and headed towards the canals.

From the row of closed-up vendors' stalls, he passed through the streets to the district of outdoor markets, also all closed for the night. Here in the sanitary markets, mice scurried along the doorways, around dismantled market tents. Nikolai brushed up against an old stall which left a streak of tar on his shoulder. If that wasn't enough, he noticed a light rain was beginning to fall from the newly returned clouds. He hoped Nadja had already made it inside to her house. But of course he knew she had. Certainly she had reached her house by now, was sitting dry in her living room. Surely she was happy now, waiting peacefully for him. Nikolai smiled with great love in his chest for his Nadja who was now so far away.

Walking along, he clutched his book of myths under his shirt to protect the calfskin cover from the rain that came falling heavily now. The rainwater felt like strands of dirty rough cloth as they slid across his bare neck. He passed through the lower quarter, the tight mazes of streets. He noticed a boarded-up shop with a painted sign hanging over the worm-eaten door. The sign read: V. CHERVYAK – BLOODLETTER.

Once the Lower Quarter was behind him, he climbed the misling hills of the rose garden, head bowed low. Only did he look up when he passed the gazebo in the arboretum. There he thought he saw a couple seated together, arms around each other. He heard the man's voice talking quietly to the woman beside him. Nikolai quickened his pace and passed the gazebo without looking to see if there were in fact people there.

At the stone archway leading into her garden, he stopped and noticed the gate was shut as usual for the night. Using the key which she kept on top of the rock wall, he opened the gate and went across the garden. A lantern on the porch was burning gentle flames; eager spring locusts fluttered around it. Nikolai turned the lock in the front door and went inside.

"Nadja?" he called up the stairs. Her name echoed through the empty house. The rain poured heavily outside. He had taken a detour in finding that book, he knew. Still he'd returned by the same route she would have come herself. Was she on the terrace? The terrace was flooded with rain. "Nadja!" he yelled again. Where could she have thought to go if not straight home? Or had she come and left? A new hope was born: maybe she had worried about his taking so long in retrieving that book and had gone to find him in his room in the Lower

Quarter. But he had not taken long! And anyway, their paths would have crossed. Now he was worried that she was lost, or somewhere, wait! There was a sound in the kitchen! "Nadja!"

Nikolai ran down to find her.

There was no Nadja in the kitchen. There was a trembling open window, its damp curtain slapped against the pane. Splashes of rain bounced on the marble counter; and there, beside it all, he saw the struggles of a broken crow, drenched with flapping wings, cawing on the window sill.

"A bird, not Nadja! And this was not her doing? An open window?" No, he realized that he himself had forgotten to close the window before the two left the house earlier this evening. There hadn't been rain earlier.

Nikolai freed the bird into the night, and feeling fully lost, he sought the sofa and flung himself down, tossing the book he'd brought for her on the immaculate table. In the center of the glass table sat a crystal cruet filled with wine – now it was filled with drinking water. For hours, it must have been hours, Nikolai watched the dark window that looked upon the midnight yard. He could not see through it, for the lack of light and the violent rain, so he watched the vulgar water drops streak across the window pane.

"The way those dark drops run over the glass," he uttered sorrowfully, "...one would say they are worms squirming in the sod. One would say they are worms slithering to find the surface of the dark earth."

CHAPTER XI

When Nikolai finally heard Nadja coming in through the front door downstairs at half-past four in the morning, he leapt up from her bed where he had been lying awake in waiting, and he ran to the banister. Nadja froze by the door and trembled. She was drenched from the rain. Her hair was wet and lay draped heavy on her shoulders. Her lips were swollen and damp. The hem of her dress was torn. The residues of dirty water formed blotches on her forehead.

"Where did you go, Nadja?" Nikolai asked firmly. His voice was angry.

"Just for a walk," she answered listlessly. She then passed her lover on the stairs in silent indifference.

"A walk for the entire night? You were by yourself?!"

"I don't know, Nishka," she said. And with these words, she drifted away like wet linen. Trembling, Nikolai seized her shoulders and stopped her. She looked closely at him.

"Why is it, you say you are going home, you send me to get a book, and when I come to find you, you are gone? You are gone the entire night! It is nearly dawn! What am I supposed to think?!"

"I just went for a walk, Nishka. Don't worry, I was by myself."

"But you could have said something! Why did you leave on your own like that?"

"Sometimes your Nadja is a bit wooden, Nishka. I am a little bit made out of wood."

CHAPTER XII

There were things he would always remember about Nadja. The way her lips were swollen in the morning when she woke up. The way her mouth pouted as she sat drinking tiredly from her cup of morning coffee. The way he would leave the bed where they'd slept to wash and shave and begin the day, and come back thinking she would be awake and dressing, only to find her wrapped in the blanket, sleeping like a stone. In the beginning, she drank tea in the morning. He taught her the pleasures of coffee. She now preferred coffee, just as he preferred sweet pomegranate wine. There were many things they taught each other, and many things he would remember about her. When, on this day, she awoke again with swollen lips, she quickly turned them inwards to shade them from the sun coming through the window. It was midday now and the rains from the night before had stopped and the sky was a light crystalline blue. The air was humid.

Nikolai awoke the first. He was happy to find Nadja cradled near him, her head draped over his naked arm. This short-lasting joy was replaced, however, by a hollow feeling in his stomach when he recalled the events of the night before.

Leaving her to sleep, Nikolai stood and walked out onto the

terrace. The sounds of birds came from the over-reaching trees. He could tell by how hot the stones were on his feet that it was now mid-afternoon.

Nadja was somehow distant on their walks that day in the garden. Nikolai offered to prepare food to take down by the canals for a picnic, but Nadja wasn't hungry and didn't feel like going into town. In the garden, the two sat out the afternoon on a blanket near a grove of plum trees. Nikolai tried to make Nadja smile, but in his failing, he resorted to melancholic plucks of the grass blades near his feet. He told her he brought the book from his room. "The one you'd asked for," he said, "I'll read it to you when you want." She had to be reminded as to which book it was he was talking about.

"The story of constellations?" she asked him.

"No, remember you didn't want the constellations. You wanted a story of the earth. You also wanted a hero. This one speaks of the earth, and this one has a hero."

"What kind of hero?" she asked. Her blank expression here gave way to a small smile. This was the first time she'd smiled all day; and seeing this, the emptiness left Nikolai for a time, and he felt good again. When Nadja smiled, Nikolai smiled and he stroked her cheek with his finger. She lowered her eyes so as not to look at him.

Nikolai?" she began, using his formal name.

"Yes, Nadja? What is the matter?" Why was she speaking like this?

"I was at the bridge last night and I was thinking…"

"What!"

"What, what?"

"Why were you at the bridge?" This greatly upset Nikolai.

"Nevermind, Nishka. You know, I went to the bridge and I remember before I got there I was thinking about that Tsar story. It made me wonder."

'Inconsequential,' he thought. "What did you wonder?"

"Can I ask you a question about Russia?" she asked him.

"I've never been to Russia."

"Well then a question about the world."

"Yes, of course, my Nadiushka. What is it?"

"Maybe it will sound silly," she told him, "but perhaps everything depends on it…"

"How, everything?"

"Well, Nishka, tell me honest and true . . . if you were this False Dmitry the brigand character, and you found the Tsar's crown in a hut, would you go with it to Moscow?"

"Ah!" Nikolai laughed goodheartedly, seeing this topic as delightfully trivial. "Nadja," he said, "if I were Russian, I certainly wouldn't be a brigand. I would rather be a droshky driver. Or a pamphleteer even. It's so much more romantic!"

"Romantic? No, not a driver, let's say you were a brigand. Would you take the crown to Russia and pretend to be the Tsar. Tell me true!"

"That depends, Nadja, where would you be?"

Nadja considered this question a moment, obviously wondering how to answer in such a way that wouldn't spoil the point of her questioning…

"Let's say I'm at our home waiting for you in a little hut in the east."

"Well then I wouldn't go *west* to Moscow, I'd bring the jeweled crown of the Tsar to my little Nadja waiting at home in the *east*! . . . I'd bring it as a present!"

"'That's not right!" Nadja shook her head and then dropped it as if everything had been spoiled. "Anyway," she went on, "a brigand wouldn't have a little Nadja at home waiting for him. So let's say I wasn't anywhere. Let's say you were all alone in the world, what would you do with the crown?"

"You wouldn't be anywhere? You would have to be somewhere!" he protested, "What I would do with the crown depends on where you would be. Yes, after all, it depends on where you would be!"

To this, Nadja smiled. She sat up high on her knees on the blanket in the grass and pressed Nikolai's hands as if reassured. "Okay, Nishka... let's say I am somewhere. Let's say I'm a noble lady who lives in the Tsar's palace in Moscow. What would you do with the crown? Would you ride to Moscow and assassinate the Tsar just like in the story?"

"Of course not, Nadja. I would give it back."

"What?!" Nadja exclaimed with rage, "You would give it back!" With this, she pulled her hands away from Nikolai and turned away. After a wrathful expulsion of air, she turned back around and looked at him.

"But don't look at me like that!"

"Why would you give it back? You would ride to Moscow and give it back?!"

"Listen Nadja," Nikolai said, settling on her arm, "Imagine if I were to ride into the Tsar's palace to return the jeweled crown the Tsar had lost in Siberia. I would be a hero! The Tsar would make a nobleman of me, award me with a title. There would be banquets in my honor. He most certainly would give me a room in the palace as a reward for my deed – and money too! Then finally, as I would be in the palace, I would court you and we would be married – certainly you wouldn't refuse me, being such a hero and all, having returned the Tsar's crown!"

Nadja seemed perplexed. She sat lifelessly. "Give it back..." she mumbled faintly, "Give it back..." she said this with a voice empty of all hope, void of all passion. These phrases carried neither the upsweep of interrogation nor the force of exclamation. "Give it back..." her voice trailed away.

"Well?" Nikolai asked, "Is that not right?"

"Listen, Nishkushka," she said as though she were speaking to a child, "If you were to give the crown back, of course you would get money and a place in the palace and people in Russia would read about you in the paper and for a week or two you would be a hero to some people . . . But if you were to *kill* the Tsar and pretend you were him, then you would be *The Tsar Himself!*" Nadja seemed confused as to why Nikolai didn't think this was a better solution. "Wouldn't you want to be the Tsar instead of some little tiny man who fetches the Tsar's crown?"

"I would just want to be with you, Nadja. Not to be the Tsar. And if we were both in the same palace, we could be together."

Nadja's eyes then lit up with a new idea...

"Well! . . . What if I wasn't just some noble lady in the palace? What if I were the *wife* of the Tsar? . . . Well? What then!" She was obviously happy with her new discovery. "...Then you couldn't be with me unless you killed the Tsar and pretended to be him. That way, you could be with me, but not otherwise!"

"Yes, but, Nadja, you wouldn't be tricked into being the lover of your husband's killer. Nevertheless, if you were the Tsar's wife, I would court you quietly and we would meet in secret in the palace gardens, we would have a little trysting bench there, and then you would leave the Tsar and marry me. That would be the more romantic way to do things!"

"Again with your romance! You cannot be serious! I wouldn't meet you on your stupid bench! A Tsar's wife cannot leave the Tsar! He's The Tsar!" Nadja seemed thoroughly disappointed with this whole affair. Nikolai abandoned the conversation as he really didn't understand how he could meet with approval.

I, who was a witness to this whole scene from where I went unnoticed standing in my grove of plum trees, laughed to myself... "Foolish and simple Nikolai!" I roared with delight. Still at my task, I picked a hard, green, firmly unripe plum from a low branch, and I hurled it between the trees at the two of them and it struck Nadja's naked toe.

"Aye!" she cried, jerking her foot back. She looked around herself in the garden yet she saw me not. She saw nothing.

"What is it?" Nikolai asked her. Nadja didn't respond but sat up inspecting her foot.

"A bee sting?" he asked. His words drifted out faintly and were muffled into silence beneath the clusters of fruited leaves in the high bows that shook with the warm wind that blew.

"Nadja?" he asked. But she didn't respond. She was long from him. "Do you want to go to the canals? We could spread a blanket and eat cheese and drink wine." Again she didn't respond, but just sat there in the grass looking at her toe. Finally, she looked at Nikolai and said...

"I guess I need to start getting ready. I need to buy some things. I need a new nightgown, and some other things in town . . . maybe I won't go to the canals with you today, Nishka." There was no unease in her voice, only distance. In Nikolai's own voice, there was an expression of hollow fear.

Later that evening, Nadja bathed; and while she was alone, Nikolai cooked. The air outside was still and the evening was warm and Nikolai left the large glass doors open while he worked in the kitchen. He prepared creamed breads and flour-dusted fruits with spices and oils. He lit ready-wicked candles that offered prosperous light, and he delivered all of this to a table laid with a complacent charm that made Nadja smile; though she remained cold and pensive while the two started to eat. As Nadja began to drink wine, however, her affections lost in the strangeness of that late spring day returned, and she finally dropped her shoulders and pressed Nikolai's hand and thanked him for cooking and the two kissed and were silent while the only sounds came from palm branches rustling in the warm winds that came and went and came again.

After dinner, Nikolai went to take another bottle from the kitchen. Nadja said she didn't want any more wine. He poured himself another glass and asked if he could fix the bee sting she'd received on her foot that day in the garden. She said it wasn't a bee sting and reminded him that he was going to read the story from the book he had brought from his room in town. With brightened spirits, Nikolai fervently set about preparing a place on the terrace for the reading. He fetched a tray of candles and returned to find Nadja on the cushions on the terrace. She had drifted asleep. Nikolai woke her up to ask why she had fallen asleep. Did she not want to hear the story? No, it wasn't that. She had simply been tired. She was awake now. No, she wouldn't go back to sleep. Now she was listening.

"Nadja?" he asked her with unease, "Are you happy to be with me? . . . to have me here?"

"Of course I am, Nishka," she said, clasping his arm and pulling him towards where she lay in the nest of pillows on the terrace. He reclined against her chest, her breasts touched warmly his arm.

"And you want me to read you this story?"

"But Nishka!" she said, "I have been waiting for this story!"

Nikolai smiled at this and kissed Nadja on the forehead. By the light of the candles set behind them, he began to read…

CHAPTER XIII

"The Myth of Helonius"
(as read by Nikolai)

The ages tell and will always tell of the great Helonius, singular youth, who set off from his home with courage in his heart, and braved the perils of battle in distant lands for the love of heroic glory. It all began when his baby brother Aesop...

"Aesop!" Nadja interrupted, "what a strange name!"

"Yes, well, they were simple people."

"Go on, Nishka. I'm listening."

...It began when his baby brother Aesop was stolen by giants. There were giants on the earth in those days — men of immense stature who dwelt in the eastern, hilly, untamed lands. Helonius and Aesop were born of the west, where fields of gentle crops grew in copper hues, baked by the sun. Between the east and the west, there were canyons. There were lowlands, golden with wheat like honeyed earth, and from these fields grew black spindly trees.

Now, beyond the forests and lowlands, beyond those terrifying canyons and past the fields of gentle crops, lay a little provincial village. In this village, with its little brick houses, there was a single square and cathedral tower. Nearby was a house, where lived an aged man with his two sons...

"Mmm, two sons," Nadja considered this, sitting up to pay better attention, no longer tired but happy to be hearing the story, "What were they like, these two sons?"

"Let me keep reading, Nadja!" Nikolai tugged her arm. She quieted down and he went on...

...Nearby was a house, where lived an aged man with his two sons. The eldest was grown and already had a dark down of hair beneath his navel and on his chin. This was the brave Helonius, hero of the tale. The younger brother was a tiny boy, just learnt to walk, given the name of Aesop. The father of the two was a wiry-bearded man who practiced black magic and quoted from ancient texts.

...Aesop was a feeble child who often suffered grave illnesses with bouts of fever. His father chanted prayers for his child and called upon the heavens. One day, during a bout of illness, the child fell unconscious with a violent fever and was dragged into coma. The father built an alter in the yard and there he stayed up all night summoning salvation for the lad. The father fell a tree and built a fire and prepared alchemic solutions. he drank bitter tonics and spoke to the clouds that passed before the moon. It is said that God flew down like a gyrfalcon and appeared before him in the form of a man, standing in the yard. God told the father that if he wanted his son Aesop to live, he needed to take the boy twenty versts away from the village. There he would find a freshwater spring and a stream nearby. He would then need to leave the child by the spring for twenty hours. God told him that when he would come back, the child would be well and would live many and lengthy years, and have several offspring and blessings would befall each generation to come.

...The father heeded the vision and went to carry out the task. In a blanket of cotton, his child he wrapped. Poor Aesop, deep in a coma, rested

in his father's arms. The father carried him twenty versts away from the village. There, sure enough, he came to a stream of freshwater near a spring. The father bundled his son well to guard him from exposure, he poured stream water over the boy's feverish forehead to cool him, and he placed him on the banks of the stream near the spring. He crossed himself and said a holy prayer and left.

...After twenty hours had passed, the father returned to the spring and the stream nearby. To his despair, he saw his child was gone! "Where art thou, Aesop my child?!" cried the father, as he searched the spring and the stream, "Hast thee drowned?!"

...Sick with desperate fear, the father threw himself to the wasted earth. It is said then, just as a beam of sun cracks through well-built clouds with welcome shards of light, so then a great hope passed over the face of that aged man.

"He hath not drowned! He hath come to feel better! Lord!" cried the father in revelation, "He hath been cured, as saith the prophecy, and in wellness started off on foot for our home in the village. My son hath been led back by an angel, thus took a different route so our ways ne'er crossed."

...This, the father's hope, did not last, however. Despair came to the banks of the stream when he saw a horrible sight: an old black-hooded woman appeared at the stream carrying a bucket with which to fill with stream water to take back to her nearby hut to water her animals. When the old woman saw the father kneeling by her stream, she shook her boney finger and cackled at him...

"Your child has been stolen!"

"What speakest thou, old woman?!"

...The black-hooded witch then answered him in morbid words... "You are the father of that little youngling, that sleeping boy! That was your child, was it not? I will tell you, man. He was taken, robbed by bandits!"

...All the while she was cackling this, her hands were busy at work: one, pulling her black shawl around her body; the other, dipping the bucket in the stream to fill with water.

...The old black-shawled woman went on to tell him that some men had come. Hefty men, mighty of stature, hailing from the east; these men

were dwellers of a fortified city built on seven hills, overlooking a harbor and a sea...

"Like ours?" Nadja interrupted. She was excited by this detail, "Our city is built on seven hills! Our city is fortified and overlooks a harbor and a sea!

"Yes, Nadja, just like our city, but whoever first copied down this myth surely had never heard of our city. Many cities are built on seven hills. Can I go on?"

"Yes! Yes!" Nadja pulled tightly to Nikolai's arm, and listened as he retook to reading...

...*These men were dwellers of a fortified city built on seven hills, overlooking a harbor and a sea, in a region where all the humans were immense in height and physical strength, built like demi-gods. The origin of these half-men, half-gods, was revealed, the black-shrouded woman claimed, when they committed an act of hubris by bragging about their purpose: it was to return the infant to this hilltop city in the east, wherefrom they hailed. There, they'd claimed, they would cut him into pieces, cook his flesh and eat his roasted limbs...*

"Aye!" Nadja gasped, "Roasting limbs!"

Nikolai continued...

...*Upon these words of the old black-hooded woman, Aesop's father was struck with fury. A sound like thunder poured from his chest. He leapt and tried to strangle the old woman and throw her body in the stream, but before he could grab her, she was gone in a puff of smoke!*

...*Now the woman was gone and it was just Aesop's father standing by the empty hut, by the empty stream; all the while, his beloved son Aesop was gone. Deep in despair, crushed and defeated by the cruel heavens, the old father of Aesop turned and walked the twenty versts of misery back to his village home. And when he arrived, he fell into a long and sorrowful mourning...*

"What happens next?" asked Nadja.

"I'm reading..."

...Now, Helonius, the eldest son, who was built of brave bones between which flowed heroic blood, told his father he would go find his little brother Aesop in the city of the giants in the east, and bring him back alive and well. Helonius had a hero's glint in his eye as he imagined the odyssey he would take...

"Wait!" Nadja interrupted again, "What kind of young man was this Helonius? I like him."

"Nadja, I'm in the middle of telling you! Do you want me to finish?"

"Of course you need to finish! I just want to know what he looked like, Helonius. And how old was he?"

"I don't know. But it said he had hair on his chin, so he was at least a teenager. Maybe he was older though if he was strong enough to travel and fight. Maybe he was twenty-five. Maybe older, who knows?"

"Mmm," Nadja bowed her head.

"Why?"

"It all just reminds me of this boy I once met when I was traveling once with my mother."

To this, Nikolai frowned and shut the book. "How can he remind you of anyone, Nadja? I haven't even said anything about him yet!"

"Don't be mad, Nishka. It was just that 'hero's glint' you mentioned. It reminds me of a boy I met who lived between here and the West Islands. He too lived in a village like in this story, a village with just one square and one cathedral. And there were fields nearby, honey-colored fields with black spindly trees. He was very dear..."

"Nadja!" Nikolai growled, "I'm not going to read you any more of this story..."

"Nishko!" Nadja squeezed his arm, then drew off to say, "I'm sorry if I'm making you jealous. Don't be! I was just a girl then. Sorry, Nishkoo. I'll stop." Though she kept going... "It just reminds me of a time years ago . . . you have to listen to my story! . . . I was traveling with my mother to see my father in the West Islands . . . Why are you frowning? Don't you want to hear about my life?! . . . Okay, thank you. I'll go on...

"I was just a girl, a silly little girl . . . barely a woman . . . well, a very young woman. And I met a boy who also wanted to travel to the east to be a hero. Nikolai! But don't be jealous! Certainly that boy was no Helonius! He wasn't heroic like a man, he was more like a brother to me. He was the same height as me even! They were all short in that village. Maybe he was one centimeter taller, but that was all. They were so short there! Anyway, he had a way about him that I knew one day he'd be heroic."

Nikolai was not impressed, but Nadja went on. She explained their meeting:

It happened while the young Nadja was in her late teens. She was traveling with her mother to meet her father in the West Islands where he was waiting for them. It was summer. Nadja was on vacation from school. She remembered those fields with the smell of ambrosia, and how bright and yellow they were – and how dark were the leafless trees! The two women stopped over for lunch in a little village halfway between the Minor City and the West Islands. They had eaten a strange salad, and after the meal the mother started feeling ill. She decided she couldn't travel on right away and needed to spend some time in bed.

Young Nadja and her mother took the largest room in the hotel near the cathedral overlooking the square. The mother had been helped to the room by the concierge, and Nadja was left to bring the suitcases up. Little Nadja was terribly upset that there were no porters to help carry the luggage. It was then, while standing in the square in front of the hotel, that she met a boy her own age who lived in the village. Nadja recalled the moment...

"I looked at him and I said, 'Hey, boy! What kind of place do you live in? Your village hotel doesn't even have porters! Can't you get off your silly stone and help a young lady with her luggage?' . . . I guess I was a little brat," she smiled.

The boy she was yelling at was to become her companion. The two of them were to wander around together for all the while her mother was resting and getting well. Nikolai asked Nadja what the boy's name was and Nadja claimed she could no longer remember; though at the time, she spent every hour of every day with him, several days at that. Meanwhile, her mother's illness had turned for the worse. In addition to the food-poisoning, the poor lady caught a chill and was bedridden with fever in that hotel room for nearly a week. During all of that week, the boy never did learn Nadja's real name, as she told him it was something other than Nadja. "It was all like a game," she explained to Nikolai, "An innocent game. I was young and was traveling and it seemed a romantic life, so I invented a persona to make it even more romantic. No one in that little village knew me and my mother was too ill to talk to people to spoil things, so I was free to tell people whatever I wanted. I remember I made up some name that sounded majestic and romantic, and I told the boy that was who I was..."

Nikolai frowned.

"Not to be naughty," she said, "just for the romance. The name Nadja sounded so common. I wanted a name like a queen. I wanted to be greater than I was, more mysterious..."

She told Nikolai that the two took innocent walks together out to the fields surrounding the village. They spent the afternoons lying on a blanket, darkening their faces in the sun and telling stories about their separate lives. Nadja recalled that she'd discovered that the boy had an older brother whom he didn't want to run into in town, for fear that he'd be made fun of.

"You see?" she laughed, "He was such a boy! Still, there was something brave about him." She told Nikolai how he had told her he was a well-known adventurer. A famous adventurer, he had said; and how she had believed him. "Maybe he *was* a famous adventurer," she said, "He seemed like it, always talking of his expeditions to foreign countries..." As she told all this to Nikolai, the latter listened, listlessly resting his hands on the closed book he'd been reading from. He listened as though he didn't like the story yet still wanted to hear it, as if some revelation would come from it, for good or for bad.

Nadja continued... "He promised that once he finished his business – he had some new voyage to take – he would come find me in the Minor City. He'd never been to the Minor City, though he said he'd been everywhere." Nadja recalled how he had described his adventures... "Always traveling with a blade and a string. Why those things? Why *'a blade and a string,'* I wondered? Strange things! '...I've been on every beach on Afric's shore!' he would brag, puffing his chest. Even so, he still didn't know the first thing about traveling to the Minor City. 'How does one get there?' he asked me. I told him, 'One must cross fields and canyons, saltwater lakes and forests.'"

Nadja talked again about those fields of sun-cooked honey with black spindly trees growing up to the blue sky. She had told him how the Minor City had a harbor. She described the medieval walls that fortified it; and how, nowadays, giant ships of steel passed from the harbor into the inlet and disappeared in the sea. In the center of the city, she had said, one can have anything . . . fine meals, and there are shops where one can buy everything there is! . . . That was fine! the boy had told her, he knew of such places! He'd visited all kinds of large cities and foreign towns! "'So when will you come to the Minor City?' I asked him.

"'I'm taking off on a long and dangerous expedition,' he told me, 'A voyage that will take several years. But once it is over, if I am still alive, I will come to the Minor City to take you away.'

I laughed! I told him I would wait for him for seven years, and then I would find some other adventurer to marry if he didn't come."

"And has it been seven years?" Nikolai asked gloomily.

"Oh..." Nadja stopped to consider, "No, not seven. I think

about five . . . yes, it's been five years!" Then she burst into blithe laughter, "But, Nishka! Anyway, can you imagine a man traveling to meet a silly girl from his boyhood? It was just a game!

"...Still, he was sweet. He was so shy when we spent those afternoons on the blanket in the fields. I would have let him kiss me but he didn't try. Still, he was . . . But stop, Nishka! Why do you make that face! . . . Okay, I won't say things like that. I'm sorry I did. Anyway, as expected, the day came when my mother was well again and it was time to continue on to the West Islands to see my father. It was a sad time for the boy and me . . . Okay, Nishka! I just want to tell you one last thing because it was so meaningful to me then...

"...We were walking together back from the fields where we'd been lying. He was carrying the picnic blanket under his arm. He knew my mother was feeling better and I had to leave his village. He looked so sad. Me too, I think. Anyway, he helped carry our luggage to the edge of the square, and I went behind the cathedral to say goodbye to him. 'Hurry!' I said, 'My mother is waiting for me by the edge of the square!' It was then he leaned to kiss me on the mouth, but he missed my mouth and just touched the corner of my mouth! Poor boy! I helped him after that, and we kissed and I felt so much more sad since he'd missed my mouth; and it was right at that moment, I knew I would miss him terribly. I said some silly things, I'm sure . . . but Nishka, stop! I was a foolish girl! . . . I said some foolish things and I said he was my brave hero and if he didn't come to find me in seven years there would be a big emptiness in my life forever after, and that he had to come or else! . . . The whole time I was fumbling with a piece of lace on my dress that had gotten torn earlier in the day when the two of us were lying on the blanket together. I don't know how it got torn! But I noticed the lace was half pulled off, and I decided to tear the piece off completely and give it to him – something to remember me by. So I did. I tore the strip of my lace from my dress and I put some of my perfume on it and I gave it to him and kissed him on the mouth and that was it. You know, I was his first love, Nishka. I was the first girl to ever kiss him, I'm sure!"

"I don't feel like reading this book anymore," Nikolai quietly said in a pathetic voice.

"Oh Nishka! I'm just telling you a story from my past that happened so long ago . . . from when I was just a young girl. It might have well happened to someone else, I was so different then . . . well no, I won't say that. It was me then too. But still, please read the rest of the story!" And so she implored him to continue reading. Nikolai tried to forget Nadja's story that had injured him, and he started to read and stopped again, but now she had begun to cling to him more and more tightly. She caressed him now with more affection than she had shown the whole day previous, so soon he felt good again and happy to be with her; and so, with Nadja beside him, close and quiet, he began again to read…

…Now, Helonius, the eldest son, who was built of brave bones between which flowed heroic blood, told his father he would go find his little brother, Aesop, in the city in the east and bring him back alive and well. Helonius had a hero's glint in his eye when he spoke of…

Nikolai stopped reading.

"Why aren't you reading?"

No answer.

"But Nishka, why are you making that thing with your eyebrows?"

"I just didn't like that story you told, Nadja. Now you think the hero of the story is that boy from your past."

"But no, Nishko! That boy was so long ago, I don't even remember his name! And I'm pretty sure it wasn't Helonius…"

"But of course it wasn't Helonius!" Nikolai growled in annoyance, "Why would it have been Helonius, of all things?!'

"No, rather it was something simple," Nadja added, "Something biblical. Oh, I don't know. Let's stop talking about it. I was such a girl!"

"All right. I'm going to read."

"Okay, my Shooshka-Nishkachka!" Nadja purred as she settled in the crook of his arm to listen.

...*Helonius had a hero's glint in his eye when he spoke of the odyssey he would take to save little Aesop from the giants of the east. He approached his father who was sunk in despair in his old-fashioned chair, and he told the aged man he was leaving to find his little brother and bring him home again. The father paid no heed to his son, Helonius. So grief-stricken was he that he simply remained in his chair where he shuddered with sadness. But Helonius was not to be discouraged. He set off anyway with great bravery in his heart. He traveled a long distance and experienced many strange adventures on the way. Many were the adventures in the little villages where he stopped to take respite. Finally then, after many weeks of travel, Helonius came to...*

"But, wait!" interrupted Nadja, "It's not going to tell what kind of strange adventures he experienced in the villages?"

"No," Nikolai answered dryly, "This is an old tale. Quixotic literature didn't come until later."

"I'm not sure I understand."

"No, I see that you don't," Nikolai said, "No one knows who originally wrote this story or why, but it was probably a man who wrote it for a woman – and so he skipped the adventures and went right to the point."

"Oh," said Nadja.

"As I was reading..."

...*After many weeks of travel, Helonius came to a great fortified city in the east, built on a harbor near the sea...*

"Like ours!" Nadja interrupted again.

"Nadja!" growled Nikolai, "As I was saying..."

...In this eastern city lived a people of immense stature. When Helonius arrived in the city, he found he was more than a head shorter than every man and no taller than any of the women. But Helonius had bravery in his heart, and so he searched this little hilltop city without fear of killers or thieves. Around nightfall, he found his brother. The prophecy, it appeared, had been correct. The brother was alive and conscious. But he was locked in a cage awaiting to be cooked for a midnight feast. Helonius hid himself in the nearby hillside and looked on at the giant men guarding the cage. They were picking their teeth with goose quills and discussing the feast that was to take place. Aesop, they were saying, was to be roasted and eaten, his limbs cooked and torn from his body, the inward parts tasted. Helonius waited in the hillside until when, in the dark of night, the men opened the cage to lead their prisoner to the cooking pits. It was then, when the cage was opened, Helonius sprung from the hill, and flung two swift stones which struck the giants in their throats. In one heroic dive, he swiped his tiny brother from the cage and returned to the hill where he hid him in a discreet nook. His brother being safe, he then climbed down and finished killing the two guards, as well as the men gathered by the cooking pits. All of their bodies, he tossed angrily off the cliffs. He fought many men. He fought with stones, with bare hands and with sticks, which he tore from the soil. All of these giants he killed. All he flung with great agility from the tops of the cliffs. He spared no man, all were slain. After, taking his brother from the recess in the hill, he carried him in his arms into the heart of the city. There he looked for the most beautiful girl to take with him to be his bride. He found a beauty that was very short for a woman of this region — measuring exactly the same height as him. She was magnificent in her beauty. Helonius took his new bride and his little brother and the three traveled west through the canyons and fields.

...When Helonius returned to his village with his new bride and little brother, his father was almost dead with grief. Seeing his eldest son return with his other son in his arms was his salvation. Happy tears tumbled from his face. The way water spills over a mountain ridge when the snow melts in the springtime, so spilled his eyes with joyful tears.

...So in the end, the village took Helonius to be the greatest hero who had ever lived. His new wife was the most beautiful girl anyone in the village had ever seen. And Helonius lived happily with his wife and father and brother. The brother Aesop grew up to be a great poet and Helonius became king of the country and his beautiful wife ruled as queen.

Nikolai closed the book.

"Oh, it is so beautiful, this story!" Nadja cheered.

"It's not beautiful," Nikolai frowned, "It's schmaltz! The whole thing's poorly written, and the ending is ridiculous . . . king and queen! . . . blah!"

"Why do have to ruin something beautiful, Nikolai? There's a reason this story is still around after all these centuries. It is beautiful. All of it is beautiful. Except there were some very gruesome parts . . . the part where they said Aesop would be roasted and his limbs torn and eaten by the giants."

"That's the only part I like," said Nikolai, "But you must admit it ends poorly . . . the beautiful bride who reigns as queen of the village?"

"Nikolai," Nadja addressed her lover thus, pulling away slightly, "Do you remember back at the start of spring, when we began to meet? Back then you would have liked a romantic story like this one."

Nikolai said nothing. He tried to kiss Nadja in the faint darkness. She did not bring her lips to his, but looked away with half closed eyes. She looked up into the night. The night was lit by tiny stars which punctured the thin membrane of sky. Her lips were full of dreams, her eyes were for the heavens. Nikolai mumbled ruefully to her, almost unaware that he was speaking... "Our lips," he said, "are full of stories. Our eyes are for the past." Yet, Nadja heard nothing, for she was already asleep.

CHAPTER XIV

"The Summer Solstice"

The season of spring had folded fast, now the nights were hot at last. Summer, alone, watched its first day, while the two lovers, together, saw their first summer night. The strange and unhappy distances that had separated them only days before were gone. The two had repaired themselves. Now again they were close in their walks in the garden. Now again they were close in their place on the terrace. The garden was agreeable in the mildness of morning, though the afternoon was often too hot to stay on the lawn or linger on the paths of the rose garden. On the terrace, the couple ate fruit with ice and wine and rested beneath the shade of the palm branches. In the night, the brittle pods and browned leaves crackled – not with the swaying wind, for there was none; but with an air that was dry and thirsty. That first night of summer, Nadja turned to Nikolai as the two lay outstretched on the terrace beneath the dark purple sky and she asked him, "If you…" and stopped.

"If I what?" he asked her, heeding the worry in her voice.

"Nishka? . . . Do you think people can only be in love in the springtime?"

"Not at all," he replied, pulling her in close, "The summer is a perfect time to be in love."

"But Nishka, it is strange. Something changes with the thoughts in summer. It is an all together different time than the spring."

"How so different?"

"I don't know 'how so,' maybe nothing." Nadja turned away. Then she looked back and told him she did not feel the same as in spring because she did not feel young in the summer. She mused on the idea that the only kind of love one should have is spring love.

"But we have spring love, Nadja. Even in the autumn we will have spring love."

She was not at all reassured by his words.

"I don't know," she said, "I guess sometimes your Nadja is a little wooden."

"What do you mean, wooden?"

"I guess I am made out of wood."

The two lay silent a moment, outstretched on the light bedding on the terrace. The cotton quilts of early spring had been discarded in favor of summery muslin sheets. In the darkness, Nikolai listened to Nadja's irregular breathing as he himself grew tired. It was late in the night. While his arms were wrapped around Nadja, that he felt her unclasping them so she could get up.

"Where are you going?" he asked her shadow.

"Just away for a minute. I'll come right back."

He waited for her on the empty terrace, trying not to wait. Fortunate sleep came without his knowing. Nadja was still gone when he awoke again.

Downstairs, a beam of silver moonlight cast through the open glass door leading out to the garden and fell across the surface of the table by the sofa, which Nikolai passed looking for Nadja. She was neither in the house, nor in the empty yard. "Goodbye, Nadja," he mumbled solemnly, silently, not knowing what he could or should do. "Goodbye,

Nadja," he said and returned to the terrace and fell back asleep alone.

In the blue hour before dawn, Nikolai woke to feel her anew – her damp skin against him. She had returned from her voyage and he was happy and he pulled her in tight and felt the joy in his breast.

"Where did you go?" he asked her, pressing his heavy eyelids to her shoulders.

"Mmm," was all she said.

Nikolai crooked his neck to look up at the sky to judge its quality. It looked as though the aurora was seeping in over the trees.

"I walked down to Otchajanie," she told him, "to the bridge."

To this, Nikolai opened his eyes wide. Had she gone all the way there? And alone? In the middle of the night?

"You know, Nishka! The heavens were there! And there was so much blackness! I could tell you of the blackness..." A strange tone was in her voice.

"It is dangerous at the Otchajanie Bridge at night, Nadja. Even in the day! But you know this, Nadja . . . You know this!"

"I know this, Nishka . . . but I wanted to see the heavens."

"There are thieves in the alleys around that bridge. You are lucky you weren't hurt!"

"But you go there sometimes."

"Yes, but I was raised in that neighborhood. I know which parts of it to avoid at night. Anyway, I am a man..."

"I want to be a man," Nadja said. She paused after and added, "No, I don't. I want to be a woman. Still, Nishka, nothing would have happened to me there..."

"But you don't understand, Nadja, something would've happened to you. That's what you don't understand."

"But Nishka! Nothing would have happened to me there. You wouldn't have let any harm come to me!"

"How would I know if someone is harming you if I don't even know where you are? Next time you go to the Otchajanie Bridge in the middle of the night, tell me first so I can make sure nothing harms you there."

"I'll try, Nishka. I cannot promise, but I'll try. I'll really try."

CHAPTER XV

As a summer mist of sweat gathered on her sleeping forehead, Nadja's nocturnal words passed inaudibly over her trembling lips, telling the stories of sleep. Her eyes were full of darkness and her lips were full of dreams.

Nikolai lay often awake watching her on those first nights of summer, feeling the imprint of time pushing folds into his own weary face. While her lips were full of dreams, his eyes were for the passage of time to remain with them, there, in that far secluded place that was soon to leave them.

When the two would make love, Nadja would not move. She lay like stone, outstretched like a long, drawn bow, ready to receive the passing flèche, letting it skiff across the hard bones of her hips. She would not move in the heat, but lay silently there to receive him. He fell upon her with joy, pouncing the way a child's cat pounces on a pile of streamers; and after he was done, he spoke and tried to have her speak, but she would not respond. He would ask her this and that as he caressed her supple skin; as he caressed her taught belly and resting breasts, rising and falling with uneven breaths; still, she would not answer his requests.

Eventually she crooned his name, "Nishka."

"Yes, my Nadja."

She did not answer, but muttered again, "Nishka." And again, "Nishka, Nishka," ...quicker now as though coming to him from a faraway dream.

"What is it, Nadiushka?"

Pause.

"Don't touch me," she said.

A sorrowful stretch of time passed.

"Do you want to be alone?"

"Yes."

"I will leave then," Nikolai said, getting up.

"Stay with me until I sleep and then go back to your room in the city."

Supple-limbed Nikolai replied not a word but lay back down beside her and let his forearm rest against the warm mound of her nightshirt, he did not come closer. He listened to her sleep and in his grief he could not sleep, nor did he want to; for in sleep he would have been even farther away from her. At one point, he breathed her name loudly into her ear and listened. She did not answer, though her breathing slowed down.

"Nadja," he repeated.

"Mmm . . . What?" she breathed.

"Do you want me to sleep here?"

Silence.

"I'll go back home to my room and you can be alone here."

Again she didn't respond, yet when he got up from the bed she jerked suddenly and turned to him in the darkness and said, "Wait! . . . Please, Nishko!" Then, "...Let's go downstairs together. It is so dark this room! And there are strange noises coming from out on the terrace!

95

"...Go downstairs and wait for me, Nishka. I will change first. Let me be alone to change."

Outside the large pane of colonial glass, the shapes of the trees swayed black against a sky the color of coal smoke. The summer trees ruffled up and sank themselves down again with the passing gusts of wind. Nikolai tapped at the surface of a large sandglass on the living room table. Meanwhile, he studied a crystal cruet placed neatly in the center. Thoughts passed quick and left him bewildered, letting him wrestle with the reasons as to why Nadja was different now. She had become strange. 'What if she is insane?' he wondered. He pushed the sandglass away from him, taking one of his books from the table. It was a leather-bound book with a black cover. A thought flashed through his mind. He though to clutch that book tightly and run away with it into the night. It was a silly thought. "Why do I care about a book?" he asked himself, "To hell with books!" He flung the book back on the table and turned his eyes to the banister where he noticed Nadja descending the stairs, dressed in unfamiliar clothes.

She sat herself on the same sofa as Nikolai, but kept well away and didn't move for a long time. She just kept seated, staring straight ahead. Outside the open window, the limbs of the trees rubbed together like the brittle legs of crickets. Nadja watched them through the glass. Nikolai turned to her, but she kept her eyes fastened to the night. Time passed and a cool damp wind came through the open window. With it, came a thin and bluish light, creeping as a shadow does to absorb the darkness in the dim room. It was a hollow, blae-black, and misty, ominous light. Nadja turned suddenly away from the window. She tore her eyes from the window and looked at the table where sat the cruet and the book. Her eyes grew wide with alarm. As she caught sight of Nikolai's book on the table, she turned to him and demanded...

"Nikolai!"

"Yes?"

"What is that book?!"

He didn't answer.

"What is that book, Nikolai, with the black cover?!" This she demanded louder now, with urgency.

Again, he didn't answer.

"Nikolai, tell me! What is that book with the black cover?! That thick, black book!"

"Why do you call me Nikolai all of a sudden?"

"Please!..." she turned to him imploringly, now, "Nishka . . . Tell me what that book is, please..."

Nikolai leaned slowly forward and took the book from the table. He opened it, creasing over the light onionskin pages.

"It's an ancient text," he told her, "A religious scripture. One that never made it into the canon of the bible. It's a story that speaks of God's lament for having created time. Do you want me to read a little?" Nikolai looked up to see if Nadja was listening, which she was. He then began to read from the book...

> *And so God went forth and created time. God created time so that the closed buds on vernal trees would bloom and yield petals as glorious as mortal skin. He created time so that fruits would ripen and moisten and be fleshy and sweet to the tongue. He created time to make iron from the pale limbs of youths, to make wetness of dry groins, and hips like fertile kettles from the fragile strands of maids. He created time so that the breathless glimpse of desire would lead unto the breathy fulfillment of that desire. But then he saw that time would destroy in turn the beauty he'd created. He saw it would wither the sweet golden age among his vernal groves; and for this he lamented his creation. God dropped tears for the time he had made, and was torn by the scythe of despair.*

Nikolai stopped reading. He looked up and saw Nadja seated, unmoving. "Should I continue reading, Nadja?" he asked her, "Should I go on?"

"No, Nishka, stop!"

"I will keep reading."

"No, stop!" she cried, "It is so dark this book you are reading! It is so dark this book! And its cover too!"

Nadja kept trembling. And terror-faced, she spoke thus unto him... "Look outside, Nishka! Look how dark it is out there!" Her eyes held tight to the window, "Just look outside! . . . No stop, Nishka! Quit now!" She then inhaled and exhaled and her chest rose high and fell and she stopped. She paused and then added more calmly, slowly...

"No. Don't read now, Nishka. It is very late."

"But it isn't late," Nikolai replied, looking out of the window, "It isn't late, Nadja. It is early morning. Dawn has broken."

CHAPTER XVI

That morning, heavy clouds swelled with damp light. After what would have been the sunrise, had there been a sun to rise, Nadja turned to Nikolai where the two were seated on the sofa and said, "Nikolai, I'm going to bed now. Go back to your room in the city, please."

Hearing these cold words issued from Nadja's lips, Nikolai took his book from the table and stood to leave. He looked once down at her where she sat, unmoving, but she did not meet his glance. After a silent moment, he turned and walked away. He went out the door and out through her garden, and walked along the ivy-strewn walls of rock, quickly now, along a brittle and dew-laden sorrowful morning.

Back in his cellar room, Nikolai fell to his wretched bed. "Goodbye again, Nadja. Thrive in your hilltop garden. Here I will let these crude blankets smother me. I'll let the tenements above fall and crush my bones . . . There is no reason to keep these blankets from smothering me!"

Nikolai's bed did not usher in sleep that morning, but kept a foul watch. Outside in the city it was a barren morning, full of clouds and steamy rain.

CHAPTER XVII

"Summer and the Final Days of June"

It showered everyday for the next few days. Sultry rains swept the city, over the wet hills in the distance, over the sea. In my wanton strides, I found her one morning. She was sitting on the edge of the Otchajanie Bridge, feet dangling over. Slow blasts of foghorns bellowed in the distance from the vessels of ships that passed their heavy bellies through the steel waters of the great harbor beneath us. She wore her thin grey rain jacket, its hood pulled up over her head. As she sat thinking or looking out, her eyes passed from the abyss of water beneath to the distant shoreline.

Speak now of that sandy golden strip of shore that appeared this day as iron ore. The grey mineral sands stretched sadly beneath the steel supports of the Otchajanie Bridge. I passed where she was sitting, walking quickly, as if I were just another ordinary citizen tramping along in the rain. It was after I passed, when I turned around to look at her, that she saw me. Her eyes flashed and I read fear in them. I gazed down at the harbor below and mused to myself... How far it would be to fall from this bridge, gentle girl! All the while, she sat like wild game stalked in the wilderness. I remembered clearly our last conversation, and how she'd looked at me when she realized exactly what events must come to pass. She had the same look of fear in her eyes then as she had now.

While I was occupied with these thoughts, the girl was making haste to stand and leave. Throwing me a cautious glance, she began walking hurriedly down the slick edge of the bridge. Of course, I followed her. All the while, I looked beyond her at the city's Lower Quarter looming in the distance. The filthy alleys of Otchajanie awaited with their hot grey clouds. As she walked, she held her jacket tight to shield herself from the rain and threw glances frequently back over her shoulder. Her strides were small and many: merely a pebble crossed with each footfall. My strides were few and long: a continent passing beneath each step. When she reached the stairwell at the foot of the bridge on the Otchajanie side, she descended and disappeared into an adjoining street that led into a dusky alleyway.

"Go on, dear one!" I laughed. Another lost doe in the forest hoping to eschew me . . . "Go on! Run and sink into the folds of the city and we will find each other upon the bridge again another day, or in the lost crowds of the marketplace – amid the filthy stalls and the odorous fish stands – another day!"

Not long after, I found Nikolai tramping along Fishmonger's Row. Though disheveled in face, he was dressed well in clothes, wearing the brown topcoat Nadja had bought for him. His path led him through the grimy warehouse streets of the Shipyard District to the foul rows of Nesretan: that singular haunt of gambling dens and ramshackle bordels where worn-out women sit in windows lazily munching prunes while younger whores giggle like children in pleated skirts on nearby steps.

Nikolai's miserable hunt for Nadja took him through Krasota – several times to the Anchises Hotel. He then went to the arboretum. In the rose garden, the rain stopped and a thin summer light dawned from the clouds. It was a light with a buttery orange hue that lit upon the pebbled path and rose bushes with a peculiarity Nikolai had not seen for a long time. It seemed like something from his youth. Not since then had he seen such a light. Observing this, his sadness momentarily dissolved. Now it was summer, he thought to himself. He was strong in years. And he had his Nadja after all.

When he reached Nadja's garden, Nikolai took the key from the top of the stone wall and entered the gate. The gardens were strangely empty of birdsongs. The residues of rain dripped from the leaves on the trees and one heard the plying apart of the wet shafts of grass on the lawn.

In the afternoon, the birds returned. New summer magpies piped on the branches beyond the rail of the terrace. There, Nikolai sat in a heap, waiting for Nadja to return. She never appeared in the garden that day, nor in the house; and finally darkness came, though late it was, as the sun's course was high and long overhead. And when night finally came it was black and pure and formidable. It followed the obese moon on its low track from the garden's edge to places yet unknown.

CHAPTER XVIII

Dawn passed copper strokes on the stone streets of the city's Lower Quarter, where I was walking, as was my custom. I had been to the Peninsula at the blue hour. I had watched the morning pass in the Upper Quarter. I'd observed the summer sun falling majestically on the harbor. Now to tell of the night before...

It was late, sometime after midnight. I'd found the girl anew at the Otchajanie Bridge. The slick railing gleamed with the light of the low moon, passing steady and swollen. She sat alone, humming a little song to herself. Her legs were pulled in tight to her chest, her knees against delicate breasts, her left cheek resting against a sacred thigh. When she heard my loud footsteps approaching on the bridge, she stopped humming, but did not grow afraid. She did not run from me. Rather, she turned to look at me and stood up calmly. She met me.

"Very nice song, little summer thrush," I laughed.

She smiled coyly and dipped her head, agreeing to go wherever I would take her.

To my wise house in the Upper Quarter, where heroic colonnades stand wrapped in summer ivy, I took that girl and laid her down, and she gave herself easily. She rose and fell before me, panting like a cat watching prey among the ferns. I slept with her wet skin upon me and woke to feel her hot breath against me.

Later, I came down the stairs with an empty burlap sack in my hands. "I'm going into the city," I said, "I will be back later in the night."

"If I want to walk, myself?" she asked timidly, "…to leave the house and the garden?"

"Take the key to the house and gate," I said, "It is the only key." And with that I was gone.

I returned late in the evening carrying the burlap sack, now filled with heavy rocks. The heedful girl was home, yes; but gate was locked. I saw her on the terrace, among the leaves of the ivy that appeared as shards of emerald and jade beneath the lanterns lit in the darkness. That brazen lamb was leaning against a fluted ivory colonnade on my gifted terrace, silently observing my homecoming. Calmly, I set a brutal hand on the latch of the gate. The sack, which was filled with ready rocks, I let hang low by my side.

"Open the gate, good girl!" I called to her. Silently, she refused. Feeble latch! I shook the gate with my free hand. Then laughing aloud, I left the entrance and began to course the perimeter of the gate around the eastside of the garden. As I walked, my burlap sack of rocks clanged against the copper bars. Feeble bars! Between them, the lush and ready fruit that grows within my garden pushed out and hung on their stems, fresh for the swift drop to the earth. I laughed again and peered through the bars at the forms among the colonnades on the terrace. The girl stood staring steadily at me now, less afraid.

"My lady!" I called with fueled words, "let me into the garden for that which is mine within!" And then, "Heed my words for that which is within the garden belongs to me!"

With soft passivity, the girl refused again. "Speak then!"

She replied by yelling across the garden that she was frightened of me on this night, and that she would now like to sleep, and should I not please leave?

From the back of the locked yard, my scythe I took; and returning then, I, to the side of the gate that led around to the front of the house, I began slashing with might at the heavy stems which grasped the lush fruit. Weighted were they, like heavy drops of lead, dripping, dripping, pushing through the copper bars. Rich red ovals of ripe fruit fell again and again to the ground as I slashed at everything growing within the garden that was pushing outwards. So the fruit fell and landed on the dark earth like garnets flung wildly upon a violet midnight shore.

When I'd finished my holy task, I emptied my sack of rocks and filled it with the fruit. I then turned and left, ignoring the girl at the colonnades. I would head to the Lower Quarter. I would visit the Otchajanie Bridge.

From the cliffs of the Upper Quarter, I could see the bridge in the distance. How gloriously it stretched across that harbor! There, on that magnificent bridge! I knew what I'd find on that bridge. I knew what I'd find, and thus I hurried... On my way, the warm summer storms began again.

CHAPTER XIX

To tell of the moment when, late at night, Nadja returned to her home...

Flimsy-eyed Nikolai awoke to a stirring downstairs and ran to the banister to see if she'd come back. "Nadja?" he called, "Is that you?"

She stood like a hooded pilgrim, wet and drooping from the rains that had come and gone. She looked now different than he had ever seen her. She was sheepish, apparently traumatized, with her head hung low.

"Are you wounded?" Nikolai asked, descending the stairs to approach her. "What have you found? What is in your hand?"

Nadja looked at Nikolai with cold indifference. In her hand, she clutched a cloth sack, tied with a string. Some objects appeared to be packed inside.

"Nadja, talk to me!" He tried to grab her arm as she passed him on the stairs. She would not answer him, however, and as she passed, he took hold of her arms and pressed her to the wall on the landing. He tried to bring her face to look at him, but she kept turned away and remained silent.

"Why won't you talk to me Nadja? What is it in the bag you are holding? What have you found?"

Nadja clutched ever more tightly the cloth sack and refused to answer. Nikolai grew fierce in words and tore the sack from her hands. "What are you hiding from me, Nadja? Show me!"

The sopping burlap cloth ripped in the struggle and the objects that had been packed inside rolled out.

Three damp pomegranates.

They rolled down the stairs and only stopped when they hit the closed front door.

When the pomegranates rapped on the door, Nadja's eyes flashed upon them with a sudden and hysterical gaze. She looked at them, but remained silent.

Nikolai took her wet wrists in his hands and urged her to speak...

"Where did you go, Nadja? Where were you all night and all day?"

In reply, she merely looked at his hands as though angry that they were gripping her wrists. He let his hands fall then, but urged her again to explain herself. She looked at him blankly, as though she didn't recognize him; she then turned and walked up the silent stairs.

"She *is* insane!" Nikolai panted in a loud voice, "Go on then!" . . . And with that, the feeble man turned and went for the front door to exit through the dark garden.

Outside, no rain fell from the sky that had became ever so clear for all its darkness, ever so known for all its vastness. On this night Nikolai would return alone to his basement room in town. He would search for no one and no one would come to find him.

CHAPTER XX

When the watery morning's peach light flushed the streets of the Lower Quarter, when the costermongers set up their daily stalls and wheeled in their foodstuffs and hummed their homespun tunes, when the summer children in short pants began throwing their idle toys from the steps in the crumbling streets, Calico the flower vendor began work dying his roses in the shop above Nikolai's cellar room. He would come to receive a message just before noon from a young lady; and, as was his fashion, he would scrawl it with his childish pencil and hobble off to the alleyway to deliver it.

Nikolai had been sleeping in sorrow since the night before. When he heard Calico's knock at the door, he was filled with a hope of the greatest kind. He opened the door to greet the flower vendor.

"Beautiful girl! Beautiful girl!" chanted Calico, hopping up and down with his foolish grin. And what hope there was! A note in Calico's hand. Nikolai thanked him, tore the letter away and began to read...

"MEET ME AT THE THIRTEENTH-HOUR, AT THE ANCHISES HOTEL."

Signed:

"Your Nadja."

So Nadja wanted to see Nikolai that very afternoon – and not an afternoon longer. What hope filled gentle-hearted Nikolai. He dashed inside to dress.

Nadja was early and waiting for him when he arrived at the hotel at one o'clock, fresh and happy, bearing no traces from the traumatic night before. She greeted him with a little tear in her eye and embraced him.

"What happened last night, Nadja?" he asked her.

She just smiled and didn't answer. He asked again and finally she said, "You know, Nishka. I'm a little bit wooden. Your Nadja is a bit wooden. But, you know this!"

He knew it, and he didn't care anymore. Let her be wooden! She was back with him now, and he didn't care to ask about her woodenness or any other questions about where she'd gone the night before, nor did she herself speak about this or offer any information – although in passing she mentioned that she'd been at the Otchajanie Bridge.

The two drank wine together, fresh wine, but only a small carafe. After, Nadja wanted to leave.

"Take me away from here," she asked him as the two walked out through the streets of Krasota. "Nishka, will you? We will walk as far east as we can, to the end of the Peninsula. Then we will take a boat and cross the ocean. We will make a home in the desert. We will have a house in the sand with pomegranate trees beneath our windows. Please, Nikolai . . . If you don't take me now, we will never do it!"

Nadja's words were fervent. But to this, soft-skinned Nikolai merely shook his supple head… "No desert, Nadja, no boat. Let's go to your house. That is where we need to go."

So saying, Nikolai drooped his hand over Nadja's arm and urged her to walk towards the Upper Quarter.

"No, Nishko!" she resisted, "We are almost to Otchajanie! Let's cross to the Peninsula. Let's find a boat!"

"No, let's go to your house."

"Not there!" Fear stole across her face, "There are too many people there!"

"But it is just us there, Nadja."

Nadja looked into Nikolai's sponge-colored eyes with her own that were icy-grey like frozen pebbles. Now all fear vanished from her face and was replaced by a new look – one of mocking disgust. "So you *are* afraid!" she said with scorn, "You are afraid to take me away from here!"

"Take you where?"

As his question drifted over her, she drew away from him like a sheet drying on string bound to a drying-pole, as it's tempted away by the wind. "I want us to leave this city," she said, "I want you to take me away from here, Nikolai, for another life, elsewhere . . . that is, if you want us to stay together..." Her glance flashed back and forth with rapidity as she said this. She was searching in his eyes; yet, as his own eyes were blank, she resembled someone looking for furniture in a clearly empty room. Finally Nikolai spoke in ardent words...

"In all seriousness, Nadja, we can talk about leaving. We can dream about it and imagine it and even pretend in our heads that we are doing it – that we are leaving the city together and running away to start a new life together . . . but in all seriousness, we cannot leave. We cannot, you see! We must stay here . . . we are bound here! So let us go to your home now." So saying, Nikolai took Nadja's arm anew, and pressed her to take backwards steps with feet that were firmly planted in the direction of Otchajanie.

"Bound here?" she asked with horror, "Why can we not leave?" She pulled her arm away from his.

"Because, Nadja... I have no money to take you away, that is why. You know the situation. I get a very small sum of money every month. It is not enough to travel on. And if I leave the Minor City, I will no longer have that money!"

"I have money," Nadja said.

"Your money," Nikolai said, "...Anyway, your money comes from your father, and he won't permit you to leave the Minor City with his money. Not with me, at least!"

"You see," Nadja said, "you *are* afraid! You are not a heroic man, Nikolai. Do you realize this? Do you realize that you are not heroic?"

"What is that to say? You are trying to say that I am..."

"...A coward!" Nadja cried out, "You are a coward!" Her words cut across her lips and shot Nikolai with a sting. They caused an unusual flush of anger to seize him. He raised his hand as if he were going to issue her a slap on her face. He brought his hand high above her head. Nadja stood still unflinching, waiting to see if Nikolai would do it. But his hand just hung there, trembling slightly, like a balloon on a feeble string. Then, finally, he dropped it. Nadja watched as his hand fell to his side. And as it fell, so did all his strength, and all their joy.

"I will forget that you called me that, Nadja," Nikolai said, meekly. "Let us go now to your house." He took her by the wrist as if to lead her away the way one leads a child.

"No!" Nadja cried, repelling him. Then, more softly... "We are not going there, Nikolai. My family is there now."

"You family is there?" What a perplexing new notion. "But I thought they weren't coming until autumn!"

To this, Nadja covered her face with cupped hands and then quickly tore them away and shouted in a new furious spree... "They're there! I'm sure they are there!"

"Please calm down," Nikolai said, trying to soothe her, pulling her into him. Nadja allowed Nikolai's grasp but fell limply towards him, uncaring. With his palm he brought her chin up, and then brought her lips to his and stole from them a kiss. There was a strange taste of metal on her breath. He kissed her again. He pulled her swollen metal-tasting mouth against his but she was gone for him. He felt her breath on his lips but she was gone. While his lips were for her breath, her eyes were full of dreams. Her eyes were full of gamey dreams, while her thoughts were for the passage of time to remain elsewhere, among others, in those remote places far gone, looked for but not found, found but never held for long.

CHAPTER XXI

Nadja eventually consented to return to her house with Nikolai. At first she walked silently beside him. When they reached the arboretum, she began to speak, and most freely. She even seemed to take delight in mocking him. It was a new pleasure…

"How could anyone love you, Nikolai?"

"I don't know, Nadja."

"You know what," she laughed, "Maybe I love Helonius."

"Helonius!" Nikolai gave a comic sigh, "But that's silly, Nadja! He's just a character!"

"Yes, but he's not afraid," she said remorsefully. Then she laughed… "Do you understand that Helonius was not afraid? He was an adventurer, while his foolish brother, that stupid Aesop, was just a poet. He was a weak little poet! A foolish dreamer! That's why he was an infant who got stolen by giants."

"That's not why he was stolen by giants, Nadja."

"Yes, that's why, Nikolai!" Nadja laughed sardonically, putting particular emphasis on Nikolai's full first name. She then explained to him that brave Helonius had explored the world, and for that he became king. That he didn't just live only for a woman, that he lived for...

"Are you listening? Why are you looking away?"

"Because I can't believe how seriously you're taking this, Nadja. It's a damned story!"

"But it is serious! Helonius didn't just live only for a woman. He wanted something great out of the world, apart from that . . . and for that, he was rewarded with a beautiful woman. And she loved him and admired him...

"...You know actually," she continued after a pause, "I'm jealous of her, this woman! She found a great hero. She found a hero who had a silly poet for a brother. She found a king!" All the while Nadja was speaking, Nikolai listened to her in a listless and flimsy manner, standing before her half planted to the ground, half being brushed aside by her words; he resembled a soiled and flimsy piece of trash that rests on the sidewalk and is every now and again stirred up and pushed a few inches by the upturned soles of hurried pedestrians' shoes. Nadja continued...

"Since a king strives for power, a king knows the world; therefore, he can love a woman. A poet just seeks love, but he doesn't really understand what it is. He knows only his dreams so he can't love a woman, he can only love himself. He doesn't live *in* the world, he lives...

"What? But don't make that face at me! Nishka, what I'm saying is true! The king dies among the people, the poet dies alone. Nothing. Nothing..." Nadja added no more, but finished letting out a final gasp of discontentment before sinking down to a drooping weight that seemed about ready to deflate completely and lie on the ground.

"What your saying is not true, Nadja," said flimsy Nikolai, tugging at the unresponsive sleeve of Nadja's dress. They were now walking slowly along, though gaining no more than a single pace per minute. "Listen, Nadja, I know both dreams *and* the world. And I can tell you which a person can love with. The world, I tell you, is where we are beaten. It is where our rent is collected and our teeth are pulled. It is where we wake with nausea and burn with fever. It is where people suffer and where love goes dry like dead autumn leaves. Spring, on the other hand! ... Oh, why did I say spring? I didn't mean to say spring ... Will you please just turn to look at me, Nadja? Yes, just turn your face a little. Okay, there. I promise I won't touch your chin anymore. Okay, I won't! I promise...

"So that is the ugly world, Nadja. The world is sugar drops on a plate at a fine hotel on the waterfront. The world is adultery for the sake of boredom. Poetry, or dreams, rather ... that is where love is, Nadja. Poetry is where love is. It is our nights spent on the terrace where palm branches sweep back and forth across the stones as I lie with you adoring your every breath. Don't you remember how perfect it was back in spring when we would hold each other? Dreams and poetry. Dreams and poetry are the moon coming through thin clouds over a midnight bridge as the harbor lights dance in the distance and black waves lap against the shore. Poetry are your words to me when we are together – when you wake beside me, as when you are falling asleep. Nadja, do you know how sweetly you talk to me as you fall asleep? At that time when you no longer know what you're saying. How you talk to me then, that is all dreams and poetry. There is nothing of the world in that, it is all dreams ... poetry and dreams ... two people beneath an eternal sky, and the words they offer only to each other..."

So he spoke, and she turning to him said...

"It is pretty what you say, but it is completely absurd. Anyway, Nikolai, you don't know the world as you say you do. You've never even left the Minor City. Maybe you know poetry but you don't know the world and so you can't compare the two."

With Nadja's fueled words, Nikolai recoiled as if stung by a wasp.

"Well?" she asked expectantly.

He then lashed back...

"You think I don't the world, little Nadja? This simple, little world! You think because I haven't traveled to every country like you have? You think because I've never summered in a luxurious villa in the West Islands with my rich family, or swam in salt springs, that I don't know the world? Are you really as shallow as that? I'll tell you the world I know, Nadja! My world is a cellar room in a basement with one little window of warped glass up in the corner, a window where spiders spin dirty little webs. My world is what is found down on Fishmonger's Row with the laborers slaving away and the drunks pouring liquor down their wretched throats. My world is what is found late at night in the basement bars in the Shipyard District where people gamble to buy flesh and bad wine; or in the dirty alleys Otchajanie where thieves hide in the shadows. Mine is a world that ages the flesh and turns the skin yellow with jaundice. Mine is a world of men whose eyes are punctured in the veins as they crouch in their hovels tossing dice, hoping to throw that throw which will win it all – to win the thing that can never be had and which doesn't exist, and when we each take our last breath of life it will be to ask aloud... 'Why doesn't it exist? ...And why did it never come? ...And why did we spend so much time looking for it when we could have been doing other things?' . . . What those other things are, I don't know. Who does know? No one in our company as we wander alone. Sick and alone, it makes us, this world. We throw the dice and whatever comes up makes us sick and alone. The world throws life on a pair of scales and weighs it up against a stack of filthy coins . . . And I'll tell you, sweet Nadja, the balance never stops wavering! That is what the goddamned world is, my dear Nadiushka. Poetry and dreams don't do this, can't you see? To hell with your salt springs! . . . Before I met you, my life was an actual gamble where everything was at stake! Everything! If I didn't strive in the race with the fools around me, I'd starve. Never parents to help me, like you, or a house and garden to be my sanctuary, like yours. So don't tell me I don't know the world or that I am a coward, you damned child! Do you hear me?!..."

"Nishka! Stop, Nishka!" Nadja breathed hysterically and cried, "Please! You're being so violent, Nishka. Can you stop shaking your hands like that? You are trembling!"

"There . . . Good," she said, seizing his hands, "Don't be ruined. Let's sit down a minute."

She led him to a doorway where they sat silent for a long time.

Finally Nadja spoke...

"I know these dreams you mean, Nishka." Smiling, she said no more but looked away as if she were now thinking of something that had been hidden and now revealed itself. Her eyes grew wide and became coated in a glassy texture. Nikolai, meanwhile, sat flopped in a miserable heap beside her.

"I know these dreams, Nishka," Nadja whispered, drawing out her words like thin wisps of wool. "They fall out of the moon, Nishka. They slice up the moon right in front of you. Then, you are left to watch it! I have dreamt this! You watch the moon being chopped up, and then someone comes along with a scythe and slices the moon and it bleeds and you have to watch the blood gush from it, and red seeds fall out!..."

To this new and peculiar spectacle, Nikolai pulled himself up and gave a loud laugh. It was sorrowful for a loud laugh, but it was a laugh nonetheless. He then felt a large tear tumble from his eye. It plopped down and soaked his shirt. He turned to Nadja and asked her what she meant by the seeds in the moon. She told him he was pretending not to know. "You know all about the seeds in the moon," she said, "They are bloody, these seeds! . . . and they drip all night long out the moon!"

Her new and strange words upset him. He felt as though she were drifting indifferently away from him. He had picture of himself in his mind sitting beneath a cold overcast sky on a little island, while she was on a raft, floating away from him, uncaring. And each sentence she uttered was a new lapping wave coming to push the raft farther. He saw one of her paintings in his mind: a girl sitting nude on a ledge of clouds dangling her feet. Large tears flew from her eyes and her hair swirled with streaks like tails of comets. Nadja had begun this painting a week ago and worked one night while Nikolai was sleeping, and when he woke missing her, and went to go find her, he saw her downstairs perched on the easel, swiping swift brushes across a hopeful canvas. He saw her own eyes were crying. Her swollen lids dripped, now silken tears, now nothing, but blinking dryly with wild fascination as they looked upon the moon outside the window.

"You no longer feel free with me, Nadja," said Nikolai, gloomily.

Nadja then hid her face from him and admitted that she was beginning to feel different. or that she *didn't know* . . . or *wasn't sure*, was what she said; which-upon she issued forth a sort of pained groan.

"I feel I want to fly away from here," she said with glass-colored eyes. "I would go with you, if you could, but you are too afraid to take me. I will go with Helonius."

"Helonius again!" Nikolai roared with joyless laughter. "Helonius is an unreal character, Nadja!"

"Yes," she issued forth lifelessly, with mechanical apathy, as if she didn't believe her own words, or wasn't sure or interested anymore, "...He is just an unreal character. You're right, Nikolai . . . Let's go home."

That night, Nadja gave herself limply to Nikolai. She didn't look at him or care to resist. He, who was fervent in the lovemaking, felt as though she had returned, but she was gone. He looked foolishly at her after the two had finished and were strung on the terrace, lightly clad. He inhaled deeply and touched her naked shoulders...

"You see, Nadja, poetic love creates liberty. A cantankerous world does not. I will tell you truthfully, Nadja. I prefer my liberty over all, but I prefer you more than my liberty . . . Wait, don't speak . . . I know you will say otherwise, that you prefer your liberty over me, but that is fine. You *should* prefer your liberty over me. A woman *must* prefer her liberty over a man. To be happy, she must. A man to be happy, however, must yearn for his woman more than his liberty. This is the rightful order. You look like you don't believe me."

"I do but..."

"No listen, Nadja. Listen so that you know who your Nikolai is..."

"Who is Nikolai?" she asked.

"He is a man who adores his liberty, prefers it over all. Still he prefers it less than his Nadja. He wants to find his liberty in her – has found it. He once sought the world in stories and tales because the world of the foul city he was living in, while it gave him poetry and dreams, was ill and poisonous. He once wanted to choose the world. Finally, he chose . . . But what is it, Nadja? Why do you cast your eyes downward? Why do you look so…?"

"It's just that…" she began.

"Just what?"

She turned away and looked past the terrace rail and off into the night. After a moment, she looked back at him, looked into his eyes, and said, "It's just that…"

"Say it, Nadja."

"I want you to decide."

"Decide what?"

"This Nadja you speak of in the third-person, is it me?"

"Yes, of course it's you!"

"Well, then this Nadja wants you to decide. She wants you to either to choose her or else to choose the world."

"I choose you," Nikolai said, firmly looking at her with great love in his eyes. He took her chin in the palm of his hand, and said it again…

"Nadja, I choose you."

"No," she uttered with dark veiled eyes, "Don't choose me. Choose the world."

CHAPTER XXII

It rained that next morning. Nikolai was alone in his cellar room, lying on his bed, listening to the drops that pounded hard against the dirty glass windowpane. "Long drops of rain crease down the soiled window, sorrowfully..." Upon his sunken chest sat a folded note he had received that morning – delivered by Calico the flower vendor. "...Drops creasing down the window, one would say they are worms slithering through dirt to eat a buried cadaver. Yes, they are not rain, they are worms! It is madness to call them rain!" The news had been taken solemnly to bed and now the note rose and fell with Nikolai's feeble breaths. In the note, Nadja stated she was leaving immediately by train to visit her father for the remainder of the summer in the West Islands. "The time has come," the note read, "...You knew the time would come, Nikolai, but you didn't believe me... Farewell."

This rupture led him first on a despairing jaunt to the train station to search for her. No avail. He went to the Upper Quarter after, broke in through her gate and walked through her abandoned garden. He went to the Anchises Hotel in prayer of finding her at the patio restaurant, but alas, the patio restaurant was empty of patrons. Vladimir had greeted Nikolai warmly and said he was surprised to see him there. "Weren't you going to travel together?" he asked. "Surprising!"

It turned out Nadja had been to the Anchises early in the morning, briefly, to see Vladimir and say goodbye. She hadn't mentioned Nikolai, however. Vladimir had just assumed. She was radiant and excited about her trip, excited to see her father and to go swimming. Of all of this, Vladimir recounted to Nikolai assuming that things were different between them. Yet now that Nikolai's pained face was read clearly by Vladimir, the latter changed the tone and direction of the conversation. Nikolai realized then both how much despair was being displayed on his face and how much of it was being clearly communicated to Vladimir; yet for all his hopeless despair, he truly believed now that he had found a pitying comrade in Vladimir, and that Vladimir in seeing the sadness and despair, was feeling benevolent towards the young man as he considered the best way to help him. To Nikolai's grievous astonishment, however, Vladimir's reaction became remarkable cold, quite quickly, and the distinguished hotelier merely outstretched his hand to shake Nikolai's hand goodbye, while bidding him a pleasant continuation and profitable summer. It became instantly clear all that had been revealed to Vladimir in this meeting and whose side Vladimir was on. As Vladimir turned away coolly to resume affairs, Nikolai gasped at the emptiness before him. He, himself, then turned away to leave the hotel. Above him, the pods of the carob trees planted along the patio streams crackled loudly. Outside, the shoreline on the harbor was damp with misling rain. Nikolai's placed his last hopes of finding her in the slick railing of the Otchajanie Bridge. There, however, he would find her not. He would find no solace in the crowded empty city. He would return alone to his room to swim immersed in the cold quilts of pain.

CHAPTER XXIII

"July and a Visit to a City in the South"

The month of long-dead Julius: I found her again at the Otchajanie Bridge. She was not sitting but was standing, looking out. When she saw me, she turned, yet she did not run. Seemingly unfrightened, she did not hide her face this time, but turned to me as I swept towards her and she fell across my arms like a blanket folded over a banister.

"But you do not run from me?" I asked, seeing now all that I possessed in her. Her eyes told me that she would follow me anywhere.

"Why would I run from you?" she replied, then pressing with emphasis, "...*And how could I?!*"

"No, this time it is different," I agreed.

"Why *this time?* I don't understand how I could have ever run from you!"

"Come," said I, "let us travel together." With her head pressed against my chest, I looked out from the Otchajanie Bridge over the great harbor steeped in fog.

"You see…" she said pointing down at the shoreline at the base of the bridge. "Look there at the strip of grey and golden sand. I want to build a tent there with you and live with you for eternity. Right there on that field of shore."

"We shall, my love," said I, as I held her tight, "We shall have our tent and our eternal camp on that field of shore, our bodies wrapped in iron ore. We'll listen to the endless lapping of waves on the dark sand, we shall! But first... we travel!"

Beneath the dirty glass roof of the Minor Station, I clasped her moist hand and led her amid the clamor of trains. We boarded then a rail-bound vessel and began to travel south. "You have never been to the capital?" I asked, "It is a city like no other."

"No, I have not. But you will show me."

Unadorned by harbors, unadorned by outlying forests, though well-wrought with concrete and electric lines, the capital greeted us with its multitudes. I took her to an old hotel and laid her down upon the bed. We made love to the sounds of subterranean trains coursing beneath us. Violent horns blasted out in the street below and the window rattled with the commotion. She gave herself easily. Her gamey eyes watched me as I came down upon her. While she gasped with pain and turned her face, her upturned breasts pressed hard to my chest, and we glistened with warm summer sweat.

After, when she lay torn and beaten like a weary animal, catching her breath, I kissed her long. I kissed her long and thin thighs, those well-spent thighs, until I stood and left the hotel.

I went out to buy a gun.

When I returned to the hotel room, I put the gun in the cupboard and walked over to the bed to where the girl lay. Life was returning to her...

"Come down here and I will rub you," she said, pulling gently on my arm. She took oil from her traveling bag and rubbed it on me. She offered me her lips again and again.

"Good lips," she said, "And good eyes too. Wandering eyes."

"Our eyes will know the heavens if our lips stay for each other," I told her.

In the night, the basement trains kept their furious paths in the tunnels below the city. In the hotel room, we lay naked and did not sleep. She turned to me often, now beginning to speak but afraid to finish, now asking questions that had no end.

"I am a little afraid of you," she admitted.

"Afraid, you are?"

"You are like someone who has always lived."

I did not speak, but listened.

"You are like the immortal gods."

She paused a moment, then added...

"Be careful," darkening her eyes like a forest lynx, "I think you should perhaps be afraid of me too."

"Afraid?!"

This idea made me laugh.

"Anyone who lies with me gets a bit black."

"I am not afraid," I said, adding then with a sardonic smile, "But you must be a little careful yourself, for she who lies with immortal gods is never left unharmed."

"But *I am* afraid of you." She insisted this like a frightened child, "...Frightened, I am . . . Oh! What is that?!" She pulled in close to me, "Frightening is that noise beneath us!"

"Those are the trains below ground."

"Frightening are the lights beyond us!"

"Those are the neon signs out of the window."

"Frightening are those flashes of fire!"

"Those are the cable sparks from the tram cars running."

"Frightening is that crying moon!"

"The moon is silent," I told her, "It is not crying."

One night, after we had returned to the hotel room, I asked her if she wanted to leave the capital.

"No," she replied, "I want to stay with you here forever."

"But don't you miss our little city in the north?"

"No. Do you miss that place?"

"I miss only the hues of your eyes when your eyelids fold upon them."

Later, when I was getting ready to lie in bed, she asked if she could shave me.

"Yes," I said, looking over by the window, "By the lamp is my razor. Fill the sink with hot water."

The girl stood from the bed, wearing my shirt, no underwear beneath it. I admired her grateful well-made legs as she crossed the room.

"I've never shaved a man before," she said, looking at me for help while holding the razor.

"Fill the sink with hot water and soak the razor," I told her, "Add some soap to the water."

"But the sink is rusty!" she cried, looking into the basin.

"No matter," I said, "Fill the rusty sink with hot water and shave me with the razor and the water."

"But I can't use that sink to shave you! . . . It's rusty, it's filthy!"

Growing annoyed, I walked over to the sink and stood beside her. One of my hands, I set on her small naked shoulder; the other I used to take from the windowsill a small penknife that I'd set there earlier. I took my hand off her shoulder and took the knife in my hand; and with it, I pried one of the diamonds out of the ring I wore on my left-hand middle finger, leaving one lonely diamond, two sapphires and an empty setting.

I took the loose diamond and dropped it in the sink. It clinked with the sound of an old spoon tapping a crystal cup and disappeared down the drain.

"There!" I told the girl, "Now it is a rusty sink with a diamond in it!" With that, I went back to the bed and sat down. "Now, fill the sink with water and prepare the razor and bring it over and shave me."

The girl obeyed and prepared a cloth in a sink of hot water where she had soaked the razor. She brought it over and stroked my chin. Carefully she worked, not cutting me once. She was proud of her work and had amazement in her eyes.

"Look at me," I said. She cast her eyes down. "You have the eyes of a feral fawn," I told her. She kept them downcast and brought her small body, so long, to bed, and I took it upon myself.

The next morning I awoke to find her sitting near the window, staring blankly out. I went and stood beside her. "What are you looking at," I asked.

"My heel," she replied, "it's bruised." She held her foot up and I looked at the bottom-side. It was true, she'd bruised it. It was swollen and rippled – purple like the foot of an aged dancer, too old to leap and land without rupturing veins on mortal skin.

"So it is," I said, "bruised."

That afternoon, after we had made love, I lay on the bed looking at the ceiling. She, meanwhile, stood naked at the glass by the sink looking at her reflection. She remarked that her hips had grown wider. They were strange to her, she did not recognize them.

"They are good like this," I said, "no longer a girl, they are the hips of a woman."

"And what will happen next?" she asked.

"You will see," I said. And I stood to wash her hands at the sink.

That night she was crying. She whimpered calmly the tears of mortal lamentation.

"What have you?" I asked her, "Why are you crying?"

The girl undid the clasp of her bra and held the lace in her lap.

"It is yellowing my bra, and my panty's strap too."

"It is the grime of human bodies," I told her, "The dust of the flesh."

She cried harder now, dropping viscid tears of regret for all that was left behind her. For all that she'd had in the garden in spring was no longer real. Now she sat in this worn hotel room with me, and the sound of trams and trains raced by the window as she clasped her underwear in trembling hands and soaked the cloth with yellowing tears fallen from slender eyes.

"My thighs hurt," she told me, "and they tremble like one who has grown old."

"It is the breaking of flesh, the dust of the world. Now, lie down and sleep. I will tell you, dear girl, that fruit we so happily ate from the trees this last spring, that fruit you so happily tore from the twigs, uncaring for the brittle skin of the branches, nor wise trunks coated in bark – for you had the soft and fleshy fruit – I will tell you then as now that you, yourself, were the twigs bearing fruit, that the world so happily tore."

"I don't understand," she murmured tearfully in a low voice.

"Lie down and sleep," I said.

The following morning, about five o'clock, before it was properly light in the capital, as I was lying awake with eyes closed, I heard the girl stirring in the bed. She was checking to see if I was awake, and believing me to be sound asleep, she crept silently from the hotel bed and pulled her suitcase from the corner. I watched her with close-fastened eyes. Over her shoulder, she peered again and again, breathing quickly, afraid that I would wake up, trembling like a child; she filled her suitcase with her strands of clothes and prepared herself to leave. Once I heard the door click shut, I stood and dressed and left the room to follow after her.

At the train station, I walked discreetly around near the tracks. As expected, I saw the poor girl buying a ticket at the counter. A bird had flown into the station and was now trying to pass through the dirty glass roof to escape to the sky. It was only a matter of time, I thought to myself, let her go, let all come to pass.

Back at the hotel, I inspected the room. All that I had brought was still there. She hadn't opened the closet where the gun I'd bought remained on the shelf. The gun was still there. It was then the middle of July.

I stayed two more weeks in the south. When I think back on those last two weeks of July spent in the capital, I am surprised at the calm patience with which I conducted myself. I stayed by myself and let one week slip into two, trusting she would wait for me, believing that I would take the train north when I felt it was time and there we would be reunited together – there we would return to the garden to pass another season together. Perhaps I enjoyed fooling myself like this. This, at least, brought calmness. Calmness in abundance, to me and everything around. That is what was needed over all: a period of soft wetness before the eternal flood; a moment of dry peace before the endless drought.

I spent those final two weeks in the capital drifting through the quarters of the city, wandering the electric tunnels of the basement trains, watching the inhabitants gather in their groups on street corners, shadowy citizens flooding in and out of tram terminals. Everyway were the signs of life in its midst. I observed people who coughed with death and disenchantment. I observed others who smiled with lingering relics of love, the last residues of youth and discovery. At the square of the marble capitol, summer feasts drew crowds at night. Powder blasts filled in the evening air flashing carnival delights. One afternoon, I observed a parade. Masked revelers gathered in the streets and squares. I kept always on the outside. hovering around the fringe. I kept in the shadows, in the outskirts.

It was unseasonably cold the last week of July. A wind traveled down from the far north and chilled the summer air. I had to keep the windows closed at night while I slept. This kept out the sounds of the trams and the underground. Those noises, I craved while awake, so I kept the windows open a crack in the evenings and bought a coat to wear as I sat at the table and worked. There I drew some sketches, created what I could, I didn't know what else to do. I had always taken up the occupations that I had wanted to, that pleased me, seeing these wants as my sole obligations. Now I desired only contemplation, a little creation, over all, a world where I was the sole participant. I was disillusioned by my past work. The sound of the pendulum on the clock aggravated me, and so, with a single gesture of an outstretched hand, I stopped it from ticking. I dismantled the electric light in favor of a lamp that sat on the table where I worked burning kerosene. Moths flew into the flames, singeing their wings. All of this was of no consequence. Over all, I was perfectly calm and at ease.

I decided to return to the Minor City on the first day of August. As time drew near, I considered changing my plans to remain in the capital a little longer. I was conscious, however, of the obligation I'd created for myself long ago; and I knew I must be in attendance when things came to pass.

When the time came, I took my suitcase, my clothes; I took the revolver I'd hidden in the closet, as well as the few items the girl forgot to take with her when she left, and I started off through the capital streets. I waited beneath the soot-covered roof of the East Station for the overnight train. I studied the time table. Soon the great cast-iron engine came, docked and dispatched its weary passengers. I boarded and took a private cabin. Within moments we were chugging off through the steel grids of the industrial north.

CHAPTER XXIV

At last in the Minor City. An end to the month long sojourn in the south. From the station near the Otchajanie Bridge, I walked to the Great Canal and crossed over to the Peninsula. It was early morning and bright and hot with clear sky and vibrant sun. A friend of mine had recently built a house atop the rocky cliffs on the eastern side of the Peninsula. I wanted to pay him a visit, to see his new home and to find out about all that had happened in the city since my departure a month before.

After I entered the gate, a maid ushered me into a house furnished with cherry wood and laid with stone. There, my friend came to greet me, still in his bathing robe. He had let his beard grow. The two of us went out onto the terrace and sat awhile. From there, you could see the ocean view in all its splendor. The horizon line curved majestically and the ocean was as vast as the sky. You could watch the sun's morning haze sweeping across the inlet, evaporating in a whirlwind of swiftly vanishing fumes until all that was left in the sky were tiny cloudlets sailing quietly. Cloudlets, one would say pellets of bleached wool dropping dark spots of shadows like beauty marks on the skin of the crystalline waters of the ocean. We sat at the table and drank from a fresh pitcher – water clean and newly drawn.

"The woman you were traveling with, she left the capital before you?"

"Yes," I replied, "Two weeks before."

"Do you know what happened to her a few days after she returned?"

"No idea," I lied. I was sure I knew.

"She died."

A long pause.

There was a poplar tree planted in a box in the corner of the terrace and its leaves rattled as the wind swept over the patio stones.

"Suicide, they say." He looked at me firmly, dispassionately, "There was no sign of a struggle. She was found nude, washed up on the shore beneath the Otchajanie Bridge."

I stayed quiet. My friend poured some more water into our glasses and went on…

"Her clothes, or rather specifically, a grey raincoat, was found neatly folded and set on the bridge near the place she had leapt from…"

I'd heard enough. Raising my hand, I signaled to my friend to cease speaking. A few more words about other things and I took leave of him.

CHAPTER XXV

That was all early this morning. I recall these events now at midday as I stand on the Otchajanie Bridge looking out over the harbor. Ash-colored clouds have overtaken the clear skies and a hot fog begins to descend upon the great basin of water. I watch as the disoriented boats push towards the bridge, sounding their foghorns in even blasts that echo under the humid grill of sky. Once these boats pass beneath the bridge, they'll trail into the deep of the ocean and be gone. This same harbor that carries heavy ships of steel, so swallows swiftly the tilted buoyant sands of time. Men and gods fear such a harbor.

The temporal fog thins to a haze, dropping down to smother the waves, only to be destroyed again by the sun which shines with fiberglass splinters of light. The water is once again stained with icy blue dye. How the sun burns with cruelty on this day!

How the wind whips across the bridge with perfect stillness. Where there was water before, there is water now. Where there is water now becomes a silver puddle of mercury sliding down a steel spoon; lost in glass, lost in sulphur, lost in grass burnt brown by the sun – a field burning with summer fire!

A flash of cold feverish swells within me, while mortal sweat beads upon my forehead. I find I have been walking for a long time through the disjointed streets of the Lower Quarter. Again and again I find myself returning to the Otchajanie Bridge. I am surprised at the calmness I feel now, looking out from this bridge, as though my being here will come to alter things, reverse my fortune or at least unclothe the mystery and crown it with . . . with what? With justice? Nay!, such is merely revenge and our blistering month of August permits not such youthful occupations; justice merely sets out to agitate life with nausea, as it did on the day some divine or otherwise said word set this dying world in motion. Here, in maturity, we could have walked in complete calmness. Meanwhile, glory refracts from the irises of our eyes and coloured blooms of springtimes past wither in the cold shadows we cast in our wake. To speak then of calmness. Calmness! As if one can merely . . . remember walking away from the Peninsula this morning? How I then calmly took the news. Passing through that gates of his house, remembering clearly every word he'd said to me as I started down that lane away from the house. While I walked, I tried to explain to myself what all of it meant. I felt not even a flash of fever then, only complete calmness. Suicide, they say? Did they not know it was old age! The girl had died of old age! Hurrying through the Lower Quarter, I saw the bridge looming up ahead. I wanted to come here to look out to the place where she'd been found, rolled up on the shore . . . As if being here would stir me to desperation. But here too I feel now only calmness. So what of death? While I was soaking my hands in a rusty basin, she was soaking herself in her own abyss. So it was this bridge she'd leapt from? Consider that! To leap from the Otchajanie Bridge, of all places to leap from! I had loved her, had I not? As though she were the only thing I'd created. I remember clearly all those times she would be here sitting at this very bridge waiting for me, or else not waiting, and surprised to see me. Then ready to run from me as soon as I approached. Always sitting on the edge of the bridge as though she were perched on the edge of the world, perched on a ledge of clouds. Always wearing that light grey rain jacket, the hood pulled tight over her head concealing her long hair. That jacket was "folded up neatly on the bridge," my friend had told me.

I remember the way he waved a single finger as he said it. Washed up on the shore, had she?

One remembers easily those times. One remembers easily then, yet one remembers even more clearly that first day back in early May. The time when we were new: It was a vibrant afternoon when we made love to each other for the first time. We had come from the vineyard and were crossing through my yard into the neighbouring garden. We didn't know the people who lived around us back then. We knew some people who lived down below the arboretum, but the people in our quarter were strangers yet. I remember clearly that first day, I took her hand and crossed with her into the neighbours' garden; and once on the other side of the archway, I leaned her up against the wall of the garden and kissed her long and hard. We continued walking after that. We spoke idly of this and that. Then, not far off, we noticed a girl who was knelt down beneath the canopies of apricot and fig trees picking the fruit that had fallen on the ground. She was naked, and when she heard our voices walking in the garden in the cool of the day, she flushed with shame. She flushed with shame for being naked and she dropped the fruit she had been picking and hid herself amongst the trees. We looked at each other and smiled about this strange girl who stood there trembling amongst the trunks and branches, one of her hands cupped over her breasts, the other cupped over the dark-coloured mound of hair between her legs. She never did see us though and after a while she stopped searching with her eyes to find the source of the noise that had frightened her. She began looking up at the bows of the trees overhead, apparently contemplating the leaves and the limbs. We decided then to leave that garden and give her a chance to run away.

We went back through the arch into my own yard and waited as the naked girl left her hiding place in the trees to run back to her lover where he lay on the lawn. I could hear her talking urgently to him, explaining that she was cold and needed him to take her inside. He listened to his lover, and stood up and covered her with the blanket, and then he covered himself, and the two headed into the house.

Once both gardens were empty, I felt a slender hand reaching for mine. It was her. I took the hand and led the girl back through the granite archway, back to where we'd been before. Walking beneath the bowers of trees, we came to the hiding place and walked past it to a sunny spot in a grove of apricot trees. I then lowered her down on the grass and made fresh love to her for the first time. Our bodies were hard as they were naked and wrapped in passion and we trembled together. How her body was warm and wet and alive then. To think that it is now cold and dry and empty of marrow, as the memory of her breath slips from my mind.

One forgets easily her scent. One forgets easily her scent and the feeling of the drops of wetness on her skin, yet one still remembers that garden and how permanent it seemed then. And one wonders how it could end. Yet, that it did end, was that not also part of my design? Did I not know all along how it would end? And just *why* it would end? And that I changed nothing, nor even thought to try? Back in the springtime, I watched her become that woman for whom a man can shed all his past and forsake all time. While he looks into her eyes he sees her change into that first soft woman, lost in vernal dreams...

What was that?

...For a moment just then, I remembered the way she smelled. It came fleeting by, but now it is gone again. What regret I feel now for that woman lost in vernal dreams who was born of me, and I of her. We were the only lovers then. We walked holy through the days that ripened like spring fruit. Summer fruit grows bruised with the casting of shadows. Wrinkles form on the skin, while the sun and moon revolve around each other, and the terrifying stars fade one by one and drop ten by ten into the dingy film of time, stream of space, a streamer blowing in the wind and the touch of sun on the tip of the breezing leaf caught by the late jade light of the sun, and with it comes that last memory of the first day in springtime long ago...

A young boy lost in the grass. Walking past the rhododendrons in the warm tincture of spring, with a fresh-washed head and dilated eyes. A god in a garden. A garden, a dream. Garden gleam and garden stream. All the light the garden knew, left violet prints on leaves astrew; the chance alone that we would fade, brought all the light to amber shade...

All youthful nonsense!

And why, so I ask, why of all things, why this calm?!

One last long look out from the Otchajanie Bridge: the damp salty air brings a strange chill as the August sun is extinguished, as if grasped by a wet cloth. Gone are the days of youth when the sun was clean – its rays round like discs, wafers of gold tumbling over the tops of the trees. Now the sun burns dirty with an absence of heat. I look below and see that strip of sandy shore stretching beneath the Otchajanie Bridge – a leaden strip smudged with gold. So it was there on that strip of shore that she made her eternal camp. There, where the waves of the harbor lap on the rocks while the early foghorns sound.

CHAPTER XXVI

I find I have been walking for some time in the Lower Quarter, returning again and again to the same places. I've wandered the deserted streets along the harbor, the packed alleys of the markets, fragrant with dead fish and spices, I have made my way up the hill several times, as if there, in some hidden crease in the arboretum, I will find the answer to all my questions – find the frayed thread of the mortal cloth, so to speak.

When I was walking along the market streets a while ago, I heard the bell of the Bastion toll. It was that time of afternoon when sun's rays scorch through the ether unhindered. Through scalding streets, vendors were passing with their carts. Aged men, hunched over stands, threw ice upon the fish they were laying out for sale. Passing the flower vendor's shop on Fishmongers' Row, I listened to the continuing tolling of the Bastion bell and the shouting voices. I watched a rat scurry from beneath a semolina cart. I followed it with my eyes to where it ran up a passageway. There in the passage way, I saw a sorry figure coming out into the open street. It was Nikolai. He was almost unrecognizable, so wretched was he, dressed in the dirty clothes of a beggar. His hair was matted and tangled. His hands were scratched. He hobbled slowly as he walked, slightly hunched over with a look of illness. He clutched his gut, his face was twisted in agony. I suddenly thought of that pistol I'd bought when I was in the capital. I'm not sure why I thought of it just then, but I then remembered that when the girl left me in the capital, she'd left several articles behind. One in particular, I put in my pocket before I went to the train station yesterday. Now, standing on Fishmongers' Row, watching the miserable figure of Nikolai as he crouched down to grasp his stomach in pain, I felt for the article, touched it, and looked back at him. I smiled with pleasure at my new idea. Why should there not be anguish for us all?

    The vendors bustled around me, crossing between us. At one moment, Nikolai stopped and turned and looked at me. He looked directly at me. Tears were streaming down his cheeks. He resembled a feeble child trying to summon pity through choking tears. He turned his face back down to hide it. Looking coldly down at the wretch, I felt in my pocket through remnants of anguish, and drew from it that folded item the girl had left, and pulled it out and pressed it to my forehead. There it soaked up the beaded sweat, tingeing the once white material to a sallow yellow. Following this exercise, I walked over to the doorway where Nikolai was huddled over; and, with a sweep of my hand, I let the item drop upon him. His body collapsed on top of that stained article and the wounded man sobbed with long-flowing tears. He lifted his eyes once to me. They were gashed like the bloody surface of the August sun. He raised his trembling hands. In them he held a torn piece of paper. It was a note from his departed Nadja, which spoke thus...

    Dear Nikolai,

    I told you it must end and that it would end and you didn't believe me but now you must. I am in the West Islands. I am happy here. What we shared in the spring was beautiful, as you know, Nishka. It was a unique time. I will remember our nights on the terrace. Are you happy in the city without me? Nishka, I won't call you that anymore, Nikolai. Simply put, I don't think I'm going to be coming back to the Minor City for a long while. I will be traveling with my father. He has plans for me and is very excited. I am sitting outside by the sea now and the sun is very bright. My father will be coming down in a minute so I have to hurry with my letter. He is so serious my father. He wants me to go study abroad and he wants me to marry. Sometimes I wonder how he can be so serious! – still there is a lot of pressure to be a young woman, moreover the daughter of someone like him.

"You need to marry before you are too old," he says to me. Oh, Nikolai, I told you how serious he is, my father. If you only knew! Anyway, what you did know is that I could not remain with you forever at my father's house in the Minor City – though sweet it was with our terrace and our garden. We were playful like children. Oh, to remain as children! But you knew that we could not remain! Only one word from you and I would have left, Nikolai. You know this! I would have run away with you. It is you to blame now, I believe, for all that is gone between us. Only one word from you and I would have left and gone anywhere. I would have traveled to the south with you, we could have lived together... married or not, money or no money – it wouldn't have so much mattered. I loved being with you and I would have left with you but you were a coward and would not take me. You were afraid to take me and take the world at the same time. You wanted only me without the world. Oh, Nishka, poor Nishka, if you only knew! I cannot explain this now but I don't need to. You know – or you didn't know but you should have! – that it couldn't have continued in the way you wanted it to. We are from different worlds and I couldn't have brought you into mine. I was depending on you to bring me into yours (did you ever realize this?) . . . but you didn't. You refused to, and so we must give up on that. I will be traveling with my father and another family – my father's good friend, his wife and their son (a young man of my age, whom I knew when I was a girl). I have spent a lot of time with him and his family since I have been here and we have shared some beautiful things. It too was beautiful what we lived, Nishka, you and me. It was. I was a little girl for you at first, or so I felt. Then I felt I became a woman alongside you. It was as beautiful for me as it was for you, but now it has come to pass and I no longer long for you. I have been very happy here. My father and I are getting along well. He is getting older and is beginning to

treat me like an adult. He doesn't tell me to stop after one glass of champagne anymore . . . but enough of all this! I will be traveling with this young man and his family for sometime and I shall not return to the Minor City for a long time so please don't go any more to the Anchises Hotel looking for word from me, for there won't be any. I know you went there looking for me or else you wouldn't have received this letter. But please don't go there anymore. I am leaving you now, Nishka. But you know I will cherish those memories of the past, those nights we had together, our tales of the terrace. I will cherish those memories even more for the fact that they couldn't happen again neither for us, nor for anyone. With farewell to the past, I bid a happy adieu to you and remain always,

One who loved you deeply,

Your Nadja.

Nikolai trembled on the last words: *One who loved,* again and again; such horrid sounds clashed in these words! Nikolai's throat began to swell and he felt his body dropping once again. He caught his weight and stumbled a few steps forward. He then took the note and refolded it and tucked it into the pocket of his wretched clothes. This-upon he lurched down the steps towards the harbor, swaying in utter despair, until his body collapsed on a bench. There it remained unmoving, slightly breathing, slightly.

The sun slid slightly across the sky. I passed Nikolai where he was curled up on his broken bench, his hand outstretched towards me the way a beggar's does, seeking alms. I cared as much for his despair as a child in a garden cares for the despairs of a crawling bug. I flicked his miserable hand from my sight and continued on my wanton path. To tell of my own anguishes! I was determined to wander until I could sort things out in my own mind, once and for all.

CHAPTER XXVII

I have been wandering through the bleak quarters of the Shipyard District for the better part of the afternoon. I am in the mood for nothing clean like the rose garden, nothing pastoral like the sweeping paths of the arboretum, soon it will be evening and I will remain in these dismal streets of the forgotten quarter. If nothing leads me away, I will stay here all night.

Now it happens, quite by hazard, while walking along a row of shabby houses past meal counters and drinking-dens, that I run across a man I once knew. He recognizes me immediately and calls me over to him. All the while, he taps a rolled-up newspaper he keeps tucked under his arm. The two of us duck into a tiny little hovel of an eating house, where we sit at a corner table. There we drink from a pitcher, unclean water swimming with insects. He shows me the newspaper he has been holding. I spread it out before me on the table and the man begins to fade from view. I am arrested at once by the article in the center of the page which talks about her death. I begin to read. A simple suicide, it claims, quite a routine occurrence, nothing out of the ordinary: a girl throws herself off the Otchajanie Bridge in the middle of the night. Her body was washed up on the shore and was found the next morning.

There is one detail, however. One thing mentioned in the article that keeps returning to my mind over and over. When the girl had jumped into the harbor, she was nude. Her rain jacket was left up on the bridge, neatly folded. She had taken it off as well as her other clothes. But this was not the detail that struck me. What struck me was that she hadn't been completely nude. There was one thing that she was wearing; when they found her body washed up on the shoreline, there had been this: a strip of old cream-colored lace tied in a bow around her left wrist.

BOOK II

Songs from the Cellar

CHAPTER XXVIII

Let me sing now of the descent into the cellar... On sultry August nights, flitting about like passionate bats, we breathed the fumes of the underground. Ours was the loftiest of oblivions, the basest of companions, vile men and women of the sacred summer. In those depths, we sang our nocturnes and danced the bacchanal. Feverish blood battered in our veins like clock pendulums. So sorrowfully we perched on the longing for all that had wilted. We sat drenched in wasted memories of the forsaken spring and dreams of far gone afternoons. Such gamey nights give way to rueful mornings.

Cached in the tenebrous shadows of Nesretan Street, I stood observing Nikolai as he approached the old Nesretan public house: singular place, a squalid drinking-den named for that sorrowful neighborhood where the inhabitants remain with traces of poverty and the visitors leave with inflictions of madness.

It was early August and I'd returned from the capital. Nikolai, likewise, had just received the fateful letter from Nadja announcing the death of their affair. Leaving his basement room after nightfall, he began wandering along the poorly-lit walkway that coursed the polluted Minor Canal. When he reached the Shipyard District, he could hear the clanging of industrial cranes swinging their loads at the far-off piers. He passed beggars lying in nests of damp rags. He passed street urchins selling counterfeit stamps. He passed gamins hunting in garbage cans; stray cats. Around the bars, girls in cheap high-heels walked like painted doves on stilts on the arms of ruddy-cheeked military men. Amid the squalor were festive scenes, strung-up lanterns of torn paper. At little inexpensive restaurants with tables that spilled out onto the sidewalks, young couples sat and drank cheap iced wine. Two youths began to fight in the street and some bleary-eyed policemen came to settle things.

After the Shipyard District, Nikolai took a detour to wander alone through the grim streets of Otchajanie. Here, there were no military youths or policemen on patrol. Besides the whores and junkies, the streets of Otchajanie were populated merely by passing shades and shadows. Abandoned by the law, these streets were adopted by wild-eyed cutpurses who hid in doorways waiting for that one lost traveler who had wandered the wrong way with a purse full of money after leaving the train station.

He thought of Otchajanie and that letter he had tried to write to Nadja before leaving his room. He knew he would never send that letter, nor could he send it, having no address for her to send it to. It was a teary and pathetic plea he had tried to compose with a hapless bottle of wine that had turned to vinegar. He had torn the paper finally and decided to go outside to take a drink, or take a walk, to clear his head.

He thought of Nesretan, that despairing part of town where those cast-away from the Shipyard District came to drink and play cards in underground cellars. There was a public house there where he would be welcome, he thought. The idea to go to the Nesretan public house provided a brief spark of joy, a strange feeling that relief could be found. He counted the money now that he'd taken earlier from the large plywood box which he kept in a the crawlspace behind the cupboard in his room. He had enough to buy a few liters of wine; perhaps some stupefying plants or pills, above all: oblivion.

Nikolai had frequented the Nesretan public house at a time before he knew Nadja – back when he worked as a laborer on the piers at the shipyards. Often, after work he would pass by with a coworker, or by himself, to drink until he was tired enough that he felt he could sleep immediately once he'd returned to his room.

That sort of life, however, had changed when he met Nadja. She caused him to forgot completely about his friends from the piers, this drinking den, this life in the sad lower-class district. Nadja presented a new kind of life for him, a glorious one. She was a clear-eyed girl who'd never dwelt in smoky caves; who'd spent clear-eyed evenings on her ivy-laced terrace overlooking flourishing gardens. He had met her and she brought him into her life. Theirs were nights of good wines at the Anchises Hotel; days of sweet coffees on the banks of the canals, morning picnics in the arboretum amid scents of blossoms, never cavern smoke nor liquor fumes. The fear that such a life of beauty would come to an end had haunted Nikolai at times when they had been together, casting shade on his joy. But such fears he'd always chased away by living the passions of the present and keeping optimistic thoughts for the future. To come to the realization that such hopeful times had fallen so swiftly, and into such utter wretchedness! . . . with all those joyful days behind him, it pained Nikolai to think that he had lived so naïvely. He realized now he had been blind. He had done no more than to dance through the spring like a fool in the silk blouses sewn of the threads of tragedy.

Something of a romantic idea that Nadja would be waiting for him at the Otchajanie Bridge kept creeping into Nikolai's mind as he walked towards Nesretan. She would be waiting with some explanation as to why the cruel letter she had sent was wrong. Tearfully, she would explain, it was all a mistake. She had been in a delirium. She would tell him she loved him, that she would always love him and never leave him. She would tell him he was silly for believing that note where she spoke of that particular 'young man' in the West Islands. There would be no 'young man.' There would only be her and Nikolai and she would kiss his skin everywhere it was damp with lips that were hot and swollen. Yes, she would be there! She would be at the Otchajanie Bridge, otherwise –

well, otherwise, he would leap from the bridge and end it all!

"What a night!" he cried, clasping his hands. He then began to wring them in feverish self-mockery. "I'll find Nadja at the bridge, or else I'll leap into the harbor!" A nearby policeman on the street turned and looked at Nikolai suspiciously then. Sallow-skinned Nikolai kept on. Soon he arrived at the public house.

"What are those, eagles?" he asked, looking up towards the rooftops. They were two birds: black vultures with shriveled heads. They had been perched on a rooftop scouting for carrion, hissing in the night; and now they took flight and soared eastward across the Nesretan sky with wildly flapping wings. In their talons, they clutched long tendons of meat that dangled down. Nikolai again clasped his hands and saliva glimmered on his lips. "Eagles!" he cried foolishly; and knowing such a sight to be a good omen, he knew and believed now that good fate was to be his. He smiled at the omen and went into the public house.

CHAPTER XXIX

In the cellar, burned a brass candelabrum. Three black-eyed gypsies stood huddled in the corner, tuning forlorn mandolins. Glass lanterns had been strung from the arched stone ceiling and they emitted sly red light from wicked bulbs. As the gypsy band prepared to play, patrons with swollen eyes and burnished hands arranged themselves at tables of hearty wood adorned with gluttonous bottles, which were used to fill cups that were quickly drained. A little pockmarked waiter was busy ferreting back and forth, taking money in exchange for uncorked wine. At this time, Nikolai entered unnoticed and took a lonely seat near the crowds of patrons.

"What will it be?" asked the pockmarked waiter.

"A liter of wine."

The wine was dark violet and acrid-tasting, having known the cork for too long. Nikolai drank quickly and watched suspiciously the people around him. Some boatmen were gathered at a nearby table speaking words in an alien tongue. They had coerced three young ribbon-haired students to share their earnings; and the girls, not understanding the boatmen's words, drank the men's wine and laughed and talked amongst themselves. Nikolai observed and began mumbling aloud...

Mole-faced girls! Look how they speak a vulgar dialect. Ach, city peasants! The clothes they wear wouldn't serve as rags to clean my Nadja's terrace floor. Why 'my Nadja?' . . . whose Nadja is she? Some clever monster in the West Islands has caged her. He serves her water in crystal cups and shoots venison in the wilderness with her father. They give Nadja the deerskins to wear as coats and let her out to tan on the beach once a week. Why am I talking like this? Perhaps I am the monster, gorging stale wine in a cellar bar in the pitiless Nesretan district. Vile Nesretan! I remember this bar from happier days. Remember, Nikolai? . . . Remember those olden days when you would twirl girls around on this floor? What kind of phrase is *olden days* ? . . . All the while, this same gypsy band whined and whistled with their well-worn fiddles. That it should end and end now? Yet, there is no ending. I am here again where I was, though older and now it's said, having known the joys of hope, the life one finds in the bright coolness of spring. I remember we used to gamble here. Only tossing out stray coins, small sums. When we won, our friends always pressed us to pay the bottles and so we usually left with nothing. Better to lose and drink the winner's wine then win and pay the losers' wine! . . . Though sometimes a clever player would win the pot and sneak out of the place to spend the money alone, elsewhere. Where would he spend his money? Oh who cares! At the Anchises Hotel? Ha-ha! Imagine one of these creeps at the Anchises Hotel. In the laps of whores eating prunes in Otchajanie, that's more like it! . . . Ah, there were more than enough whores in this place in those days – good whores who accept the payment of a handful of words and a cupful of cheap wine more often than not. Look at these drinking girls! Pink-faced teenagers! I used to enjoy such girls as these, smelling of cheap powder. Respite from the labors of working on docks. A bridge-worker is what I am, am I not? Nikolai, you are merely a dirty-knuckled bridge-worker. Nothing else! A working-class man, a coward and a drunk! Who are you to be lying with a brave goddess whose skin is tempered by the salt springs of the West Islands. A bridge-worker you are, yet still you've read many books and have little patience for illiterate city peasants. Good wine . . . it's starting to make my head dissolve in the red lights around me. Holy wine! . . . Why is that man in such a shabby coat? But look at the beauty he is caressing! . . . Oh, she is a mule, Nikolai! . . . You would have never said that girl is a beauty having Nadja to compare her to. After Nadja, you cannot touch another woman. Oh, yes I can! I certainly can! . . . and a devilish one too! I'll touch a woman with shabby thighs! Shabby thighs spotted with red marks, sweat stains and mattress burns. But how could it be? How could she have changed her mind? Tender-lipped Nadja, she wanted a hero? What is a hero? A man who travels far and wide? What we had was so beautiful. I was her man and she was my woman. We traveled without leaving her terrace. We explored the land of each other's flesh. Ours was immaculate love in the springtime. Such good fortune spills like milk from a ladle. Such good fortune spills like wine from a jug. We fed each other on overripe figs. Now I drink alone this sunken and nasty-toothed wine from spoilt grapes. How rancid everything has become! Look, now they're beginning to play cards. Just like it used to be! Watch this, some clever fool is about to open his drunken wallet and throw a sum on the table and call the other men cowards, and they will laugh and get their own money and the playing will begin. There were always so many stupid men among us gamblers, unlearned types. Though I had some good friends here. Who did I know? Let's see... A painter, an impoverished photographer who carried a tin camera around his neck, a few low-rung office clerks, some of the good men who worked with me in the harbor driving bolts through sheet metal. We had joyous times drinking, gambling and playing with the girls, twirling them around. The Shipyard District is full of fresh, impoverished student girls. Here the student girls were always different. Here there were those curious students who would stray from the Shipyard District to come to Nesretan just for curiosity's sake . . . high-school or university girls. They would sit in the corners in their groups of three or four, perched on their stools like groomed mice, eager and curious. Always the young men would drag them out and dance with them and take them home to their beds. I was a young man too then. Perhaps I still am young. Am I young? No, I am no longer young. Though it wasn't so long ago, a year? Yes, I was young with Nadja and grew old with her, and now she is gone and I am finished. 'Only one word' she had said, and she would have gone with me. But *which* word? Now she is traveling with some family of noblemen with a son she wants to marry. But is that noble son me? Ha! It is me! A clever snare! Good, little Nadja, with your letter, written to lure me to you. Why did she write that letter? She wrote it so I will hurry to come to find her! That is it! There is no other man, she just wants to try to force me to travel. A feminine game to force me to travel! Force Nikolai! Force Nikolai, the coward! She wants me to come to slay her father and roast his limbs like in the heroic stories she likes. Is that what she wants? I will find some job that involves travel, I will go to her and she will take me . . . No, it is hopeless. Let me accept gracefully that I am finished and life has gone past. Why do I need to be among the living, anyway? It is to be dead and yet still alive which one cannot bear. Who is this gypsy with the long black mustache? I have enough money for a liter and a half more after this. I will drink to the soporific music and when I return home I will sleep a dreamless sleep and be in peace and oblivion until I wake to the summer rain dripping, dripping, dripping – what horror it will be when winter comes and people hide in pairs in their homes, roasting together like meat beneath their happy blankets! . . . And all I will have is myself and my rancid cellar . . . my rancid cellar and my own rancid . . . No, not now Nikolai! Now just the dreamless sleep and the soporific music of the lonely gypsy band. They too, these gypsy players, they have known lonely lives of loss, traveling with nostalgic guitars and sorrowful violins. Still they have traveled. The devils! Nadja is only a child and she is confused. The salt is clouding her perfect skin. Why can't I get a bottle in here? Is there anyone I know in this barroom? They are beginning now . . . a slow ballad. It resembles a lazy duchess reclining on a chaise longue.

Nikolai stopped his soliloquy at the call of the gypsies' choir. He succeeded in ordering more wine and began to drink it almost violently. The public house was filling up with the music and new revelers who'd come to celebrate. A bride was feasting her wedding. A poor couple, the groom was ugly and thin, dressed in a hired suit. The bride wore a ratty homemade dress. The matrimonial pair ordered bottles of the cheap wine for several tables of their families and friends and the bride danced on a hearty bench to the gypsies' songs and twirled the tattered frills of her dress. The family of the groom all had thick black beards and the bride's family stamped their feet like bumpkins as they danced. Nikolai, having blurred his eyes from wine, felt free to talk in feverish words to the groom and his entourage. He addressed himself in an almost brotherly way to the strangers' union of marriage and gave a rummy word of thanks as someone poured him vodka from a private bottle. All in the main hall danced to the tramps' melodies; the groom thanked his friends in a final speech and took his bride back to their apartment. Nikolai had offered to dance with the groom's little sister and he recalled a sensation of her flabby cheeks pressed against his. The red lights overhead turned for him into little horsemen carrying scythes. He saw a wild-eyed boxer riding a wooden horse when a moth flew into his salty mouth. A mouthful of sour gall, a gut drenched in cutting acids. He woke alone in his bed. Ill, he groaned aloud...

"Misfortune's disgust! What time is it and how did I get home last night?"

Morning it was. Nikolai's memory from the night before was gone. He pulled himself from bed and dressed to go visit the chemist.

CHAPTER XXX

The sunlight fell clean and bright across the bricks of Fishmonger's Row. The street was wet from having been hosed down early that morning. As Nikolai left the apothecary with a bottle of headache powders, he struggled to recall the night before, lest he be not aware of some disgrace he had committed. He vaguely remembered dancing with some girl who'd touched him with oily lips. Some strange words were spoken to the bar owner. At one point he had stolen a half glass of someone's wine from a table after his money had run out. The man had caught him and shook a fist at him… "Keep your hands off my wine!" What else? Something about a broken watch. Was it his, or someone else's? 'Such a flimsy thing, my memory!' he thought. Ah, but then he remembered that he'd shared friendly words with one of the gypsies who'd remembered him from when he used to come in to drink long ago – back when he'd had friends and had known the people drinking there.

Nikolai observed of the grey-haired chemist at the counter in the apothecary. 'He is suspicious of something!' he thought to himself, 'The way he claims to be out of antiemetics!'

Back on the street, Nikolai found Calico sitting on the bricks, cutting stems for the roses he would peddle to the amorous men in city's barrooms that night to come.

"No messages, Calico? No visitors?"

"No," the old flower vendor shook his foolish head. Nikolai took a gloomy expression and walked off into the bustle of the fish markets. He would come to spend the afternoon wandering back and forth across the Otchajanie Bridge, hoping to find a spectre of Nadja. "If she does not come to this bridge by midnight," he told himself at one point in the afternoon, "I will cover my face and go into a dark alley in Otchajanie armed with a knife, and I will rob a man, some lost traveler who'd wandered the wrong way from the station. I'll take his purse and set off on a voyage to the West Islands. There I will find my Nadja waiting for me to do that 'one thing' she wanted."

Yet feeble-skinned Nikolai robbed no man. Nor did he stay at Otchajanie till midnight. Only in the evening did he once consider going off to ask here and there for work so he could fund some heroic plan; but alas, he knew all plans were beyond him. He could not go forward, he knew this; but he could not go back to his sad cellar room to waste the evening away either. He feared a lonely night in that squalor would lead him to suicide. After abandoning the bridge, he returned home to pick from his own stash of dwindling money. He took as much as he thought he could ration so as to buy a couple liters of wine at the Nesretan public house.

Nikolai's fortune seemed to take a turn when he ran into Mikhail, an old friend of his. Mikhail was a dull-witted laborer, but he was honest and never had an unkind word to say about his friends. Neither was he ever to be found without either liquor or a laboring tool in his hand. His drooping eyes reflected a chronic sadness that his optimistic smile did its best to conceal. He was host of many personal miseries and his face was aged far beyond its years.

Mikhail and Nikolai had worked together on the piers a while back. Often, at the end of the day, they finished up at the public house where they drank and nurtured a friendship.

"Good Nikolai!" cried Mikhail, standing to embrace his old friend. "Where have you been? I haven't seen you since the weather was bad. December was it? Or rather it...." Mikhail had a habit of not finishing his phrases.

The two installed themselves at a back table with some other of Mikhail's friends. They were devil-faced people whom Nikolai didn't know. One was a lean student with a dark pointy beard. The student accepted Nikolai's company with cold disdain. Wine was issued into corpulent glasses and Nikolai quickly emptied his own. Mikhail then drew close to Nikolai to speak to him in hushed words, he tapped the rim of the glass with calloused thumbs and repeated over and over, "No good, no good...."

"What is it?" Nikolai asked.

"My old beast...."

Mikhail began to tell Nikolai about his illness, some mysterious stomach affliction, that had become ever more worse. Drinking helped to ease the pain. Mikhail said he'd been drunk most every night for the better part of a year. "We will drink together and forget," said Mikhail, "You look strong though, Nikolai. Your clothes are better than before."

"They are tragic times for me as well, Mikhail. I was in love with a girl."

"Where did she go?"

"She left."

"I'm sorry, my friend. You do have a glint of death in your eye. That will pass. We need just to drink. There are girls here. Do you want to play cards?"

"Are you playing?"

"My friends are playing."

"You're not?"

"Sure I will."

"I didn't bring enough money to gamble."

"I'll lone you a bit if you can pay me back later."

Nikolai accepted the offer and was dealt a hand. The first card he was dealt was the wounded rabbit. The second was the blind beggar.

CHAPTER XXXI

Let me sing of that night I ventured myself into a place as dissolute as the Nesretan public house. Though I had not crude wines, nor companied with the common patrons, but sat in a princely place drinking nectars of the finer sort...

It was while I was studying the newspaper I had been keeping with me that I saw Nikolai enter and join a table of shabby companions. I observed him as he quickly drained stupefying cups of wine. I decided then to dispatch a good friend of mine, someone whom I knew would help. He was a wise and devilish man the patrons called Nestor. Nestor caught Nikolai off guard in the first game of cards...

"Why are you trembling so much?"

"I am trembling?" asked Nikolai.

Nikolai began winning a happy stash from Mikhail's friends, and now had a good portion of the money in front of him and another lucky draw in his hand. Nestor welcomed himself to a chair, joined the game and was dealt in. Nikolai was growing confident and now dared to place all his cash in a straight run against the stranger, Nestor.

"Why not?" Nestor laughed, throwing crisp bills amounting to six-hundred crowns on the table. Nikolai shuddered with drunken delight when the cards were overturned. A smile stole across his face. He had won. Nestor laughed again and surrendered his money.

"You are victorious," he told Nikolai, "Let's go to the counter and buy a bottle." With that, sallow-skinned Nikolai nodded and stood and the two went across the hall.

"A liter of wine, Mitia," ordered Nestor. He then turned to Nikolai and said in hushed tones, "You are a sad creature and it shows, Nikolai."

"These are hard times."

"Do you want some powders?"

"Powders? Of what sort?"

"Powders of godly spirit and joy."

Nikolai nodded carefully.

"Pay me four hundred crowns of what you won from the game," said Nestor. Nikolai reached in his pocket to furnish the crumpled bills. So doing, Nestor gave Nikolai a packet of silvery powders. Once the wine was paid for, Nikolai disappeared to the bath stalls to enjoy the sweet relief. He returned like a god to the table, descending upon it as a drunken satyr descends on a flock of ewes when hungry evening drives them into his feasting place.

"These are empirical times, Mikhail!" Nikolai cried joyfully, embracing his friend.

"For the time I seem to be making enough money," said Mikhail, not understanding Nikolai's sudden euphoria, but accepting the repayment of the debt Nikolai was handing to his friend. "I was working on the cranes all spring," said Mikhail. "I might go to the capital this fall. I was offered a job working on the underground, repairing the rails. Have you ever been to the capital?"

"No," said Nikolai, "I've never been anywhere. But who needs to travel? One travels well enough in one's head. Actually I was thinking of going to the West Islands. Do you know how I could get out there?"

"No," said Mikhail, "isn't it..."

Pause.

"Isn't it what?"

"I'd like to sleep with one of those two girls over there." Mikhail said pointing over to two young students who were stabled like sheep in the corner. They were meek creatures perched over tepid cups of wine, looking around with unease at all the predatory stares coming in from the darker sex. The fairer one seemed to Nikolai to resemble a small wet mouse. The other had a large nose and resembled a forest mole.

"They're only children," said Nikolai, "seventeen perhaps."

"Let's go drink with them," said Mikhail, refilling Nikolai's glass.

The two joined the girls and Nikolai spoke with the mousy one. She was a first-year student at the university and sat in rapt attention listening to Nikolai. Sensing her awe, he began to tell wild stories that had no bounds. He overheard a bit of Mikhail's conversations with the talpine girl and noticed the gloom in Mikhail's voice.

Come the late hour, the schoolgirls had become drunk and were speaking sloppily and wanton. Nikolai and Mikhail too were drunk and Nikolai felt fire in his glands. At one point, he bit the mousy girl's wrist and she squealed and asked him if he were crazy.

'But this is the true life!' Nikolai concluded happily, floundering in his wine, '....Unknown flesh beneath my fingers. And if I want more unknown flesh, I will flutter off and get it!'

"There are pelicans on the canal," Nikolai informed the girls. The mousy one didn't know what a pelican was. Nikolai and the forest mole explained what it was and the four decided to walk to the nearby canal together to look.

Outside, Nikolai took his girl and the two ran ahead through the night, jumping over puddles and stones on the edge of the Minor Canal. The young girl seemed to be happy to be drunk and with a stranger in the dilapidated darkness of Nesretan. She told Nikolai a story that he found childish, but he ignored it and sat her down on the bricks to kiss her. Her mouth was moist and cold. Mikhail all the while was talking to the mole-girl, though he was not caressing or kissing her. Soon Mikhail's girl stood and approached Nikolai and her friend. It turned out Mikhail had become ill in the stomach and was off vomiting behind a wall. The girl was upset and wanted to leave. Nikolai kissed one last time his mousy girl and said he would walk them to wherever. First he had to find Mikhail to help him. He looked for Mikhail but couldn't find him. Nor could he find the two girls again when he looked for them. He found himself alone later walking along the canal talking aloud about pelicans. Some man began shouting at him to keep off his front gate. "I'm only trying to get home!" Nikolai cried, and woke up late, disoriented in the head and ill in the gut. He had bits of memory here and there but didn't know how they attached, and wasn't sure if he should be happy about the events of the night before or not. What events were they? In the smoky clothes of yesterday, covered in canal grime, Nikolai left his basement room to buy some pills from the chemist.

CHAPTER XXXII

The August sun was bleeding over the treetops in the arboretum, where Nikolai came strolling in dirty clothes. In the gazebo, he sat and wept like an orphan. Later along the path, he stopped and decided to conceive of a heroic plan, some act to return himself to Nadja. But again, all acts were beyond him, and so he gave up the idea. He wanted only to drain his time away; yet he knew he couldn't keep going to the public house in the night. If he continued spending his money on wine, he realized, he would be in ruin after a fortnight.

He managed to pass the afternoon hours, and spent the evening at some cheap meal counter in the Shipyard District. He wandered until the moon burned steady in the hot sky over the harbor. Soon it was night, and in lonely despair he returned to the public house.

I myself had been spending much time as of late drifting about the city's more dismal haunts, and was down in the cellar in the public house when Nikolai arrived. I watched him saunter to a table in the corner, near the card players. I watched him spill his coins on the table and began counting them to buy libations. Observing him, I uttered aloud…

"You poor wretch, Nikolai. You are not considering at all your fate!"

I went unheard.

Turning then to Mitia who was preparing the kegs for the night, I bid the barkeeper give us the wine… "The base wine, Mitia! I will put my fine nectars away." So saying, I tucked the newspaper I'd been reading into the bench and went to join in at cards. When Nikolai saw my arrival he began to tremble, as if he'd seen an apparition in the night.

"We'll start with a quick hand, Nikolai."

"Is that Mikhail?"

Mikhail had indeed come and was in good spirits. He'd had dinner and drank vodka with his meal and was in a fine fettle. He joined the table and soon the other friend of Mikhail came – that strange soul with the pointy beard who'd dealt the cards the night before. There were now some girls at the table. Six women in the youthful or the worn years. Spinsters painted rouge sitting alongside poorly-dressed rascals.

"Tonight we'll have real women!" Mikhail whispered to Nikolai, "Not like the schoolgirls from last night. Mine was a scared virgin."

'Virgin,' Nikolai thought, considering this word. It was a pretty word, like so many he'd known. He thought then off Nadja and chased all thoughts away. "Mikhail," he said to his friend, "let's split on the first liter. I have to watch my money. I am hoping to win a little tonight."

"We are all hoping to win a little," Mikhail laughed, "then we will take these loose women at our table and go down to the capital and rent a room so that…."

'The capital,' Nikolai thought, 'Why there? I should rather go out to the forest beyond the Minor City. Alone, I will live in a little shack. I will bring a pot of ink and write the story of the end of the world…' With these thoughts, his mind began to wander further:

Yes, Nikolai, you will go to the forest beyond. Yes! There I will grow radishes and fell trees and skin the bark and use the hard flesh of the trees to build a great house. I will live to see the dawn rise over the far harbor in the distance. I will scorn the city I am in now, visible then only as a smudge in the distance, lining the harbor. There by the murderous sea. Why murderous sea? Is it not by a sea that Nadja is taking sun right now? There is no sun right now, anywhere. Now it is night! I imagine her long body as she reclines on the sand – no longer pale of skin like she was when we were on her terrace in the spring, but now she is dark and burnished from the summer sun. I see her glistening bronze body, back arched, looking absently out over the water, squinting in the bright afternoon as she studies the light's effects on the waves rippling across the sea, or else looking blankly in thought, or else thinking of nothing at all. All the while she allows the healthy oil-dark sun to play on the surface of her skin. Is she alone? Does she think of me? Had she been swimming so that now her hair is made slick and straight with a semi-matte sheen from the saltwater. Every few moments, she'll take her gaze off the sea and put her golden chin to her collarbone and examine her tummy which is small and firm and goes in a gentle slope to where it disappears beneath the elastic of her bathing suit. Her gentle mound I knew so well. Gentle, holy mound! As she breathes her breasts rise and sit firmly and beautifully on her chest – one would say drops of sweet honeycomb wax are dripping from a candle . . . But, Nikolai, this is suicide to think like this! I must not think of her, no! Out in the forest! The forest beyond the city! . . . There, I will be alone to read books and think of high things. I will read all of the ancient texts. Maybe one day I will teach myself to write and I will write new versions of the ancient texts. I will write poetic letters that declare my solitude and send them to the home of Nadja's father to say that I am a hermit in the woods and I will not look upon another woman or soul until I see her. 'Nadja,' I will say, 'Come and find me!' . . . But no, let her be damned. I will write the end of the world after all, with a pot of ink. She showed me life just to take it away. Gave me hope to drop me in despair, she has killed me, the wicked girl! I wonder how many times this man at the table is going to win at cards. He is collecting all the money and these filthy girls with gapped teeth just giggle at everything he says. And this one has the sores of syphilis eating her face off. To touch beautiful, firm breasts again! Firm and gently-sloping breasts with tiny nipples like seeds fallen on the soft and fertile earth. What is this world? Remember the wine we drank at the Anchises? . . . How sweetly that fell on the tongue! Ach! . . . This wine, it stings like urine-stained panties sting the thighs of a tiny child. It is a feeble world I have entered!

As Nikolai gave his silent soliloquy, he helped his mouth to swallow many a glass of wine; and this wine it cast shade upon his head, so that when he started speaking to Mikhail, his words slurred and jumbled and tripped around each other, and a fiery knot grew in his throat; but Mikhail sat happily on his left, playing away at cards. He had drawn the dying soldier and the seven sisters. On Nikolai's right, a new girl came to sit. With the wine and drunkenness that was befalling him, it felt pleasant to have her at his side. She was a crude specimen, dressed in strange bohemian rags. She had rather tiny, round teeth, was plain, but not overly ugly. She wore heavy rouge and a scarf to cover her tangled hair. Despite this and the pungent odor of tobacco she emitted, Nikolai found her pleasant, and his hand, he often pressed hard against her thigh as she herself watched the card game and chugged wine with happy enthusiasm.

Once during the game, this scarfed spinster turned to Nikolai, and laughing said, "I myself wouldn't even have bet on that!" She was talking about a silly gamble the man with the pointy beard had waged against me. I had put a stately sum on the table and he raised me two-hundred crowns. I happily checked and he showed his cards: two prosperous fishermen and a louse-burdened dog. I smirked at the bearded man's foolish misfortune and pocketed the money from the table. Nikolai meanwhile filled his glass from a new liter that had arrived and began to talk to the girl in the headscarf. I, who was amassing a fortune at cards for the mere pleasure of sport, ceased to be of interest to Nikolai as he pinned his blurred eyes on the hussy beside him. She was heavy in the bust and her low-cut bohemian top revealed thick creases running from breasts to arms. She had wrinkles on her eyes from age and drink. Nikolai boasted some clever talk about having lived in the Upper Quarter once…

"There," he told her, "one drinks good wine – sweet wine, or else dry red wine with the taste of seven spices – spices tilled on seven lands!" He went on to concoct a story about his old life in the Upper Quarter. He had owned a house, he said, with the terrace and a grand arcadian

165

garden. So vibrantly he told the story, one can imagine he even believed his tale to be true and was at one and the same time living in his invented world where he was a king. The spinster hung on all his words. She said she had once had a job babysitting for a family in the Upper Quarter, and they had had beautiful bottles of wine on their shelves. Nikolai was disgusted by her anecdote but continued on with his own story while pressing more and more her well-worn thigh with his wayward hand.

"But now I live on Fishmongers' Row," he said sadly, "For at last, tragedy struck me…"

"What kind of tragedy?" the spinster asked, startled, accepting Nikolai's hand on her happy thigh. "Oh, you are like a little boy with big eyes when you tell of these things. How much did you drink tonight?"

"Drink? I didn't start to drink!" …and thus he was off in some direction until his ears perked up to hear that the gypsies had begun to play. Their songs rose and fell as the mustached mouths spouted sounds like the whining of the un-oiled wheels of marketplace wagons selling tchotchkes.

The heat in the cellar was sweltering now as the dancing had begun and sweat rose off the gesticulating bodies in a warm rancorous mist that filled the room. The scarfed girl bent towards Nikolai, smiling a silly smile, gaping into his eyes. Nikolai noticed she was pockmarked, a feature rampant among the lower-classes in the Minor City. Still, he liked the shape of her nose and the gaps between her teeth. Her bosom was full and her blouse hung down off her shoulders and her shoulders appeared smooth and shiny. Nikolai had the sudden urge to touch them, and he did. It was then she told him her name and where she lived.

Now Nikolai felt as though he had been kicked in the throat. Where she lived was Otchajanie: wretched neighborhood near the bridge, of no consequence. That wasn't it. It was her name! Her name, it was, that blew the wind out of him. That name! Why *that name?!*

"Nadja. I am called Nadja." When she said this, Nikolai felt as though a screw were turning in his Adam's apple, as though worms were gnawing at his lungs.

Then the wine spoke to Nikolai and he said to her, "You have the name of a queen!"

She laughed.

"But it is not to laugh about!" Nikolai said, sloshing wine along the barrier of his teeth, "You have the same name as the only woman I ever loved. The noble Nadja. Bejeweled girl, she exists no more." Nikolai bowed his head with deep grief and said, "She exists no more . . . for she is dead."

"Dead?!"

The new Nadja pressed her hand to her breasts, deeply alarmed.

Nikolai went on with a fantastic story…

"We were married young," he lied, "my Nadja and I. Our house sang of happiness,. Our terrace was a field of kisses. Our garden was an overturned bowl of cream, spilling gentle beauty. It was like a . . . but did you say your name was *Nadja*? You did? But how can it be?!

"…She was young and beautiful and we lived in a large house in the Upper Quarter with colonnades and endless groves of citrus trees. I remember the springtime: We had been married for five years. We had just learned she was going to give me a baby. A child by her! Can you imagine? My perfect Nadja!…" All the while Nikolai was telling this tale, the new Nadja pressed his hand to her tear-ridden cheeks and she drunk his words. I, myself, seated across the table, listened with amusement. I shuffled the cards and laughed with sinister pleasure. Go on, Nikolai! Tell your tale!

"…My perfect Nadja!" Nikolai continued, "Her belly swelled and she walked in the spring garden picking hyacinth. We were ready for our child. A month passed and there was a summer storm. Lightning struck and fell the dark branches of a cypress tree beyond the terrace. Nadja was gasping in pain, crying, for the baby was trying to be born. I sent for a doctor and helped her onto the bed in our bedroom. She screamed terribly, my Nadja, and that little child caused all sorts of ruptures to her trembling body and then…"

"And then?!"

"She died."

Nikolai bowed his head and then looked up solemnly and brushed his moist lids with his thumb. "The infant died too. And I ask, how can it be? . . . I ask you this! The woman you cherish more than anything in the world is killed trying to give you a child you yourself helped to create! As you can imagine, I couldn't go on living in that house. I sold the house and basically threw the money away, not caring – so dead was I inside. I moved then into a tiny cellar room on Fishmongers' Row, below Calico's flower shop, you know him, he comes in her selling his flowers sometimes. I purposely chose a room as dismal as my soul. How empty I have been, Nadja!

"...Oh, why do I tell you this? You think I am a foolish and drunken man! . . . You don't? . . . You mean you like it that I am telling you all of this? What a precious creature you are, little Nadja. Sweet little Nadja. Let the world spare you. Oh, but my Nadja, you see, I never could believe she was really dead. Even after I moved from our house to that cellar room on Fishmongers' Row, I kept waiting for Calico to come downstairs with a note from her saying she is waiting for me . . . I kept waiting for Calico to come downstairs and knock at my door and have a note from her saying that she was waiting for me at the Anchises Hotel, or that she was waiting for me at our home, with our new baby girl; that all this about death was only a dream. That we are still together and have our life – just the way it used to be!

"...You see, Nadja . . . Oh, you have the name of a sacred queen! . . . She and I would drink wine together at the Anchises. Have you heard of this hotel? You have? Surprising! It didn't matter how much of that sweet wine we drank, it was paid for. You know, you look like her? You look just like her!" . . . What drunken lies was Nikolai telling? As if the sound of the hopeful name that beckons this withered creature before him could grace her skin and tone it, and give her the beauty that belonged to his fair Nadja, long gone away!

Suddenly, a warbled chant came from across the hall... "Flowers for ladies! Flowers for ladies!" It was Calico the flower vendor, sent by swift dispatch, making his rounds to try to push flowers on all the men obliged to women. His famous chant, he emitted with a squeak from his foolish throat and toothless mouth... "Flowers for ladies!"

I who was occupied at cards, sent the waiter for more wine and began to deal another hand. A sly smile played across my lips as Nikolai recognized the warbling and turned around to see Calico. "Is that you, my friend?" he cried, "Come here and drink something with us!" Calico hobbled over to Nikolai, and smiled a stupid grin. He accepted no drink, for he never drank, but stood gaping as Nikolai asked him desperately, "Do you have any notes from my dear Nadja, Calico?"

Calico stood looking blankly around, while Nikolai repeated himself with tears in his eyes. Soon Calico turned away and began again his toothless chant with dumb gaiety... "Flowers for ladies! Flowers for the ladies?"

"No flowers for them!" Nikolai shouted, growing angry, "They are just whores here in this place! Filthy whores!"

"No, he's not!..." the new Nadja could be heard saying to someone across the table in Nikolai's defense, "He is just sad about his wife who's dead."

"Fine," growled the gambler with the pointy beard, "but have him keep his hands off the cards!"

Nikolai was now standing and Mikhail asked him why he was leaving so soon and where he was going. Moments later, Nikolai found himself out in a cloud of smoke and night, out on the street. The spinster Nadja with her bohemian rags and warped and creased skin stood beside him, lighting a cigarette. She asked if he would walk her home, for it was late and unsafe.

"Oh!" laughed Nikolai sardonically, "You will do fine in this neighborhood, you!"

The spinster Nadja seemed to take no offense to this remark, however; showing only pity for him, she clasped Nikolai's hand and the two began to walk towards the Minor Canal. Nikolai agreed to show her along the canal, but not all the way to Otchajanie. He would turn off in the Shipyard District and go alone to his own place on Fishmonger's Row.

The new Nadja talked incessantly while the two walked along the foul-smelling corridors of the Minor Canal. She kept abreast with him. Her thick peasant hips swung in their torn stockings. A large knit bag was slung over her shoulder. Always the same complacent grin, eager to hear Nikolai's tales. She mentioned she too had lived on Fishmongers' Row once when she worked as a laundress near Calico's flower shop. She said she hadn't known there to be rooms beneath the flower shop. "There aren't rooms!" Nikolai barked in annoyance, "There is only *one* room!" . . . and it was his. She asked if she could go with him there, but he said "No." And then, "Not tonight." He was feeling ill from the bad wine and wanted to collapse. The new Nadja took his hand and dragged him on.

At one point, she mentioned that she'd be traveling soon.

"Traveling?" Nikolai wondered.

But no, it was not real traveling she would be doing, just going to the countryside near the Minor City. A mere half-hour away by light-rail. Something about a seasonal babysitting job. Taking care of an infant at the summer home of some rich family. Nikolai had heard enough about this girl's odd jobs as a laundress and a servant and the whole affair disgusted him and he kept on, but when she continued tugging his hand he finally gave in and veered off towards the rock walls of the embankment and felt himself pushing her hard against the wall. The two embraced and he put his mouth to her sour lips and noticed she trembled before giving herself fully to him. He felt her breasts like large sagging cushions floating beneath his hands, escaping his grip the way rubber balls escape a child's hands when floating in a swimming pool. He tightened his mouth shut and she tried to open his mouth with hers. When he finally opened his mouth, he felt her film-covered teeth with his slick tongue.

After the embrace, Nikolai stepped back away from the wall and let the spinster Nadja fix the bag slung on her back. He again held her damp hand and started walking again. He hated this vile woman, and he thought to hurry off alone. But he felt also pity for her, and continued to hold her hand as he walked, trying not to smell her, All the while, she walked close beside him, clenching his hand and patting his hair with her other hand and saying she pitied him for having lost his wife, Nadja…

"And your Nadja died and left you all alone in this world," she said again and again, "You poor, sweet man! I'll be your Nadja, I'll be your Nadja, you poor, poor, sweet man…" But thinking of the real Nadja and hearing her name said aloud made Nikolai sick with desperate longing and when finally the wench beside him stopped saying how she was now going to be *his Nadja*, she persisted in talking about how beautiful the rooftops looked from the street in this part of town, once the two had surfaced from the corridor along the canal. As if it all wasn't too much! Nikolai hated these putrid roofs in the Shipyard District. He told her he hated them. He told her that they were made cheap in a nearby factory and then he mumbled something to her about a crime he wanted to commit, or was about to commit; and she laughed with disbelief while he gasped with a shortage of air to his lungs and a painful stinging in his head; as soon it was morning and the creamy viscous light of the sun pushed itself through the tiny window in the upper corner of the dreary cellar room where Nikolai was waking up – sick again with wormholes of a memory. His memory was flimsy, however, he could remembered clearly the False Nadja of the night before – that vile brigand! False Nadja, that dishonest wretch, who had killed his true and noble Tsarina and had stolen her crown. He thought it time to climb from his wretched bed and go find the chemist to buy relief.

CHAPTER XXXIII

Good fortune, I was sitting in the Nesretan public house a few nights later, playing a heroic hand. I had won the purses of more than a few men by means of a gambler's clever trickery, but was beginning to tire from that pursuit. Before me sat a liter of holy wine, such was my fare, and had ordered a couple liters of spoilt wine for the other men. There too were women with us at the table: wenches and students from working-class families, seamstresses and other slaves. Nikolai too was there. He'd been drinking to the crooning gypsies' songs for some hours and was taking foolish delight in their fiddling tunes. He sang their words with a gaping mouth, tossing wine across the barrier of his teeth.

  A new girl was sitting by him now. A thin specimen, with brittle hair and large black nostrils. Nikolai refilled her glass often and the two drank and sang while the gypsy band whined and whirled and the horns played. Nikolai was drunk and alive. At one point, he had the gall to turn and look me in the eyes, though sheepishly so. "Not a good move, young man," I issued forth through closed teeth, "Turn back to the harlot by your side." I myself was getting dulled by wine, and my own sad memories kept returning... Visions of a sweet beauty naked and drifting, dead like alluvion, along the sandy shore beneath the fabled

Otchajanie Bridge.

Nikolai turned back to the brittle girl beside him. Her eyes seized his like screws and her hand touched his shoulder and she smiled with her wide grate of teeth. Nikolai poured her a glass of oil-black wine and turned back to Mikhail who was seated on his left.

"Mikhail, do you have a knife I can borrow for later?"

"Why a knife, Nikolai?"

"I either need to make money gambling, or else I'll need to mug someone on the street. I'll need a knife to do that."

"Nonsense!" laughed Mikhail with unease, "It is nonsense, you speak of!" He clasped his friend's shoulder good-naturedly and added, "Come, Nikolai, let us sing and dance to the gypsies' songs...."

And so they did, the two friends. They held their mouths to the sky, which was then no more than a dusky slab of cellar stones, strung with an orbit of stars disguised as red paper lanterns. The two friends held their mouths to the sky and let fall in them dreams of drunken midnight songs.

I who was a witness to all, observed these two from my holy seat and spoke these words – not addressing the men, but rather addressing *the songs* that filled their hearts. I said...

"You poor wretches! Why do we sing you from our mortal mouths, when you yourselves are ageless and deathless? Is it so that we may grieve among you? Tell me... Why do we give you to the night?... For the night is like us. It is a sad and mortal night!"

CHAPTER XXXIV

"And why not travel?" Nikolai wondered to himself as he was walking back to his room one evening. It was late in August. He had just bought a razor and a bottle of anisette and stopped on his way home to watch the hazy sun fall into the darkness of the hills from a bench outside on the street. "Why not travel to find her? I just need a shave and clean clothes. Then I will ask Vladimir to help me. Certainly, he has received a letter from her. He knows her address. He will give it to me. Vladimir of all people will give it to me. Then, I'll just need the money to go find her. Just one lucky swing at the cards, that's all I need. Then, I'll need to leave this damned city before spending the money on wine and tonics. Those 'powders of godly spirit and joy' turn me into a beast! They gnaw at my memory. If I continue, these people will be the ruin of me!" It was true that as of recent, Nikolai had been threatened on several occasions on account of his failing memory. He was experiencing more that a little paranoia and knew things would turn out very badly, should he continue living the way he was living. "…No, I must find Nadja. I will run away with her anyway, just as she asked long ago on that mild night. We can set up a new life somewhere. Just one run of luck and a little money…" So the words of Nikolai ran on as he made his way home in the twilight.

Meanwhile, I was at my stately house in the Upper Quarter, standing by the ivory colonnades. After darkness conquered all, leaving only a sliver of a moon and the garden lights and the nest of stars above . . . after the winds died down and the only sounds coming within my garden were the whispering wings of the nightjars flitting between the trees, I left the grandeur of my home to go down into the city. By the gates of the house, I stopped to look around. On all sides of me, the garden lamps shone with their flickering flames leaping up towards the heaven of stars. My eyes settled on the terrace. I remembered how clearly she had looked when she stood there so majestically, wearing the robe I had given her. I sighed and thought of other times. I then felt in my pocket to make sure the pistol I'd bought in the capital was secure. It was there, bullets and all. Closing the garden gate, I started off on foot, down the hill through the arboretum.

It was a quiet night in Nesretan. At the public house we drank and played cards, as was our custom. When Nikolai arrived, he was already drunk. When he saw Mikhail wasn't there, he approached us timidly and asked to sit down.

"I'd like to play," he said, "I brought money."

"Sit down, Nikolai," we ushered forth slyly through closed teeth. My old companion, Nestor, began to deal. He turned two cards over. The first was the crooked tree. The second was the two-headed eel.

"Are you sure you want to play, Nikolai?" I smiled.

"I think we all want to play," said Nestor with craft.

"Twenty crowns apiece to start."

We all put in our tidy sums and the rest of the cards were passed around. Devilish Anton with the pointy beard won the first and collected the money. Having lost, Nikolai grew visibly pale and counted his sum. I poured a round of spoilt wine and sent for more. As soon as there were but a few of us at the table, one of my other trusted companions came by swift dispatch to ask Nikolai if he wanted more powders of godly spirit and joy.

"I cannot deal with those powders," said Nikolai. He was using caution. His hands trembled as he spoke.

"I have other ones for you then," said my friend.

"What are they?"

"Powders of deafening calm."

So saying, my friend brought forth a slim packet of powders and handed it to Nikolai. Nikolai tasted the powders and felt relieved of all grief. His nose drank them the way gluttonous roots suck water from rich soil; all the while, agony flitted from his face the way sorrow leaves the face of a crying child when sleep overtakes it.

Having inhaled the tonics, Nikolai sat charged in slumber, tossing himself amongst his cards. He played well on this night, as luck was on his side. Meanwhile the gypsies' songs whined their forlorn melodies. Their songs were sorrowful this night, resembling the whinnying of pack animals who, though tired of labor, are bound to the traveling road. I sat far off on my own for a while, studying the newspaper I'd been keeping, drinking my own clean wine.

It just then occurred to me that it was the last night of August. 'So tomorrow begins September,' I mused, 'month of singular sorrows.' It also occurred to me then that Nikolai had managed to win a decent sum of money. He was getting ready to take a final sweep of the table, to clean out my men's money and leave the bar intact.

"And where will you go with your fortune?" I laughed, and decided, though weary as I was, to return to the game. Nikolai looked at me with fearful eyes as I sat down near him at the table and ordered a hand of cards. I took from my pockets a sturdy sum to match what Nikolai was playing and we were dealt.

Nestor dealt the cards to each man. Suddenly there came a voice from behind us...

"Nikolai!" someone exclaimed.

It was good-natured Mikhail. Nikolai's turned to the newcomer and his face flushed with relief. He asked permission to hold the game for as long as it would take to shake his friend's hand. Upon standing to do so, he made a clumsy motion and spilled his wine. Mikhail shook his friend's hand and looked down at all the money he was winning and was glad his friend's fortune was changing. "I've started collecting things…" Mikhail began to say.

"Let me talk to Mikhail a minute," Nikolai begged of us.

"No, Nikolai. There is a lot of money on the table. Stay and finish the hand."

With this defeat, Nikolai sat back down and Nestor finished dealing. When the last card came up, we saw all was in my favor. I laughed.

"Poor Nikolai," said Nestor frowning slyly, "You've lost everything!" Nikolai was crushed. I smiled and collected the entire pot. And from the handsome winnings, I paid spoilt wine for the men. I gave Nikolai two-hundred crowns for pity's sake and pocketed the rest. Nikolai snatched the bill from me, barely observing it, and turned trembling to his friend…

"Just let me borrow eight-hundred crowns, Mikhail. Please, I need it!" He was shaking, lightening in pallor to a deathly white. Mikhail solemnly reached in his pocket and produced the money. Nikolai returned to the game at once.

I had won and thought to leave the table. I had no desire to continue playing. I was fed up with the night and wished to leave for other affairs. Nikolai pleaded with me, however, salivating over the thought of winning some of the fortune back from me. Finally, I agreed to play one more hand of money.

"Men," I said, addressing the table, "I am going to buy each of you a liter of wine. Then, I will play the thousand crowns I've set on the table to match Nikolai's thousand. But that is all. No more money leaves my pocket tonight. Are you ready Nikolai?"

So saying, Nestor began to deal. Lucky hand for Nikolai. He won the pot. Feverishly, he snatched the money up and thrust the eight-hundred crowns he owed Mikhail into his friend's hand. Even neglecting his full cup of wine, he turned all his hunger on the cards before us. He urged us on to deal again, throwing his entire purse on the table.

"We'll play another hand!" he implored, "Please! One more win and I can get to the islands! I can go to the islands in the west! There we will have our wine-colored days!" In madness, he turned to Mikhail. Mikhail, however, was getting ill with his old beast and was standing up to leave.

"The islands!" Nikolai screeched like a little child, "...The islands! The islands!"

Then it was my turn...

"I told you, Nikolai, that no more money leaves my pockets tonight. Take your miserable twelve-hundred crowns and go home."

"Just one more game!" he begged, his eyes searching around the room for anyone to match his bet. The other men had all folded long ago and no one was interested in playing.

I then had an idea.

Reaching into my slender pocket, I pulled out the pistol I had bought in the capital. It was loaded with eager bullets. With my deft had, I held up the clever pistol and watched Nikolai's eyes grow wide and glisten. His black pupils inflated. They began undulating with the movements of two poisonous jellyfish in the blood-dark sea. "Look here," I smiled, and set the pistol down before us on the table. Then, craftily I said...

"Nikolai... as I told you before, no more money leaves my pockets for the night. I will, however, play this gun against your twelve-hundred crowns."

Nikolai looked at the gun with puzzled avarice. My move had stumped him. After a moment of dumb consideration, he sniffed his foolish nose and wagged his head, tossing his money on the table.

Nestor began to deal.

"It's a nice gun," we heard people muttering over our shoulders.

I picked up my cards and found a pleasant hand. Nestor asked for two cards set face up on the table from each man . . . a kind of cock's furling his feathers. My first card was a glorious one. I watched clear bubbles of sweat froth up on Nikolai's trembling forehead. His own card was not so promising. All at the table saw I would win. I could keep my gun and Nikolai's money as well. I merely had to keep on with my hand, and concentrate on what I drew. I, however, was growing tired of the game. I didn't feel like playing with the trembling fool any longer. Honestly, I didn't even feel like winning. I was eager to leave the table, overall, no matter who the winner may be. Thus, I threw a careless card down. It was a senseless move, but I didn't care. After I threw the card down, I heard groans from the other men as they realized my folly. Nikolai, however, didn't groan but remained silent. I saw hope steal across his face, lifting his brow. A hidden smile of triumph begin to curl his lips . . . So I see he plans on winning this fateful hand, does he? . . . Poor, poor Nikolai. If anything happens to Nikolai, I told myself, I shall be forced to wander the earth and sleep in strange beds. I'll say I'm a prophet of sorts and pay a handsome sum so they'll have faith in me.

"What do we have?" clever Nestor called out to us men with gambling hands. To this, I laughed aloud and threw the rest of my careless cards down for all to see. Nikolai's eyes were the first to dart to my cards. He then looked at me carefully, mistrustfully, his lips trembling, trying to make a smile but nervous to do so. He then grew bold and set down his hand: Two poplar trees on either side. In between them dangled the drowned sailor. The card depicted his grey and bloated body hanging upside-down by an anchor.

"'Justice moved my High Maker,'" Nikolai said to Mikhail later, admiring the pistol he had won from me. Mikhail was upstairs by the door to the public house, drinking a tepid broth to ease the pain in his stomach.

"What will you do with the gun?" Mikhail asked.

"I'll sell it. Or rather..." Nikolai looked around mischievously, and then repeated his earlier phrase... "'Justice moved my High Maker.' ...Have you ever heard that phrase?"

"No," Mikhail replied.

"An old poet spoke of that. A poet who said he'd hiked through the underworld. He said 'Justice moved my High Maker.' As if God's emotions could be swayed by the lives of mortals. As if He created the world because He loves justice. This suggests that the world's condition can cause God to take action. If so, than could not clever mortals trick God into taking an unwise decision, or even trick Him into suffering some kind of condition?"

"You speak of nothing," Mikhail said, "And I am ill tonight. The broth is not helping, Nikolai. I don't think I can go on much longer."

"What are you talking about, Mikhail?"

"Are you staying here?"

Nikolai looked around the upstairs of the public house. He saw three new customers, young girls, entering. They were discussing the gypsy band that would be playing downstairs.

"Yes, I'm staying."

"Okay, I'm going," said Mikhail, and he was gone. Nikolai found himself downstairs later, talking to Mitia. He'd spoken with someone and found himself buying another bottle. The gypsies too were drinking and Nikolai kept checking to make sure his new pistol was well tucked into his clothes secure enough so it wouldn't fall out or be stolen, even were he to collapse from drunkenness on the street. They would find his liver before they would find the gun.

Later, he would remember having danced that night. He would remember embracing the three girls he had watched enter when he had been talking to Mikhail upstairs. One of the girls had had a rash on her shoulder. He would recall an acrid taste on his lips and some altercation on the street outside after the public house had closed and he'd left. Something about a constable having been called to the apothecary. Two drunken girls were running down the street with a suitcase they'd found. They asked Nikolai for a corkscrew for their wine. Nikolai recalled falling through a wooden crate on Fishmongers' Row. Stray cats were licking bones and the juices from the fish in the night and they scattered in the darkness when he stumbled, tearing his clothes. Back in his room, he felt vertigo and sickness from the hot air and needed cool wind on his face. That's fine, Nikolai, there is wind in the passage. He didn't want people to see him, however, stumbling in the passage. Why was this gate latched and how come he couldn't get in? There were horns a moment ago and now this deafening calm! "Oh, deafening calm! Finally, I can sit and feel the wind of my face, blessed doorway! Good that sweat cools vicious fever . . . You know, one cannot be mad when one is alone. Madness depends on the mirror of others. Tomorrow I shall receive word from my holy Nadja. If not, I will send madness upon the islands and strangle the messenger. I will dispatch imps to disturb his dreams. Madness! Madness, I cry, wrought in the reflections of eyes – sunken, glazed and watery eyes. Let me sink in that hole in the ground every night and every day. Every night or every day? Night or day? Why, where has day come from? And how is it already light outside?!"

CHAPTER XXXV

Nikolai woke late in the morning, surprised to find he'd been sleeping sprawled in the passageway. He climbed to his feet and perched on the stairwell leading down to his room and searched his disheveled clothes. He inspected his skin, which had become remarkably soiled and scratched. When he came across the pistol tucked in his clothes, he struggled with his memory to recall how he'd obtained it. When had he come across a gun? Inside his room, he stuffed it back in the crawlspace where he had kept his money in better times when he'd had a little to keep aside. He thought he remembered winning a small sum the night before. Had he lost it all, finally? No, here it seemed he had a few crowns in his pockets to get by. After changing his clothes and washing the grime from his hair, he left his room to seek out the familiar chemist to buy relief for his illness.

Out on Fishmongers' Row, Nikolai saw a startling sight: Calico's flower shop was boarded up. There were broken glass shards and flower stems strung about the street. Two policemen stood near the shop jotting notes. Nikolai slithered along the hot street, curiously eyeing the policemen, as well as the mess around the shop. He didn't make haste away from the shop, but slithered slowly along the perimeter. Seeing

Nikolai, one of the policemen called him over…

"Young man! Where have you come from?"

Nikolai thought of the pistol. "From over here," he told the policeman, slowly in measured words, "I live just here. Below this flower shop."

The two policemen now gathered beside Nikolai. The one began taking notes as he questioned him. "How long have you lived here?"

"About four years," Nikolai said. His dumb gaze drifted absently along the boarded walls of the shop. 'Could it have been here?' he wondered.

"Why do you have cuts on your hands?"

"I didn't notice."

"Do you know the flower seller?"

"I do . . . I mean, that is . . . Well, you see I live here, just down below. So yes, I know him. His name is Calico."

"Calico," one policeman said, looking at the other, "Yes, but it wasn't him…"

"It seems his brother," the other officer picked up, "a man named Radja. He was here late last night working in the shop, and was assaulted by someone who broke in. The neighbors heard shouting. The assailant was apparently drunk and confused, demanding flowers for his girlfriend."

"Assaulted the flower seller's brother?" Nikolai asked slowly in a flat tone of voice.

"That's right. Did you ever see him?"

"No."

"Well, did you hear anything last night? I ask since you do live downstairs, beneath the shop. There must have been a lot of noise in the night. Whoever broke-in, smashed the windows. You must have heard something. You can see the mess they've made…"

"No," Nikolai answered slowly, carefully, "I didn't hear anything.

I was ill last night with a fever. I was sleeping. Sleeping very hard."

"I see," said the policeman. "What is your name?"

"Nikolai."

"Your full name…"

He told them.

"Have you ever had problems with the law?"

"No," said Nikolai

"I see."

Nikolai asked then if that was all. The policemen said yes, that he could leave. As Nikolai started off, he turned around with a sudden calm and rejuvenation, and asked the policemen most alive and casually…

"By the way, how is he doing? The brother, I mean."

"He is in the hospital."

"Oh!" Nikolai shrugged then and walked off. All of this gave him a strange feeling. Of the night before, he could remember little of where he'd been, and nothing of how he'd returned to his own neighborhood. His memory was empty and it troubled him. Walking along, he decided not to go to the nearby apothecary as he had planned, but rather to go to an apothecary in another part of town, somewhere where he would go unrecognized and unsuspected. He walked to the Canal District and there stayed for many hours, afraid to go home. He returned only late in the evening to eat and clean himself. That night, he bathed for a long time, taking great care with his appearance. He would soon go to the public house. He didn't feel like drinking but he didn't want to be alone. He hoped Mikhail would be there. Reaching back in the crawlspace in his little cellar room, he felt the pistol he had stashed that morning. Next to it was the last of his money he'd placed in an old wooden box. Fifty crowns. He would be getting his check in a week. It was now September. He could sell some of the books in his bookcase tomorrow to scrape buy. Things were fine, he thought, so of course he could spend his last fifty crowns.

When Nikolai arrived at the public house, he found a large crowd assembled outside, though it was early, only ten o'clock. As he entered, he passed Mikhail who was heading outside. Mikhail was walking strangely, limping with a dusty loaf of black bread cradled in a headscarf.

"Why the bread?" Nikolai asked him, but Mikhail didn't respond. He looked at Nikolai quickly, with angry eyes, as he hurried away in the shadows of Nesretan street hunched over his bread, scuffing his shoes. When Nikolai descended to the cellar, he approached Mitia who was pouring liquor for the gypsies to warm their spirits for playing.

"Mitia!" Nikolai called gaily, but Mitia didn't respond. The gypsies began to talk amongst themselves. 'Why is everyone acting so strangely?' Nikolai wondered.

"How about a liter of wine?" he asked Mitia.

"Not tonight, Nikolai."

"Why not, how come not tonight, Mitia?" His throat began to swell with anxiety.

"I'm not going to serve you anything, Nikolai."

"What is it, Mitia?"

"Don't you remember when you left here last night?"

Nikolai stood dumb, wondering what offense he had committed. So it had been true! . . . For some time he had sensed strangeness was lurking in the obscurity of his behavior; felt only but not seen, as one senses the shapes of a traveler passing in the fog.

"You'd better not come in here for a while."

"But what have I done!" he cried to Mitia, turning, not waiting for an answer, afraid of what holes Mitia would fill in his memory, he simply turned away, ashamed. 'Better now just to leave!' he thought. And thus he did.

Out on Nesretan Street, Nikolai walked under the light of the gas lamps, trying to imagine what had happened the night before. If only he could talk to Mikhail. What cold eyes Mikhail had cast upon him! He had better just to forget the public house and find another place to drink.

He felt the fifty crowns in his pocket and walked away from Nesretan in search of some place that would serve him, some place where he could calm himself and piece things together. What had he done the night before, after all?

Nikolai found a cheap liquor house in the Shipyard District where he knew no one. He ordered a beer at the bar and sat at a corner table to drink it. There were few patrons in the place: fat drunks sitting hunched up on corner stools. A ceiling fan flapped noisily overhead. Nikolai drank his beer and watched flies drop one by one from the ceiling onto his table.

CHAPTER XXXVI

"Autumn at the End of September"

Nikolai never returned to the Nesretan public house. He ended his summer passing from hovel to hovel, from drinking den to food counter – places where he spoke not and knew no one. He had long since abandoned his plans to seek the help of Vladimir. He was no longer in a condition to do that. Hope having dwindled away, he fell into long bouts of dreamless sleep, waking late in the afternoon. Walking through the Canal District in the evenings, he would be haunted by strange obsessions: desires to cleanse his body by bathing in tainted yellow milk, or to go live in the bows of the trees in the arboretum. Back in his basement room, he would imagine the city flooding in a great deluge. He saw tumults of water pouring into his cellar, crushing all; and when the waters would finally recede, he would be gone; and all that would be left would be a thin film of decay on the ground. Days overleapt themselves. Outside, in the light of warm, early autumn, things were altogether different. The windows of Calico's flower shop had been repaired and Calico was running shop and his business was thriving. New crops of flowers were brought in from the country, and new harvests of vegetables filled the costermongers' stalls in the marketplace. The sun washed the bricks of Fishmongers' Row and happy mothers pushed strollers with tidy children waving pink hands . . . sweet mothers buying groceries for autumn dinners. Nikolai came out one evening at sunset and was struck by the way life was going on around him despite the dark tunnel of despair he had dug for himself. People were taking pleasure in walking, in eating in the parks and on terraces, in buying ready fruit at the markets. As Nikolai was returning home that evening, he saw Calico outside his shop dyeing flowers on the pavement. Fearing that in his delirium he had wronged the flower vendor, Nikolai hurried past, hoping to go unnoticed. But Calico saw him despite his efforts, yet showed no displeasure on his face. He smiled a toothless grin and cried, "Good season! Good season!" and resumed clipping and dyeing his flowers. In seeing Calico's stupid grin, and hearing the words 'good season,' Nikolai felt happy for one moment. The happiness came in a tender rush and left him feeling more sunken than ever afterwards, for it left a taste of what happiness is as a dead memorial. With a bowed head, he disappeared into the passage and went down to his room to go to sleep.

He wasn't sure how long he slept after that. It could have been many days. However long it was though, it passed easily. He had chanced upon dreamless oblivion.

Then, on the morning of a bright day late in September, Nikolai received a loud knock at his door. Disoriented, he looked around and struggled to lift himself from his bed. The knock came again, steady and loud. "Those the police done come!" Nikolai whispered this strange phrase into his bedclothes, then got up. "Well, if it must end, then…"

At the door, Nikolai turned the knob, expecting to find the police outside. But it was not the police who'd come for him. It was merely Calico. The little man held a pair of flower sheers and a few blooms of autumn dahlias in his right hand. He hopped on his toes and grinned. The morning sun, passing through the town, managed to shed one soft beam down the somber passageway and it reflected creamy-white light off the yellow petals of the dahlias. In Calico's left hand, he held a note for Nikolai.

"Pretty girl!" said Calico, crying, jumping on his dwarfish feet, "Pretty girl! Pretty girl!"

'Pretty girl?' Nikolai wondered, 'Of Nadja alone, he talks like that! Could it be?!'

Such a welcome sound was the ring of Calico's voice, now as it planted an anchor on Nikolai's sleep-swimming head and started his eyes flapping. As a sailor lost at sea hears the horn blasts of his old familiar lighthouse upon returning to his beloved native land, years following his departure to drift along the lonely ocean swells, such was the sound of Calico's voice to him now at this moment, upon receiving this news. Such was the joy in light-headed Nikolai's heart to hear these happy words. "Pretty girl!" He felt a large tear growing on his face. So large was it that it quickly tumbled down and called upon others.

"Good God, Calico!" Nikolai cried, and reached to the flower vendor's shoulder with one hand as if seeking to embrace him; while, with his other hand, he reached out to grasp the note Calico was holding. Such was the warmth that had entered that cellar room on this late September day. Calico faded from view as Nikolai turned in the doorway and unfolded the letter to read the words written in Calico's half-literate scrawl. The note read…

"NIKOLAI! I HAVE COME BACK! I HAVE RETURNED FROM TRAVELING. I AM IN THE MINOR CITY NOW. LET US MEET THIS EVENING AT FIVE AT THE ANCHISES HOTEL."

Signed:

"YOUR NADJA."

Such was Nikolai's pleasure upon reading these words! He clasped his frail chest with his hand and cried, "My lord, great Nadja! Today I will see you! Fruitful will be the frigid seasons! Of this I am certain! . . . Glorious will be my life!"

Yet why, he wondered, had she returned from the West Islands? Did it matter? No, this did not matter; for she had returned as he knew she would, and Nikolai was glad, for… "I will see you today, my Nadja! For today, I am saved!"

CHAPTER XXXVII

Nikolai, wrapped in sheets of euphoria, cleaned and prepared himself for the great reunion that was to take place that evening. "Never again shall I suffer!" he declared, leaving his room that late morning. There was much time to pass before he would see her, but he set off early in happy song to stroll along the sunny streets and fresh-washed banks of the canals. "Ask me again, my fair Nadja, if I would choose you or the world? For you Nadja, I will travel wide over this world with no fear of the mysteries that await us. I will capture the world and cage it. I will keep it as a pet for you! For you my Nadja! We have come to the heroic season!"

Nikolai spent much of the afternoon wandering the vibrant streets of the Canal District waiting for the hour to come when he would again see Nadja. He ate lunch at a pleasant café with a sunny terrace, not worrying that it the last of his money he was spending. If there was one day to splurge on clean food in a clean place, this was it. Now his life had returned to the way it had been; a time when all that passed his lips was good, when gorgeous were those that passed his eyes.

At three in the afternoon, he found himself nervously retracing his steps. He wondered what he would say to her when he first saw her.

"But nonsense, Nikolai!" he told himself, "I will have no speech. We will embrace and kiss. And my speech will be my speechlessness!"

He bought a little toy from a shop in the Canal District: a wooden globe on a string that one swung upwards to try to make it fall and balance on a wooden peg. It was painted yellow and green. Later, when he saw a child sitting out on the hot pavement, forming a circle of pebbles around his little shoes and humming a happy song, he gave the child the toy. The little boy smiled wide with pleasure and Nikolai continued on.

Having passed the majority of the afternoon hours, he realized luckily the time was coming near. At half-past four, he arrived back at the Anchises Hotel. Not able to concentrate on more wandering, too nervous and elsewhere-minded to drink a coffee or to go inside, he decided to bide the impatient minutes outside on the steps. The sun washed the front of the hotel and boardwalk with clean white light. The air was scented. The late afternoon was mildly warm; it was the perfect day to see again his one true love.

When the clock of the Bastion tolled the fifth hour, Nikolai turned his head to the tolling sound. Two seagulls flew in front of that glad tower with fresh-caught minnows in their claws. A great omen, he believed. It was while he was looking at the tower that he felt a soft touch of a hand to the bone of his jaw below his cheek. This was followed by a touch on his shoulder. When he turned around, he felt suddenly the splash of rain. Was it raining? It was not raining, it had merely been a spray of ocean from the harbor, spraying across the boardwalk. Yet it had sprayed before his eyes like rain. And now looking at she who had touched his face and shoulder, at the woman who stood before him now, leaning off after kissing his cheek to say hello, that the spray of mist from the harbor splashed upon him like a cold grey rain – a rain like all those morning rains he had felt over and again throughout his sad past; and again he felt the screw pushing into his throat. The screw spun like the oiled gears of a machine, turned like a shipyard crane; and as it turned, Nikolai worked to catch a breath and felt a cold wind enter his lungs. Now standing before him was the old life from which he wanted to escape, the life he thought he had escaped from, but evidently did not. Nikolai saw before him all the grey-lit yesterdays, all the smoldered sorrows – dregs of powders of godly spirit and joy, and remnants of deafening calm. He saw it in the woman's bohemian rags. He saw it in the feathered gypsy's knotted nose, in the knit bag the gypsy wore over her shoulder, in her shriveled cheeks and dusty eyes. He saw it in the country scarf upon her head, and in the gaping grin that seemed to mock him.

False Nadja! . . . Oh, why was it she who'd come to meet him?! He looked at her sunken face and understood now that it could have been only she who'd come to meet him, no one else. He had been foolish to think that he'd been saved. No, his own true Nadja was long gone away on the sunny shores of the West Islands and she would come to take no part of this new life he had created for himself. Wretched life! Such was the breathless pain! Nikolai looked at the False Nadja and tried to drive the turning screw out of his throat. He forced a pained smile and struggled for breath.

"Nadja..." Nikolai slurred. He looked away from the woman and repeated, "Nadja..." and once more, trembling, "Nadja..."

"Yes, Nikolai!" the False Nadja smiled, "It is good to see you!"

"Come."

He bid her to come, and weakly he paced along, "Why did you choose this place to meet?..." Nikolai now began to sputter words out feverishly, mingling confusion, anger, and feigned friendly pleasure, "We will take a drink somewhere in town together, perhaps..." All the while he spoke, he led her off away from the Anchises Hotel towards the Canal District. Amid the foggy confusion of his mind, there was probably that clear notion that elsewhere in town, such as in the shambles of Nesretan, it would be more fitting for people like the two of them to have a drink together.

"But I thought we would take a drink at the Anchises Hotel," said the False Nadja, following along by his side.

"Ah! It is expensive, the Anchises!"

"But that was my surprise! I earned some money babysitting in the country this summer and I wanted to treat you to a drink at the Anchises Hotel. You said back when we met at the public house that you liked to go there…" then she added… "back when you had a wife."

"A wife?" cried Nikolai, "Nadja, we will go somewhere else. Please!"

"Alright, alright…"

"So that's why!" Nikolai gasped at her in revelation, "…That's why you were traveling! . . . for babysitting! That's right! In the country! You went to the countryside for babysitting. That's why you weren't in the Minor City!"

"But I told you!" she swooned, "Are you sick? Nikolai, you're pale! . . . I told you when we were walking together along the canal the night we met…" And she began to tell him that she had explained to him that night that she was going to the country to babysit for a family for the remainder of the summer. She had left right after they had met and had only come back to the Minor City early this morning. She had said that she would send him a note through the flower vendor when she returned. Didn't he remember? She said he had told her that he knew the flower vendor on Fishmongers' Row and that he could get messages from him. She had asked Nikolai how the two would see each other again and he had said to just send a message through the flower vendor. She reminded him that he had said he wanted a message from *his* Nadja. She said she would be *his* Nadja . . . Didn't he remember? "…That little flower vendor was very nice," she told him, "He was happy to write down my message this morning to give it to…"

"I know all of that!" Nikolai barked in annoyance, interrupting the chattering woman, "…I knew that! I just forgot you were going to be babysitting, that's all!" . . . All the while, he was walking briskly two steps ahead of the False Nadja in order to keep her from taking his hand or brushing his side.

When the two reached the Canal District, Nikolai insisted on a hovel of an eating house that was cheap and dark. He led the False Nadja inside and to a table in the back.

"You sure you want to go *here*?" she asked him.

"I like this place," he lied.

They sat at a flimsy plywood table in the corner. Above, near the ceiling of the place, there was a little window covered in a grate that was even with the sidewalk. The only other customer in the eating house was an old man with dirty laboring pants. He had just finished his meal and was standing up to cough and pull up his trousers. The waiter and owner of the place, a stout, hairy-necked man, was arguing with his wife in the kitchen. False Nadja sat with her back to the wall and smiled dumbly at Nikolai, obviously pleased to be in his company. He ordered a liter of cheap wine and looked around impatiently for the waiter to return with the bottle.

"I'll pay for it," said the False Nadja, digging in her cloth sack to find her purse, "It's my treat." Then she added, "The country was nice! We have clean air there. Have you ever been out there?"

"No!" Nikolai grumbled, as sweat beaded on his forehead. He knew this was going badly and he was not going to fare well at the end, yet he thought to just drink and soak himself in wine, and so he did. The waiter came with the bottle and Nikolai filled the glasses and drank his down quickly in one swallow and filled it again.

"It's not like in the city," said the False Nadja, "Here we drink and breathe bad air. No, in the country it is nicer . . . simpler!" Then, "You don't look very good, Nikolai. You should go out to the country. It would be good for you!"

"I look fine!" he shouted back at her. He wanted to lean across the table and squeeze her neck, but he did not. He simply sat and drank the wine. He guzzled it with avarice.

"I brought you some prunes," said the False Nadja, handing Nikolai a sack. "I picked them in my employers' garden. Those people I babysat for have a beautiful house! They have beautiful baby boy, too! When I left he was able to say my name. 'Nah-dja!' he would say, 'Gurgle, gurgle!' It was so... Oh! 'Nah-dja! Nah-dja!' . . . I was about in tears all the way to the station. I'll miss him so much. Take the prunes," she said, thrusting the sack into his hands.

"Do you have any more money?" Nikolai asked with impatience.

"Yes," she smiled feebly.

"We need more wine." ... "Waiter! Another liter...." Then turning to the girl, "Thank you for the prunes. I will eat them with pleasure."

"Oh good!" This seemed to reassure the False Nadja. She fixed the scarf on her knotted hair and told Nikolai again and again how fresh her eyes were now, and how all the yard work she did helped her spirit. "I feel so much more alive after the country!"

'After the country,' Nikolai thought to himself, 'After the country.' Once a replenished liter appeared on the table, he began to pass the wine across the barrier of his teeth with fury, as though his misery were a fire and he were dousing the flames. All the while he thought to himself:

Who is this sickly woman sent by the holy name, 'Nadja?' Has she commerce with the Devil? Or is she a native of his land? Foul beasts ride along my horizon . . . Wretched foulness and this wine is spoilt! Who am I to be lured into such a farce? If this is the way the world is strung, then I scorn the world! Yes, there is freedom in that! Nikolai! . . . Yes? . . . Did you feel that flush of pleasure just now? . . . knowing there is freedom in ending the farce? You did! It is clear the Devil ascends through weak holes in the earth's skin . . . just as water leaks through the frayed holes torn in a sturdy sack. The Nadjas have fooled me! . . . both the Nadja who is beautiful and clean, and baked brown in the West Islands, married to another man by now and never to return, and this second one, ugly False Nadja with her laboring hands, her sagging breasts that nourish strangers' children, and her peasant headscarf! They both fooled me! . . . I am the greatest fool for allowing myself to be thus fooled. There is no limit to my delirium! My madness has poisoned the very marrow of my bones! Imagine if the real Nadja saw this wretched life I've been living after she left me! . . . using my meagre funds to swallow over-brimming glasses of bad wine in a cellar bar . . . And now, swallowing bad wine in a cheap eating house, with a peasant girl with toiler's hands! I shall run away with this peasant woman and we shall be servants in the country! I will be a swineherd and push peas, and she will wipe feces off of other people's babies . . . rosy-faced people, who walk tall on gentle heels....

Nikolai's thoughts went on as such, and such, until they were interrupted by the need to order more wine. He made a brazen comment that if the False Nadja had wanted to buy them both a drink at the Anchises Hotel, then she certainly had enough money to pay a dozen or more bottles at this cheap hovel of a restaurant. When he said this, False Nadja appeared to be on the verge of realizing that his words were not altogether kind in nature; and one imagined that she might even take offense, though she never did. She simply looked at Nikolai with the wide lids of her eyes and took out her miserable wallet and paid for another bottle.

"Why don't we go for a walk?" she soon bounced up cheerfully.

Nikolai didn't understand the question. He kept swilling the charred wine.

"If we leave now we can watch the sunset from the Otchajanie Bridge. We can take a bottle if you want."

'A bottle,' thought Nikolai, nodding his head. He silently agreed to leave and stood limply.

After the two were on the street together, False Nadja continued... "You know, Nikolai, it was magical for me when we first met." As she stepped across the evening pavement in her flimsy shoes, she clutched her cloth sack and the two more liters of wine she'd paid for on their way out of the eating house, along with the prunes she had offered to Nikolai. After a moment, he insisted on carrying one of the bottles of the wine so he could drink from it as they walked. "It was magical when we met at the public house..." she said once again.

'I could sleep with her,' Nikolai was thinking all the while, "this spinster in ratty stockings. A farewell to the *good* Nadja – the *true* Nadja!'

Now on the Otchajanie Bridge, the two people stood and looked out. The sun had already set beyond the western hills and the last run of red dye had seeped into the skin of the horizon.

"Thank you Nadja of the Upper Quarter," Nikolai mumbled quietly to himself, going unheard by the imposter beside him, "Thank you, Nadja, the queen of the holy quarter, who left me to this unfixable fate! Nadja, the destroyer of the poetic heart. Drunken now and autumn has come. Now drink with me forever Nadja. Drink with me, for tonight I am saved. Yes, Nadja! Tonight, I am saved!'

And tonight, he was saved. Tonight he was saved when he sang out over the bridge his lonely song. Saved when he cast that empty wine bottle over the edge to fall into the swells of the harbor and be gone – pulled by the confident winds to the strip of shore along the endless city. Saved tonight, was he, gorgeously drunk on the oil-dark wine black as kidney's gall, acrid as poison, bearing all the fumes one can consume. And so, to the False Nadja he bid goodnight.

"Thank you for the fruit and the wine, old girl. It is good you aren't away in the country anymore. We will see each other again at the public house. Soon, yes! No, I am tired tonight. Sorry, I will. No, I do thank you, truly. Yes, we will kiss..." A woman's souvenir. Sacred things, so holy to have, so monstrous to think will come no more.

Thus, Nikolai walked drunk and alone through the faded dusky streets of Otchajanie. Another lush in the alleys. Another derelict in the passageways. He held his poisoned mouth as he staggered into the Shipyard District, among the clamoring loud cranes which towered along the piers, rising and falling, lifting and dropping, heavy beams of iron clasped by iron chains. Nikolai turned into the market stalls that were closed now for night. Darkness had fallen on the empty city. And those with others were tucked away, while those who were alone were alone for the bidding.

"And what was I, but hoping?" Nikolai turned the key to his cellar room and walked into the darkened gloom. He struggled with a match to light a candle. In his pocket were the final coins that he wanted to spend no more. He knelt and put them back in the crawlspace from where they had come. From there, he pulled the tiny packet of powders of deafening calm and he placed them to his lips. And kneeling upon the ground he spoke...

"I found it upon the sink. And what was I, but hoping? . . . Upon the terrace, I lay waiting! . . . For so long, I was wanting . . . a gentle world where we may go! What do I say when you are searching? ...this world behind where I'm entombed. I spent my time as others have, to pass my night, evening in spring. But that spring, I was allowed, though evening kept beyond my reach. Although I hoped I was deserving...

"My time in spring came to an end!"

Nikolai searched the room until he found it. It was sleek and cold like winter metal. He caressed its handsome surface with his wretched hand, and put a final rag to his feverish forehead to cool the sweltering pain.

"...And I was not one," he said, reopening his soliloquy, "Why was I not one to be granted another moment to be living? Where did it go?" He reached his hands down between the rafters in the cupboard, in the crawlspace. "Ah!" he exclaimed, "Now I find it, though it wasn't by the sink..." It had been rather in the wall near the wooden box where he'd kept his desperate means.

"Another evening in spring, Ô deathless Nadja. She continued on her walk without me. She entered into the holy garden of night, leaving me behind. Remember Nadja? Do you remember? Or are you forgetting? We met in spring, you and I, when I was yearning. You walked with me, your hand, mine holding. And to our future, you were swearing. Though like a comedy in the farce we were playing, you held a mask behind your back. And while I beside a tree was waiting. In the forest, nude, you were running. I was neither hunter nor one to go with you in darkness, gone. And knowing this you went without me. I watched other men taste your skin, though it was you alone who was feasting. Now we come to the place where I am not allowed to enter. You who were busy living is still living – and gloriously so. I who was living will now die. You are exploring the throes of life, dancing in the full bloom of things, lying abreast with flowers and fields in the summer, songs in the night. I'll turn away now, and linger in past's decay. Let with this silver pistol won by holy cards over drunken squalls of a summer night, fire a autumnal blast that will shore this leprous ship at sea. Let this cellar fall upon me, and eat my flesh raw like tiny mites. This world of seasons shall bear lament, for the tired son it bore.

Deathless world, ever birthing its youthful girls, its gentle springs. An evening in spring. A temporary eternal dream. Evening in spring, I have found it! I said it was by the sink, but in fact it had been here all along! It had been..." in the crawlspace, powder and all. He found it – the pistol he'd won in our gentle game of chance. And he of blighted seed put the nozzle to his temple grim, and softly calling, he pictured sweet red turbulent winds aflame. And with swift dispatch he uttered...

"Nadja..."

It was a light and long groan, in which twice came the name...

"Nadja... Nadja."

He asked aloud...

"This afternoon, Nadja... Why did you not come yourself?!"

And with that, Nikolai placed the barrel of the pistol two and a half centimeters below his temple and saw it approaching. That sudden deafening calm. With swift dispatch it came. That eternal charge. And then it was gone.

CHAPTER XXXVIII

The singular shot echoed through the basement, and was heard in the Lower Quarter of the city. Far from the city, the new lovers lay entwined, asleep in each other's arms. No sound reached them and nothing disturbed them. While her lover slept, he dreamt of her. He felt the newness of her skin. He dreamt too of his far away home, a place he longed to take her to. She dreamt likewise of him, lost upon his holy breath. She dreamt of him and of her home, and faraway cities yet unknown. In the city from where she had come, there was an empty bed. A garden of trees empty of fruit and all green blooms. Long from that now, she would follow him, her lover, as far as he went, as he would follow her.

BOOK III

Fables from the Fields

CHAPTER XXXIX

Death traveled across the earth. The instant the gun was fired in the cellar room, its shot resounded through the Minor City. The sound seeped into the waters of the canals and the cracks in the cobblestones. It traveled beyond the city walls, echoing through forests and canyons, spilling westward over golden fields onto distant foreign lands. It pounded like thunder, enveloped the wind, shattered like glass, and then finally dissolved into a steady, slow evening rhythmic ringing of a solitary church bell at sunset.

―――

The sun was making its timely descent over the little village ensconced in the pastoral western fields. The church bell rang in the belfry, long and slow, signaling the evening to come. With the tolling bell came the scattering of a fall of woodcocks in a narrow cobbled lane where two schoolgirls came chasing an old tattered cat down the hill. They wore white tights and black polished shoes and held hands. When they passed the door of a stone village house, the door cracked open and a prim little kitten leapt out and began chasing after the girls, chasing after the tattered cat. At that same moment, a handsome young man with wild hair and a loose-buttoned shirt came skipping down from atop the same hill. He was the dreamy-eyed poet of the village, and in his hand he held a lover's tiny clover flower, bent at the stem. His old shoes flapped the stones like pilgrims as he ran; and when he reached the village house, he entered the door and ran up the stairs.

In the loft of the house, a messy room, the poet's younger brother Isaac, adventurer to be, was flopped down on his idle bed, smoking a lazy pipe. The day was cooling off and the evening found its remnants in a rosy haze of dusty light that settled on the rooftops beyond the window. The belfry of the cathedral towered proudly over all the other houses; and when it tolled, it caused a dole of cooing doves to scatter from the belfry coves and flutter about and find new places in nearby eaves.

Isaac's brother flung the bedroom door open, he ran to the far window to catch the sunset. The light of the sun flickered as its source dropped beyond the rooftops, beyond the western fields. With joy in his heart, he watched the hues change colors. His little honey-scented clover flower rested limply on the flesh of his hand. The sounds of flapping birds' wings, the tolling of the bell, and all of this brought him unsurpassable joy. He felt as though this singular bell were heralding the birth of the world, announcing the beginning of all things, ushering in the first day of life.

"What a beautiful day and night!" the poet cried over the village. Great hope flooded his heart. This was Helonius, the fateful lover who lent his name to the 'Myth of Helonius'; and what follows is the true account of his final days: the story of his life and death, and the story of his brother, brave-spirited Isaac; as well as the tale of one who is called Aesop.

The account that follows shall be told in truthful terms, so as to bring to justice all mistruths that have seeped into the legend, as well as to unfade all that is deserving of glory. Scholars dispute as to why the story of Isaac survived as myth by attributing Isaac's adventurous deeds to his brother Helonius. Some say the culture's sensibilities preferred the lover's heart of the hopeful-minded Helonius, and deemed the poetic soul more worthy of legend than the aloof spirit of his adventurous brother. Others claim that the vital change was due simply to Isaac's tendency to betray his own identity to the people whom he met on the great journey he took – for it is believed the accounts that retell his life were brought into the mythic tradition through the mouths and pens of those who made his acquaintance along the way. Whether we heed the theorists who claim that the change was made by simple error, or those who believe that the change tells something deeper about the needs of this myth-making society and the roles its heroes must play; all this needs not be speculated on. It only needs be curiously noted that the presence of someone named Isaac has dropped altogether from surviving versions of the myth, whereas the older brother Helonius, who only took a minor role in the real events, gained eternal fame as the celebrated hero. Aesop too took a vital change as we will see. All in all, the myth is a mingling of stories, remnants scattered about the cities and towns in the people's heads and the fables they read in their gardens, the tales they tell on their terraces. Let not the myth take precedence over the actual events. Heed instead the world for what it truly is, and how it came to be born, one evening at sunset...

Long, the bell tolled.

"Filthy whore!"

The bell tolled again.

"Let that noise be damned!"

Helonius heard his brother shouting but didn't respond. He leaned farther out the window, breathing deeply the air...

"There is nothing more beautiful than the smell of evening after a hot day," the poet sighed.

"Shut up, you filthy whore!" shouted Isaac.

He was cursing and swatting at a little mosquito who was buzzing in his ear, creating a din, disturbing his pleasurable pipe and the idle tapping of his dusty shoes on the wall. Finally, with a hefty swat, he crushed the whore against his skin and resumed his task of puffing and tapping.

"Oh, the bell," sighed Helonius, gazing at the glory out the

205

window, "And those sweet rose-colored roofs, lit by the sun. It is ecstasy to be alive!"

Isaac responded to his brother's words by snorting his nose and spitting a stem of tobacco on the floor.

"You don't know how happy I am, Isaac!"

"I think the whole world knows, lover boy. Listen, they're ringing the damned church bell for you!"

"It is a gorgeous thing to be alive!"

From the window, Helonius peered past the cathedral at the village houses built lower on the hill. He could clearly see her house among the others in the village. He imagined her in there in her bedroom and he smiled. In his fingers, he twirled his little clover flower. Now the sun was fully over the horizon and the church bell stopped tolling and all was silent except for the distant cooing of doves.

"I can picture her sitting sweetly there in her little room studying hard for her exams, thinking of me as I am thinking of her."

"I bet she's in there lying sweetly with another man."

"You're a scoundrel," Helonius frowned, "You have no idea how pure Alissa is – and how pure I am with her. Not even Adam and Eve were as innocent as we."

"Very poetic, brother."

"I wish you could just be happy for me."

"I am happy for you, Helonius." Isaac joined his brother at the window, "You managed to ensnare the prettiest girl in the village."

"She is beautiful," sighed Helonius.

"Yes she is, I agree… blonde locks, small plump breasts ripe for picking, and sweet youthful thighs ready for putting one's mouth…"

"Isaac!" Helonius gave his brother a slap on the shoulder. Isaac laughed on his pipe stem, and turned silent and stood by his brother at the window and yawned.

"My Alissa," Helonius went on dreamily, "I saw her just

moments ago. Think of it, she is studying night and day and isn't allowed to leave her room until after her exams on Monday. Yet we'd arranged a time when she would come down and give me a kiss. I went there and waited in the little street behind her house and, sure enough, she appeared around the corner and smiled . . . Oh, how she smiles! She rushed to me and took my hands and said, 'My Helonius!' . . . just like that, she said it. 'My Helonius! What work I have to do! I miss you so!' Then she kissed me again and whispered that she had to go back up to study but that we would meet after her exams on Monday. Now I am left with the sweet taste of her kiss on my lips and I have only the most perfect souvenirs to keep me happy till then!" Helonius inhaled again, admiring the scents carried in the warm air, the scents of dry trees. Isaac yawned and refilled his pipe.

The two brothers shared the loft on the top floor in the house owned by their father. The one staircase led from the room down to the street out back, while another staircase led down into the family's kitchen. The kitchen had jars of dried curiosities and a bookshelf where they stored things, a large dining table where they ate, and a workbench where their father tinkered. From the kitchen, there was a door leading out to a small courtyard, which led through a gate to the street out front. The last doors led to the bathroom and to the bedroom where their father slept. The father was an odd-jobber, a carpenter and handyman of sorts, always cheerfully concocting plans and half-baked inventions. He was small in size and not well-liked in the village. People called him the 'unholy fool.'

"You know what else, Isaac?" Helonius asked his brother after the two had been silent at the window for some time. His voice was waning of lover's sighs as he carried the burdens off gossip. "...Walking back just now from seeing Alissa, I was passing through the square and I saw father. He was sitting in the square talking to Aesop."

"Christ!" Isaac shook his head in shame, "Did you go up to him?"

"Of course I did not! I wouldn't want people to see me with him. When I saw him talking to Aesop, I quickly turned around and started off the way I came from and took the long way back. Already people were beginning to stare as usual. And I overheard people in the square gossiping badly about him. You know, it's going to break his heart when they tell him that they're not going to give him a place on the Village Council."

"Well, he shouldn't be surprised. A man who sits for hours chatting away with a goat in a public place shouldn't be surprised when he doesn't get voted into public office. I don't blame people for gossiping about him when he's an idiot like that."

"Yes, well I just wish he would realize that they aren't going to vote him in next Friday. It's going to crush him when he finds out. He's already practicing his acceptance speech."

"The fool!"

"Well it is gets worse and worse all the time and our family is the topic of ridicule. But it will get better. Things will be better when Alissa and I are married."

"You're lucky her parents are letting you marry her," said Isaac.

"They don't have much choice…" Helonius started to go on but then decided to leave off the gossip, for gentler thoughts were in the air; and anyway, he preferred to look out the window and imagine his sweet Alissa studying away in her bedroom across the way. He thought of how her parents didn't want her marrying anyone younger than twenty-seven because they thought such a young man would be irresponsible and make foolish decisions. Now Helonius had turned twenty-seven and had worked to save up a considerable amount of money. Further, they understood that their daughter was in love with Helonius and that they would lose their daughter if they tried to forbid the marriage.

Isaac squinted with displeasure out the window. "You've attained your happiness, brother. Someday, far from here, I will attain mine."

"Why don't you marry Bethany, the priest's daughter? She's very pretty and that would certainly redeem our family in this village."

Isaac cast a glance of annoyance at his brother. They both knew the priest would never allow his daughter to marry a descendant of Isaac's father. "Anyway, she's already engaged to a saint," said Isaac, "Why do we play this game, you and I? Trying to match Isaac up with holy girls?"

"Because that is the only way our father will be redeemed in this town. Those who don't call him a fool call him a blasphemer. We need to marry someone from our family into the church . . . I know!" he cried, "You can marry the daughter of the organ player!"

"Cross-eyed Cabernet?! She's uglier than sin! She's the sperm in the Devil's eye!"

"Disgusting, Isaac, She's not so bad."

"Brother, she's cross-eyed and pigeon-toed."

"Well, at least her father will let you marry her."

"That's because no one else will marry her, for one," said Isaac, "That, and because our organ player is deaf, he can't hear all the gossip that goes around about our family." Now, Isaac was enflamed by the distaste of the conversation. "Anyway, can we stop all this talk about marriage? You are the lover-boy who marries people. I am an adventurer who travels far and wide and makes women swoon. You make your babies. I am going to find lost fortune!"

Helonius, who seemed not to have heard his brother's last words said, "Don't worry, Isaac, when Alissa and I are married, we are going to build a house outside the village, far from all the gossip. You can come out and live with us. Stay as long as you want. Sooner or later you'll find your one true love as I have and you'll be happy as me. Anyway, brother, I'm older than you, so aren't I allowed to find happiness first?"

"*Aren't I*, you say, as if it were quite a word. Helonius, I'll tell you. My happiness won't come from my marrying a little village cream-cake. My happiness will come from something much greater!"

"What could be greater than romantic love?" Helonius asked, puzzled.

"Heroism, my dear boy," Isaac said through his pipe, wrapping his arm around his brother's shoulder. "Heroism! . . . I'm not going to stay in this town with all of these gossip-mongers. Neither will I live in my brother's shadow in the outskirts of town, as if marriage and the provincial life were the be-all and the end-all. What about heroism,

Helonius? Have you thought of that?!"

"Heroism is finding a woman and loving her."

"*Heroism is finding a woman and loving her!* . . . Ha! You talk like a peasant, brother! . . . You found your little woman here, live your little life here, but don't you realize this world is vast? Beyond this silly village there are cities where more beautiful women live, where fortunes can be had. Treasures and glory hide on distant shores. Fame and kingship! Why be a little man when you can become a king? Are you soft-blooded, Helonius? Yes, you are! Why do you look at me like that? It's true. I will have glory and the life of a king, or else I will die on the road of adventure. They will sing songs about me, Helonius! You laugh, but you will see. Your name will be forgotten, but the 'Story of Isaac' will be told for centuries to come! A great life a man can have, Helonius! We only have one life, so why be a little man?"

Helonius was growing weary of his brother's talk. "Romantic love is what makes one a great man, Isaac. Anyway, you go ahead and plan your scourge. I'm off." And with that he drew away from the window.

"Off?"

"Yes, it's Saturday. Tomorrow's Sunday and everything will be closed and I want to buy Alissa a necklace to give to her on Monday after her exams to celebrate. I have to hurry before the shop closes." All the while Helonius was saying this, he was crouched down unlocking the cabinet at the foot of the bed to pull from his nest-egg some sturdy coins to buy the necklace. Forthwith, he locked the cabinet and slipped the key beneath.

"Helonius!" Isaac shouted suddenly in a loud voice, "What are you doing?!"

"I told you. I'm going to the jewelry shop."

"When you're there, will you run across the street and buy me a map?"

"What do you want a map of?"

"The universe."

"Isaac," Helonius groaned, "I'm in a hurry."

"You'd better run, flower-boy, it's almost seven!"

"I'm going, I'm going. And cheer up, brother. Maybe we can win Bethany for you after all."

"Heroism!" Isaac shouted after his brother who had already left the room and was running down the stairs to the street.

CHAPTER XL

"My brother is a fool," Isaac reminded himself after he was alone in the room. He reloaded his pipe with a fresh knot of tobacco and began to pace... "Heroism is heroism! Travel and conquest." Stopping a moment, he looked around himself to see if eyes were tucked in the air. Then, scoffing it off, he realized no one could be watching.

At the cabinet by the bed, Isaac bent down and retrieved the key from underneath and unlocked the latch. Inside, he pulled out his brother's nest-egg: heavy coins with copper and gold serrated edges. "Hmm!" he shrugged, "It's too bad I don't have money like this! How far I would go! Clear to the eastern sea to kiss the sweet lips of...." Putting Helonius' money back where it belonged, Isaac searched below on his own shelf in the cabinet for the real purpose of his hunt. He found the old box that was made for storing knife blades. It was inside that box, that brave Isaac kept his most favorite possession: a single strip of a young girl's lace. It had long-since faded and lost its perfume. Full of nostalgia, adventurous Isaac sat on the floor by the cabinet and felt the lace with his fingers. "Very poetic, brother," he mumbled to himself. Realizing that foolish romance was welling in his own eyes, he quickly stopped and returned the lace to its hiding place at the bottom of the box, and pushed the box back into the cabinet. He locked the door and slid the key underneath.

Clever-minded Isaac lay on his bed, scratching the stubble on his chin. He thought of the leg that had once brushed neatly and so fragrantly the faded lace now well removed, and in the dry air of a warm evening in the room with the open window, he slipped into the past and spoke aloud a memory:

I remember those lips! Those impossible lips made for one thing. Oh, sensual girl! What was so impossible about that mouth? Sweet like clover honey. Like tasting the stems of clover flowers. Well, I wouldn't go that far! I've known honey sweeter than those lips. There are sickly bees with hind legs sweeter than those lips and I'm starting to sound like a foolish poet myself. I sound as bad as Helonius! Nah! I wouldn't go that far either . . . Yes, but those lips. Those lips and the way she looked at me in that square, now five years ago. Already five years have passed? Christ, the time! How the light was dusty in those memories. She was just a girl then, like I was just a boy. It was early summer. The light was shining on the square. And how she looked at me with haughty eyes as she tried to pull her suitcase up onto the sidewalk. That shirt she wore, with those little breasts. Cotton and lace. She was a girl and yet a woman. A beauty from the Minor City, from the east. I remember how she called over to me, "Hey!" she yelled, "Are you just going to stand there staring at me? Or are you going to help me get my suitcase onto the sidewalk? What kind of boy are you?!" How her lips were full and sensuous as she shouted. "Have you ever thought of being a gentleman?!" she hollered. And then, "Are you just going to stand there, tossing pebbles in the square and smoking that pipe while a young lady is struggling with a suitcase?" Was I smoking a pipe then? Yes, I think I was. But how hot the sun shone! There was no one in that square but us. Her mother was already upstairs in the hotel. I went to ask the girl who she was. It turned out she was traveling through with her mother to visit her father who was working in the West Islands. They stopped in our village and her mother got sick with food poisoning. They were forced to wait in our village until the mother was well and now she was upstairs asleep in the hotel room and her daughter was downstairs in the square struggling with their suitcases. She was surprised there was no porter at the hotel. "You don't have a porter?!" she asked again and again, "What kind of place do you live in?!" What a brat! I told her she was pretty. Beautiful, I said. I wasn't timid. "You are very young," she told me. Young? We were the same age! Indeed, seventeen. Not older. "But I like older men," she said, "...older men who know the world." Well, I told her, you bring your older men who know the world and tell them to get some pistols and I'll bring mine and I'll be happy to duel with them. Have you ever had one man shoot another for you? No? That's more gentlemanlike than lugging suitcases, isn't it? I toss pebbles to keep my trigger-finger in shape. "And you are not even taller than me," she said, "In fact you are shorter!" . . . No, we are the same height. Couldn't she see that? Actually, I am a good centimeter taller! "Where I come from in the Minor City," she said, "the men are very tall. I am short for a girl from my region. But here I'm as tall as anyone!" Well, I told her, you bring your tall men and tell them to get their pistols and I'll... "I know," she said, "you'll shoot them for me." Indeed I will. "But who are you and why would you shoot them?"

To be with you.

"To be with me? What would you do with me?"

What would I do with her, she wondered? What a girl! I would make sweet love to her over and over again. What is your name, my beauty? Victoria? Well I am Isaac, a professional adventurer!

"An adventurer?" she asked, "but I thought you live in this little village in the middle of the fields." I sure was clever in how I answered her. She drank my words!

No, I said, I am just here on a short excursion with my father. He is a famous architect and he is . . . Did she ask his name? Yes, and my swift tongue said his name was Heliosoppe. *Heliosoppe the Great!* . . . have you heard of him? No? Surprising! He has been commissioned to build a cathedral in this little village, and since I am a celebrated adventurer who has been all over the world and has seen many cathedrals – I would say most of them! – he asked me to take a trip here with him and give him advice on the design. After, I'll go back to foreign lands.

"Well," asked the clever girl, "if this here is the only hotel in the village, why aren't you and your father staying here?"

Because, I said, we're guests of the mayor! We get a royal welcome wherever we travel. Have you traveled much?, I asked the beauty.

"I have seen not a few places: The Minor City, the capital, the West Islands...."

That is all? Well, Miss, I have been everywhere! Through the southern jungles. My sturdy ship rounded the Cape of Good Hope and my upward eye caught the sun shining down from the north. I have crossed tundra and desert, and vast mountain ranges . . . The Minor City, you ask? No, I haven't been there because I've been too busy traveling to other places, but I will go there soon. Travel is nothing to me! I have gathered jewels in the East Indies. Rubies, diamonds, emeralds. Someday you will travel with me, Victoria, and I will give you all the jewels I collect. By the time I was saying this, she and I were out in the fields taking a walk together. I had helped her get her suitcases upstairs. She had brought them into the actual hotel room because she didn't want me meeting her mother when she was sick. So I waited in the hallway and she came out and said her mother was sleeping and she was bored and wanted me to show her the village, which I did; as well as the fields around the village. It was early summer and the fields were fiery red. The winds kept sweeping them over and over. I kissed her there. I'm sure it was her first time. No, it couldn't have been! She was a lengthy beauty, tall and – I didn't ask her, no. I just took her in my arms and kissed her, right in those fiery fields where we walked. And she had thought I was short! Like a little brother, she had said! But then when I kissed her, she felt how strong my arms were compared to hers. It was the first time I kissed a real beauty like that. First and last. First and last time I've ever even seen a girl as beautiful as Victoria. I took her to those fields and pressed myself against those sweet well-formed young breasts. And remember, Isaac, she didn't want you to stop. And even you saw her perfect eyes cross then, only slightly when she looked back at you as if she were made completely dizzy by the kiss and you knew then you had conquered her. Conquered the beautiful Victoria like all those foreign lands you'd said you'd conquered!

...How long were we together? Almost a week. To my good luck, her mother stayed ill day after day.

How is she this morning?, I would ask.

"Not any better," she would shake her head. Then ask, "Isaac? Do you want to take me out to the fields now?"

Of course, my sweet Victoria. We will have a picnic. You can sing me songs from your native land. I will bring the blanket. "But don't you have to help your father with the cathedral today?" No, Victoria. That is, yes, I already did, early this morning before coming here.

I remember how happily she would say that her mother wasn't any better each morning. She couldn't bear the thought of leaving me. I'm sure she even took the hot water bottle off her mother's stomach in the night to keep her sick as long as possible so we wouldn't have to part ways. Why was I nervous that time I saw Helonius coming out to the fields? If he had seen me with Victoria, he would have wanted to know all about her. I would have never kept her for myself. She liked older men, she said. Foolish Helonius would have told her that our father was no architect either. I remember we were lying on the blanket in those fiery fields, and I peered out and saw Helonius going for a stroll and I pulled Victoria down and held her so Helonius wouldn't see us, nor she him, and I tried to quiet her while she giggled, but soon Helonius was gone. Then I kissed her long and deep on that swollen mouth of hers and she grew sad and timid and it was then she said her mother was finally feeling better and the two would be traveling on to see her father in the West Islands. And how the pain came to the gut when we talked about her leaving. On the way back to the Minor City, she'd said, she and her mother would be taking another route and wouldn't pass through the village. Would I be in this village for a long time? No, I said, I had more traveling to do but then I would come find her in the Minor City. "Will you really come find me?" she asked. Well, Victoria, will you go away with me if I come for you? . . . "Where would you take me?" All over the world! To its farthest reaches. You will be my queen and we will have adventure and know the greatest life. So? Will you come with me? "Well," she said, "If you put it that way, I will!" And we laughed and kissed again on the blanket and then she said she would wait for me in the Minor City for seven years. "I will wait for seven years," she said, "and if you don't come find me by the time I am twenty four, I will marry another adventurer." Didn't we have our birthdays on the same date? I think my birthday was one day before hers. But we had the same age. I remember I asked her if she would be happy with another adventurer. Her face became sad then. Remarkably sad, as though I had become as precious to her as I'd hoped to be. It was with that solemn look she said, "If seven years go by and you don't come to find me, I think there will be a real emptiness in me – for my entire life. Something very empty will grow in me and it will never be filled." These words I remember exactly. Many times over the last five years I've repeated those words. Those words stayed potent while the perfume slowly left her lace. I think I was a little embarrassed by her sorrow. I mean here was a perfect creature who was sorrowful about having to leave me! Did I not begin our affair with just a bunch of boyish lying and bragging? And now she was trusting me and giving herself to me – and it was strange, though not unpleasurable. Oh, it was pleasurable! I tried then to soften that moment, remember? You said to her when she was solemn and almost crying with sadness about having to leave, you laughed at her and kissed her and said... Victoria, the only way I won't come to find you is if I meet my untimely death beforehand . . . if I am eaten by wolves while crossing the arctic on expedition, or if I am killed by wildcats while traversing at night great Afric's shores. Such often happens to brave adventurers. But surely you will hear of my death. It will be news that will travel far and wide. If you learn of my death, you will know that that was the reason why I didn't come to find you. "If I learn of your death!" she cried, "Well, then!... Then I will myself jump into a deep abyss, some ocean or lake." And I fell silent then, not knowing what to respond and I held her a little longer.

It came about when we were walking back towards the village on that last day – our last walk we would take together – that I noticed Victoria's dress was torn a bit by the hem. Torn from us rolling together on the blanket in the fields. She seemed upset a little, mentioning that it was an expensive dress. Then she said she didn't care and bent down and tore from the hem a strip of lace, removed it the rest of the way and gave me that strip of her ivory lace. When we reached her hotel, she ran upstairs and sprayed some of her perfume on it. Her holy perfume! It smelled like her neck, her legs, under her chin, her back, her breasts... That smell stayed strong for all of the summer after she'd left and then went away little by little. What did she say when she gave me the lace? That it was so I would come one day and give it back to her and not be eaten by wildcats or something like that? Seventeen year old girls are so silly! Still, she kissed me with her swollen mouth like a woman then, in that lace dress missing a little bit of hem which she left with me; and then she ran upstairs like a girl and came down with her mother. What a serious well-dressed dame her mother was! Remember that hat her mother wore? And how serious she looked! Then her daughter just waved a mere goodbye to me as if I were only some acquaintance she'd spoken to a couple of times during the week; and that made me very sad, but Victoria made up for it after the two women were a ways away. Across the square, Victoria turned and looked secretly over her shoulder with that loving look that seemed to say she really would wait for me for seven years, that she would really throw herself into an abyss if she learned of my death, and she blew me a kiss. When I walked home waywardly to our house – here, to this very bedroom – carrying that sweet-smelling lace, I was sad, but too worn-out to be sad. I remember that sacred week with her left me feeling like the wind was knocked out of me once she went away. When I reached the road to this room, I lay down here on this bed in the emptiness and pressed the hem of her dress to my nose and stayed all afternoon and evening in bed for a lack of something better to do. I will come find you, my Victoria! I will walk through the streets where children play and rats eat garlic. All the cathedrals are falling down and we just built them. The last cathedral has tumbled. Am I sleeping now? Why are the cupboards slamming downstairs?!

Isaac got up from his bed and went to close the window. A draft was causing him to shiver with light goose bumps. He wasn't sure if he had slept while reliving that memory or not, but decided it didn't so much matter. There was ruckus downstairs in the kitchen. Someone was slamming cupboard doors. 'I'll have a look,' he thought, and went for the door. First he made sure the brothers' cabinet was locked.

"Ho!" cried Isaac's father, a jolly little man with strands of black hair combed over his hairless crown. The old man was carrying a large block of cheese the size of a wagon wheel. "Look what I came upon!" Isaac rubbed his eyes while his father set the cheese block down on the kitchen countertop.

"What is it?"

"A block of cheese!"

"I see it's a block of cheese, but where did it come from?"

"Eleanor the old spinster owed me for a front gate I fixed on her house so I took this cheese as payment. It's good dust-mould cheese. We'll eat some tonight and save the rest for Pentecost. Lord bless us! Are you here for dinner tonight? Where's your older brother?"

"Out rubbing palms for little Alissa," said Isaac, "He's probably telling the clouds about his love for her." For some reason, Isaac's mentioning the word 'clouds' made him think of Aesop and he peered past his father to the door leading out back and saw the goat was tied up and drinking water from his bowl.

"Well that's my son!" the father cheered, wringing his hands with pleasure, "Little Alissa sure is a beauty! Their wedding will be the pride of the village. A sweet little bride like that in a white dress and veil, she'll have our priest crying like a watering can! Ho-ho! We'll invite Father Gugusse to the wedding feast so he can bless the bride and her new family in our own home! Can you see it? I've decided after I'm elected, I'll spend some funds from the Village Council to buy old Gugusse a new alter…

"You know, Isaac!" the father added in hushed tones, furrowing his eyebrows to hide the words like a coverslip, "when I'm on the Village Council, I'm going to reveal to all our citizens the man who will betray the village. Hear me, son! One man will betray our holy village!"

"Who, father?"

"Osiah the cartographer."

"Osiah the cartographer?"

"Hear me son, I'm not mincing words! And if not him then…" and here the kitchen grew quiet. Far off, the sound of an animal drinking water could be heard and a heavy door slowly creaking; the light of the crepuscule coming through the door put a strange glow in the room. Father and son looked quietly at each other for a moment. The father soon broke the silence…

"We'll have to wake up bright and early Monday to finish painting the new town hall."

"We'll see about that," said Isaac.

"Oh, we'll see nothing, we're doing! I need you to help me all this next week. I already paid you sixty francs to help me with the painting. Did you spend all that money already? The hall needs to be painted for the Village Council inauguration on Friday. I can't accept a position on the council if the walls are only half painted. I volunteered, you know. Out of my own good will, I volunteered, and I paid you sixty francs to help me. By God, I did!"

'Sixty francs,' Isaac was thinking, 'that lasted half a day. Helonius the idler blows his nose with sixty francs…'

"Blows his what?"

"Nothing."

"Oh, I thought I heard you say something . . . Listen, if I give you an extra ten francs, you'll get yourself a new tie to wear at the inauguration. I don't want you there in rags before everyone we know on my big day!"

'And when the town rejects him,' Isaac meanwhile was thinking, 'Do I want to be there to see it, holding the leash of a goat in a cheap ten-franc tie? Or perhaps now is the time to take my trip to the Minor City to call on sweet Victoria…'

"A great victory it will be," the father mumbled, taking a knife to cut into the dusty block of cheese, "Where is your brother? I'm going to cook a stew with some of this mould cheese."

"I said he's not home."

"Well when he returns, we'll eat."

Isaac took one last look at the pathetic figure his father cast as he flumped down with all his weight to push the knife through the cheese that was flopped upon the sagging counter. He then turned and left to go back upstairs.

CHAPTER XLI

Returning to the brothers' loft, Isaac found Helonius knelt down by the cabinet returning his flock of coins to the brothers' cabinet.

"Too late," he frowned, "The jeweler was closed. Not open again till Tuesday."

"Well, father has some new cheese. You can steal that to give to the little bird."

"I don't steal," said Helonius, "Anyway, I have an idea."

"You are going to write her a poem," Isaac laughed.

"I already did write her a poem! . . . But that's not my idea. I will read her my poem, but I want a gift to give her before I read it."

"Read me your little love poem," Isaac implored, rubbing his chin with delight, "Then I'll tell you if it needs a gift to follow it. It just might!"

"I'm not reading you my poem!"

"Yes, read it!"

"You don't like poems, Isaac."

"I like poems. I just don't like poets!"

"What's the difference?"

"Poets sit around dreaming fanciful things while real men act out fanciful things. No, poets are scum. But poems are good . . . if they're good poems. What do you think the travel books I read are filled with? Brave poetry!"

"What travel books?" Helonius asked, "I've never see you reading anything!"

"I read all the time! I read books of adventure and travel. And the language in them is pure poetry! If they weren't poetic, they'd be worthless. It is because they speak about the *wine-dark sea*, and the *rosy-fingered dawn*, it is because they speak poetically like that, that one wants to visit these far-away places. Who would want to sail on a distant sea unless they knew that sea was *wine-dark*? I tell you, Helonius, you think I'm some kind of underbred cretin just because I don't read the same kind of pastoral romances as you do. Because I don't read about chevaliers and soupy star-crossed lovers who drown themselves. I have a good education, you know! I read books, I just don't like poets. Do you know why I don't like poets? Because I don't like cowards!"

"Thanks," said Helonius.

"No, but these stories of yours with shepherds who run off to the woods with nymphs, they are stories about cowards. I read stories about brave men. Heroic tales! So read me your damned poem, Helonius!"

"I'm not going to read you my poem, Isaac."

"Well then tell me your idea for a gift."

But Helonius didn't tell him then about his gift. Without responding to his brother, he went downstairs to the kitchen. He would come to tell Isaac about the gift the next afternoon when he was setting off to go procure it...

The family had just attended the Sunday service, and now Helonius was going with an empty oilcloth bag over his shoulder to visit the fiery fields to pick ambrosia flowers. Alissa had never seen ambrosia flowers, though she'd heard about them. They were in the ancient myths that Helonius read to her. The gods ate them and Alissa often said she would like to have some. Helonius wanted to pick her ambrosia flowers aplenty: great bouquets to give to his fair beloved. But that was the next day. The night before, the family of two sons and a father gathered at the old wood table of planks to eat a late dinner. The soup was scalded with dusty rinds of cheese and boiled carrots.

"You have that glint in your eye, my son!" the father said to Helonius, "When do you see your Alissa next?"

"Monday at five in the evening. After her exams. We are going to meet in the square."

"That's nice, son."

Polite Helonius then said, "Tell me about your day, father."

"Oh, you asked! I was down at the printers to have invitations cards made for the post-election party next week. We'll invite the whole town to celebrate once your old man is a great town figure! But the printer was closed today. He's usually open on Saturday. Guess he's been sick. I'll check back Monday."

"Why not wait until after the election before you print invitations to a victory celebration?" asked Helonius.

"I say, why wait? After all, the Lord said, 'A king is he who hath three strong sons, and a king shall feast every eve and night and celebrate before he sleeps."

"But you only have two sons," Helonius said.

"And a goat," Isaac smiled.

"A goat!" the father cried, raising his hairy hand, "where are you, Aesop? Aesop's going to eat now!" And with that the old father stood and went out to the back where the goat was tied up and unfastened his chord and led him in the kitchen to try the dusty cheese. "You have to taste this cheese, Aesop!"

The goat licked the cheese and grew very excited, taking off to fling his hooves about the room. In his rampage, he overturned the nativity scene on a corner table by the workbench. Helonius set the holy figures back up while his father took Aesop out to tie him up. The father returned inside and inspected the nativity scene.

"Helonius! Baby Jesus is on his back!"

"Yes, father," replied the puzzled son. Whereupon his father turned the figurine of sleeping Jesus over to lie on his stomach. "So he can breath better!" he told his sons. Then, "Let's sit and finish the stew. Good dust mould cheese! The kind the Savior ate himself!"

One heard the sounds of spoons plopping into wooden bowls as the three men resumed eating. "Thank you for the food, Father," Helonius piped with reverence. This made the old man wink at his youngest son, Isaac. He said, "Look how respectful Helonius is when he's in love." Then to Helonius… "Thank the Lord for the food, Helonius. Sacred cheese! Like the holy book says:

The birthing wolf,

Her heart fed with tenderness,

Gave forth from ripe brown nipples,

Food to feed the universe.

"…I reckon that would be the correct translation from the old language. You remember that old children's bible we had in the common language? Do you, Helonius? Isaac, you were too young. But Helonius, when you were just a boy, you had that common child's bible with all the pictures in it. There were barely any words, just pictures to tell the stories. Then when I thought you were big enough to have a bible with only words, I took you and that bible and we went to the window, and I said 'Boy! You don't really want to read from this book anymore, do you?' and you said, 'No!' and I threw that book out the window!

"…Then, I needed to find you a real bible, do you remember? And just by chance, I met that itinerant prophetess at the edge of the village. She was wearing a black robe and was traveling with a baby in her arms. Someone had said a women was making her way for the village with a baby, and that it was a stolen baby, but no one with any sense believed the gossip because the woman was a prophetess. She met me and took that bible from beneath her black robe and shawl and I bought it right on the spot. Paid two hundred francs for it! There was no cover and six of the chapters were missing. The table of contents was missing too, it was so worn. I took that book and read the first page and couldn't understand a thing! She swore it was a bible in the original language of the bible and then cackled at me. I felt bad for not recognizing the original language, but I'd come to memorize that holy first line: *La sottise, l'erreur, le péché, la lésine*, and I wanted you, Helonius, to have a good education, so I bought that book and you never looked at a bible with pictures again! Long time ago it was, whatever happened to that old bible, eh? But you turned out to be a grown man, gallant and impeccable! Best of all, with a pretty goose to be your bride! Good cheese, eh?"

"Yes, good cheese, father," agreed Helonius.

"Yes, it's fine cheese," said Isaac.

The light set even farther down on the old kitchen where the three men finished their solitary meal. When all the light seeped out entirely, it continued to grow evermore dark. Two candles flickered up like carnivorous eyes.

'I wonder why,' Helonius then began to think to himself, 'I feel as though something strange is just on the horizon, something unusual is about to come slinking by...' He smelled something like searing metal. The odor bore out his nostrils. Isaac, meanwhile, filled his cup with beer and pulled out his pipe to have an after-dinner smoke. The father sat wringing his hands while looking across the table at his two sons beyond the candlelight. Outside, the goat Aesop began to bleat and sneeze. The sound stirred Helonius from his thoughts and he suddenly stood up and addressed his family...

"Father... Isaac... I'm going out. I want to take a late walk. I feel very happy tonight."

CHAPTER XLII

The following morning, the family attended the Sunday service as usual. As usual, the father tried to bring Aesop into the church; and, as usual, an irritated priest, Father Gugusse, chased the goat outside.

After the sermon, the pious villagers gathered on the church steps to gossip and scold their children. The father of Isaac and Helonius made his rounds with Aesop on a leash to ask if everyone was ready for the voting on Friday. A brazen dame in a peach hat told him to keep his 'filthy beast' away from her. The other villagers ignored him.

"Well, it's a good day to be painting the town hall!" the father chirped at last.

"I'm going out to the fields to pick ambrosia for Alissa," said Helonius with amorous eyes and an oil-cloth sack slung over his back.

"Me too," said Isaac, gazing up at the clear blue noontime sky, "The sun's going burn hot today! I think I'll go out to the fields to score the poppies. They'll drip fresh and dry nice! Tomorrow we can all go out and gather the sweet resin..."

"Oh, no! Not you!" said the father. "I know if you go out to the fields, you'll be gone for days. Helonius is going there to pick flowers for his girlfriend, but you need to be here to help me tomorrow with the painting of the town hall. We have a busy week, my son!"

"You want me to help you paint your own scaffold?" Isaac asked mockingly.

"What do you mean by that?!"

"Nothing, father." Then turning to Helonius, "Go, you little flower picker. Enjoy yourself."

"Should I cook enough for three people tonight?" the father called as his son was making off.

"Yes, Dad! I'll be home for dinner!"

'Dad?' thought the father, 'He hasn't called me that for a long time!'

With that, Helonius was gone... skipping off towards the street that led away from the village, to the fields beyond... to those fiery golden fields beyond.

CHAPTER XLIII

"The Fate of Helonius"

That Sunday, Helonius met his fate in the fields beyond the village. It was while he was picking ambrosia flowers, nectar of the gods, for his sweet Alissa, that Helonius came to an end. It isn't certain what happened, but one can imagine he was bitten by a serpent. For there while picking ambrosia for the girl he hoped to marry, Helonius fell and died. And it was there in the fields that his body rotted and was picked at by birds.

CHAPTER XLIV

The Sunday dinner brought forth a tender meal of creamed hens' eggs, boiled salsify, and sizzled beans. The father tasted the inward parts of the eggs and looked to Isaac, his son, and exclaimed, "I'm bewildered!"

The kitchen door to the outside courtyard was open and one hoped Helonius would come idling along the stones. One listened for the clanking gate. One listened for the bleating goat. "Are you sure he's not upstairs in your bedroom?"

"Nah, but he'll be around late tonight. He has to meet Alissa in the square tomorrow evening. He won't miss that engagement for anything in the world. No, I'm sure Helonius is fine. He's probably still picking flowers. Or else he's staring at the moon, seeing little Alissa's face in its surface.

In the loft upstairs, Isaac stood at the empty window. He felt the dinner heavy in his stomach and noticed there was no moon on this night. The bed of his brother remained untouched. The house stayed silent. Flopped on the bed, clever Isaac smoked his hearty pipe until sleep overcame him.

The next morning, Isaac woke to a hot, empty room. He somehow wasn't surprised to see that Helonius had not come in during the middle of the night. He pictured his brother sleeping out in the windy fields with dreams of his small-breasted virgin. 'He will come back in the afternoon to eat,' he thought.

Isaac was obliged to spend that day helping his father paint the town hall. At lunch, the two tossed their brushes aside. "Do you want to run home to see if Helonius has returned?"

"No, Father. You're only permitting me a half-hour for lunch. I'm sitting right here on these steps to eat this bread. Why are you looking at me like that?" The father didn't respond, but started away, sneaking off on the balls of his feet. Isaac settled to eat and waited and when a half-hour passed, his father still gone, Isaac decided to take a walk through the village.

Walking past the church, Isaac spied Father Gugusse. The old priest was angrily sauntering along, carrying a clunky object covered in a white sheet. It appeared to be a cross. The priest caught sight of Isaac and ran up to him…

"Where is your father?!"

"My father? Why do you ask? He's painting the town hall, I assume."

"That blasphemer! He has just painted the church cross!"

"How has he painted it?"

The priest tore the sheet from the cross and Isaac saw that where the two boards crossed each other, a little red mouth had been painted on. Isaac shrugged his shoulders. "So he can talk, I assume."

"So who can talk?!" the priest barked. As he stood there, his bald forehead seethed with red molten skin.

"So the cross can talk! Doesn't a cross need a mouth so it can talk? My father is convinced that the cross can't talk to the angels at Christ's resurrection unless it has a mouth to talk with."

"The cross never talked at the Resurrection!"

"Sure it did! My father read that story often to us… When Jesus rose from the dead, the cross climbed out of the tomb after him and spoke. The cross said that it was off 'to preach to those who had fallen asleep.' You're a priest for Christ's sake, you should know that story!"

Hearing this, the priest spat words like little flames and covered the cross back up with its sheet, "That is the Gospel of Peter and it is not canon! Your father is a dirty blasphemer and you are the son of a blasphemer and the whole town is going to hear about this!"

"I shouldn't be called the son of anything, little father! And why don't you tell me which gospel says that the cross wore a white sheet? That cannot be canon either!"

"Isaac! Your family is damned!"

Isaac stepped back and rubbed his chin, "So tell me honestly, priest, do you think my father will be elected to the Village Council this Friday?"

"No good will come to your father! Not in this village! Neither to him nor to you! Do you hear? Your brother Helonius may be saved. His blood may be purged of his hereditary curse, but you and your father are damned!" And with that, the old red-faced, nose-dripping priest ran off lugging the heavy cross covered in the white sheet and was gone. Isaac struck a match on the cobblestones, lit his pipe, and puffed happy smoke as he headed back towards the town hall to finish the painting.

Isaac heard the church bell toll three o'clock in the afternoon. 'The kiddies are out of school,' he thought. 'But, why do I care?' Thereafter, Isaac went on, speaking in a wayward phrase...

So what if our family is damned? There's not a damned thing I can do about it. All the rosy lips of distant Alexandria can't do a damned thing about it. All the swords of Persia can't do a thing about it. All the rosy lips that pout in wait for soldiers to come home from victory can't do a thing about it. Victory, I tell you, I am going to find Victoria! What did you say? Yes, I will do that. I will return with a beautiful girl, more tall and fair than little Alissa. The greatest beauty the village has ever seen. She will be my queen and where she walks, women will dive and struggle to stroke the hem of her dress as it passes over the ground. Men will cower in respect before my great Victoria; and where men cower, women cower behind them! How will you do it? Easily! Sure

Isaac, you have no great age, but you are a grown man as grown as it gets – neither village underling, nor picker of ambrosia flowers, nor eater of mould cheese! Let the poor poet dream and want. What I want is the flesh of the girl, those lips and the lengths of travel, to conquer cities and citadels afar. Heroism, Isaac! You hear that? Not a town hall painter, you are not that. A scoundrel like your old man? Go and bring back that girl who is like a prism shard in the silt of the Nile. To live as such, a hero, what a life! Victoria! Onward, Victoria!...

On the way to the town hall, there was a little crooked lane where lived the sleepy shop of Osiah the cartographer. Isaac tapped out his pipe and went inside. The shop smelled of dust and mildew. The rash on Osiah's crown was growing worse.

"I need a map of the Minor City," Isaac told the cartographer. Osiah gave a scowl and asked if Isaac had any money this time. "It depends if you have the map," said Isaac. Osiah looked through a stack of old travel documents and found a map of the route one would take to travel from their village to the Minor City. East was the way, through golden western fields – it was a hilly terrain south of forests, north of formidable canyons. Isaac paid the ten francs for the map of the route and demanded a map of the Minor City itself.

"I don't have one for sale," said Osiah.

"Why not?"

"It's just like that."

"My father wanted to ask you something," Isaac lied. This was his way to end the encounter. "He'll be in later this afternoon." Isaac closed the door.

Back out on the street, he rolled up the route map and tucked it into his pocket. 'A good use of ten francs. It looks like I won't be buying a tie! I wonder if Helonius ever came back. It must already be four o'clock.'

Isaac returned to the town hall and saw his father hard at work.

"Isaac, where have you been?"

"Looking for Helonius."

"Did you find him?"

"No, but I'm supposed to go see Alissa at five to ask her."

"Oh, he's making me worry!" the father said, "Well, let's get back to work. I want to finish one more wall by evening."

"I have to leave again soon. Oh, and by the way," Isaac lied again, "Osiah the cartographer wants to ask you something."

"Ask me something?" the father chirped, but his words went nowhere. Isaac was already on his way down the steps of the town hall. He wanted to go home and change before going to spy on Alissa at the five o'clock tryst.

'The worst of all possible outcomes," thought Isaac, 'is that my brother fell in a stream while picking flowers and broke his leg. He is just out wailing in the fields and can't walk home. He could be anywhere, really. But I say the most likely is that he is wandering around the village in anticipation of seeing Alissa at five. That is it! He wants to recite her his poem without looking at the text, so he is practicing to memorize it. That foolish lover-boy. Some day his sensitive heart is going to kill him!'

Isaac arrived at the square well before five and went to fasten himself behind a wall where he could survey the entire square while going unnoticed himself. He was still early, but a growing fear that his brother wouldn't come kept him rooted to spot. One would say Isaac was getting nervous.

Five o'clock tolled neatly and crisply in the church bell tower hovering over the town. The dusty rose light of evening fell and a hot dry wind brushed across the stone floor of the village square. Precisely at that moment, little Alissa came walking from around the corner. She wore a little pleated skirt and carried books in her hand and trembled slightly with nervousness. She settled on a little stone step and looked around with girlish eyes, waiting for her boyfriend to appear. Helonius, however, didn't appear to be coming. Isaac peeked out again and again from where he was hidden behind a wall, and saw that five minutes had passed and Helonius still had not come. He was now certain that a terrible thing had happened to his brother. His stomach grew a large unhealthy knot. He watched little Alissa, sitting on her little stone step, turning her head around at every sound, swinging her legs in their little tights. Every now and again, she picked up and set back down again her satchel of books. Isaac watched the lonesome tryst, fully certain that there had been a tragedy. He saw now that large tears were toppling down Alissa's cheek. She began to cry plentiful tears. 'How could Helonius be late?' she must have been thinking, 'Our love is so perfect, neither one of us would ever be late for the other!' Isaac watched the girl wait for his brother for nearly an hour, all the while thinking grave thoughts, wondering this and that. He decided that the proper thing to do would be to announce himself in the square and tell Alissa that she shouldn't cry, nor should she think that her lover no longer loves her or that Helonius missed their engagement because he forgot or doesn't care. But that he is not there because misfortune has befallen him. Certainly Isaac had better tell her that Helonius never came home the night before and neither this morning . . . that he went more than a day ago to the fields to pick ambrosia flowers for her, and no one has heard from him since. Isaac leaned around the wall once again and saw Alissa was still rooted to her seat in the empty square, swinging her legs with sadness, crying loud sobs into tender hands. 'What a young beauty she is,' Isaac thought to himself, 'Small well-formed breasts, long blonde locks of hair. Pity she hides her nice face in her hands to cry!' This sadness of hers brought him then a sort of sweet pleasure and sardonic delight. 'Let the little girl go on believing that my brother doesn't care anymore about her – that he doesn't love her anymore. It is good for her! It is good for them both! I will not set her mind at ease. I will say nothing!'

235

CHAPTER XLV

At rustic plates of mashed turnips and cornmeal bread, the father and his son, Isaac, sat that night and ate. The father was lamenting the absence of his more worthy son, the once hopeful Helonius, but he did not seem overly worried about his condition, for he was fixed in belief that his son was lost in the happy dazes of love. He was sure Helonius was now cast below his beloved's window singing the phrases of amorous praises which young men treat themselves to from time to time on moonless and moon-filled nights alike.

"Monday," said the father to Isaac, refilling his plate. "Monday is the day of the moon. I'm going to feed Aesop." And with that, he took his copious bowl and walked out to the back courtyard where his goat was tied up. He heard the beast licking the corn chops from the wooden bowl, sneezing now and again, tugging on his old chord, and here Isaac had an idea.

After the father returned, the two finished eating. Isaac mumbled a few words about Helonius.

"Speak up, son."

"I was just telling you that I would come wake you up if Helonius comes in late at night."

"Or just tell me in the morning," the father said, retiring to his room, "We have to wake up bright and early again, as you know. You and I have to finish the painting."

Upstairs, Isaac studied the ten-franc map he'd bought that day from Osiah the cartographer. There was a long road painted with brown watercolors leading from his village to the Minor City. There were pictures of ominous beasts in the shaded forests, and the bright copper-colored canyons in the south were decorated with drawings of slender-horned rams. Between his village and the Minor City, the map showed five other settlements along the road. When Isaac was tired, he cast the map aside and almost fell asleep, until he reminded himself that he couldn't sleep just yet; he'd made a plan that night at dinner and needed to carry it out. It was late enough, he decided, his father would already be sleeping and wouldn't hear a thing.

Isaac got up and looked at the bed of Helonius, which hadn't been slept in since the Saturday night last. He gave a pitying shake of his head and started downstairs for the kitchen.

In the fashion of homes where only men dwell, the dirty bowls and plates from dinner were still spread out on the table. Loud snores tumbled through the wall from where his father was sleeping. It was safe – the snores were even as foghorn blasts. Isaac stepped slowly past his father's room and unlatched the locked door leading out to the courtyard. He stepped out onto the bricks.

The night was warm and the courtyard stones felt mild on Isaac's bare feet. A singular smile crept across the young man's face as he approached Aesop who was tied to the gate by a chord. With a knife that he had been hiding in the cinched waist strap of his underwear, he reached out towards the goat and began to slice the chord. His left hand held the goat's snout, stroking it lightly to keep it from bleating. Once Aesop's chord was cut, he led the goat out to the gate to the street and knelt down and spoke thus…

"Listen to me good, Aesop. I am sending you out in the world to find Helonius. If you don't come back, may God be your shepherd for evermore. If you do come back, and you bring with you my brother

Helonius, alive and good in health, I will slaughter you and we will dine on your meat in a feast of celebration for his return. If you come back here alone, without my brother... I will tear your limbs apart!"

With that, Isaac let go of the chord and watched the luckless goat skip off with a wagging tongue, off into the village night, and be gone.

CHAPTER XLVI

Early the next morning, Tuesday, sleeping Isaac was woken up by a loud clanging sound.

"Who is it?!" he shouted, climbing from his bed with his head in a nest of confusion. Someone was trying to open his bedroom door from the outside, the latch was clanging. 'Is it Helonius?' he wondered, remembering the night before. He had locked the door from the inside after carrying out his nocturnal task.

"It's your father!" came a roar from the outside, "Please open up!"

Isaac fumbled with the lock and opened the door. A half-dressed, agéd man stood trembling frightfully before him.

"What is it?"

"Where's Helonius?!" demanded the father.

"Oh! Still hasn't come back. Why?"

"It's Aesop!"

"What about Aesop?"

"He's gone!"

"Gone?" Isaac rubbed his eyes, "He's gone, you say? Where to?"

"No, this is serious, Isaac, you know nothing about it?"

"No."

"Oh, despair!" wept Isaac's father, falling into a crumbling chair in breathless gasps. "Surely the priest arranged to have him stolen. That unholy priest! Why my Aesop?!"

"Why do you think the priest?" asked Isaac.

The father looked up with worry; and, while wringing his hands in feverish agony, he explained, "You see, son, I seem to have made a mistake by painting his favorite cross yesterday. Word seems to have gotten around that he wanted to get back at me.

"What's that?!"

"What's what?"

"Oh, I thought I heard Aesop calling." With that the father sunk into an even sorrier heap on the chair.

"But why would the priest steal your goat?"

"Oh, I'm sure it was the priest! Yesterday evening, after you'd left and I'd finished the painting for the night, I went to the square with Aesop to walk him and feed him some of the Pentecost cheese, you see. Just then, Father Gugusse runs up to me and he's mad about the cross. I asked his pardon as a brother – as a brother, I say! He looked down at poor Aesop with anger and I pulled Aesop to my side and I said, 'Don't worry, Aesop,' touching his head, 'the old priest is just baked-up about a cross and it isn't your fault so you just keep eating your mould cheese.' And with these words, the priest began to tear his hair out even more, and so I turned to him and said in a great religious tone, 'Forgivest, father, all wrongs that have been done upon you.' . . . Seeing then that the priest was at a loss for words with my holy talk in the common language, I thought I'd take the moment to please him and befriend him once and for all like a true erudite, so I quoted a phrase from the original language, out of that ancient bible I bought from the prophetess when Helonius was just a boy, I said to the priest: *'Mon semblable . . . mon frère...'*"

"Yes, this is very good," said Isaac as he paced the room, barely listening to his father, thinking mostly how strange it was that Helonius had not returned.

Here already it was Tuesday.

"...I finally finished like a common pious man, telling him, 'Father Gugusse, the Lord made us alike, thus – you, Aesop, and myself, we are all eaters of cheese.' . . . I thought the old priest would drop heavy tears and step forward to embrace me. At least these words I spoke stirred my own heart! . . . But no! Old father Gugusse flew into a rage after that, looked at Aesop, then back at me, then back at little Aesop, and he spit on the ground and said I should have named my goat 'Isaac' after all, and that his 'caprine neck' – that's what he called it, a 'caprine neck' – would soon find itself on a chopping block. Oh! That was yesterday! Now today Aesop's chord is cut and Aesop is gone! Oh, despair!"

CHAPTER XLVII

The noontime hour came and Isaac watched the church bell toll in the dusty belfry that towered over the village outside his bedroom window. He packed his pipe and lit it and it smoked like a furnace, and between breaths of smoke he breathed the hot noon air that carried the musky scents of dried pods crackling on the trees in the village. He peered off to the left, in between the neatly-packed rows of houses, and looked to the dusty road that led first south, then east, away from the village, and wondered what it would be like to see either Aesop or Helonius tramping down that path. Perhaps they both would come – Aesop, like a heavy shadow dragging a cut chord behind him; Helonius, like an airy puff of light carrying drooping ambrosia flowers. After Isaac expired the pleasures of his window scene, he tapped his pipe on the sill and went over to his bed to dig behind it for his voyager's satchel. After finding it and stuffing a spare pouch of smoking tobacco inside, he got up and passed his brother's bed that was made up with tight sheets and a prim blanket. Helonius had dressed the bed that Sunday before church and now it looked ridiculous sitting there, like a well-clothed table copiously covered with refreshments in anticipation of the arrival of guests who would never come. Isaac searched on his brother's nightstand and took one of his good shaving razors and put it in his rucksack. He then went downstairs.

In the old leather family chair, the mourning father sat with his hand clasped to his forehead. A single sallow lamp was burning on the table nearby.

"Oh, what's the use?" his father moaned.

"Aren't we going to go paint the town hall?" Isaac asked.

"Oh, what's the use? Aesop has gone away!" And with that, his father fell into a deeper heap. Little whimpers escaped him as he mourned the loss of his goat. Meanwhile clever-minded Isaac began to kindle a fiery glint in his swift eyes.

"I have an idea, father!" he smiled. At these words, his father momentarily rose up and looked hopefully at his son; but then, just as fast, he sank back down in his sorrowful lump and buried his head in his hand anew. "I'm going to go find Aesop, father!"

The father threw Isaac a hopeless glance. "You'll never find him. Either he is imprisoned in the priests house, or…"

"Or what?" Isaac asked.

"…Or he has been stolen by vagabonds to be sold in a foreign marketplace."

"I'll tell you what, father," Isaac said, clever-mindedly weaving well-fashioned words, "I will go sneak into the priest's house and investigate the heist of Aesop. If I learn that Aesop is no longer in the village, but rather has been stolen by foreigners, I will venture out into the world and retrieve him. Soon after, I will return with your goat and will be hailed a hero!…

"Father?"

"Oh, no, I don't believe you!" the father groaned in despair, weeping far-flung tears, "No success will come of it!" But Isaac didn't listen. Being now encouraged to greatness, he stood up straight, gathered the last scattered seeds of his plan, and left his father in the sorrowful chair, starting up the upward stair, to reach his happy room.

Back in the upstairs loft, Isaac began to dress for adventure. The ten-franc map he'd bought, he rolled and placed along with two fine shirts and well-knit trousers into his traveling sack. "Victoria!" he sang smiling as he dressed himself, "Vic-vic-vic-toreee-aah!"

After he was well-garbed for the adventurous road, a pack ready on his bed with his own sturdy clothes, his great map and compass, and the fine razor and comb belonging to his missing brother, Helonius, Isaac felt just about ready to leave on the eastward path to find his long lost love in the Minor City. While he stood at the mirror, adding soft wax to his hair in anticipation of finding again the sweet, fair-eyed Victoria, he sang to himself some crudely-spun lines…

> *A slave was chained to a townhouse ladder,*
> *By a mad goatherd with an iron whip.*
> *So he threw some lies to make the old goats scatter,*
> *And with his master in despair the slave, he made his slip!*
> *Now…*
> *Far he will travel, for his long lost love.*
> *Sweet Victoria dwelling in a far away city.*
> *He will kiss her blushing thighs and he will offer her a ring,*
> *If she will come with him, he will give her anything.*
> *When the two return together to the traveler's town,*
> *The sight of a girl so pretty will make the people gather round.*
> *They'll forget about the goat and the flower-picking boy,*
> *When they see the foreign bride with her eastern golden ring.*
> *In a fine-wrought palace they'll have slaves for everything.*
> *And the great hero Isaac will reign as the village king!*

"Listen to that!" cheered Isaac, "I'm a poet as good as any that ever lived! Oh, listen to that! . . . I'm coming, I'm coming! . . . Oh, Victoria, I'm coming! My Victoreeeeahh!!"

With that, Isaac leapt from his bed and descended upon the chest by the wall. Now he was ready to perform his last errand.

With swift fingers, he took from below the two brothers' locked cabinet, a slender key with which to penetrate the lock; he began his project. Sifting through the contents of the cabinet, Isaac found his old box made for storing knife blades. In the bottom of the box was the strip of ivory lace given to him by sweet Victoria – lace now lost of perfume and faded. With a pass before his hopeful nose in search of a trace of far-gone summer afternoons, he put the lace in the pocket of his traveling jacket; it would stay there pressed to his left kidney. Happy with his traveler's token, Isaac then began to sift through his brother Helonius' things. There was his stash of money – his incubating nest-egg, coated in bloom, comprised of heavy valuable coins. Isaac reached behind the money to see what there was that might interest him. It was then he found a little dark box he had never before stumbled upon while rummaging through his brother's things. Isaac looked inside: a little vial of liquid, liquid of the clearest sort. "Poison?" He turned the vial and inspected the label: WATER OF ABEL, it read.

"What is 'Water of Abel?'" Isaac withdrew the cork and smelled the liquid… "Ugh! Perfume!" he coughed as the strong scent swirled his nostrils. "Brother's been hiding flowery perfume from me! So the wimp picks flowers and hides perfume!"

Just then, Isaac heard a tap at the door. "What is that?" No, it was nothing. Isaac crouched back down in front of the cabinet and decided to dab a little of the perfume on his wrist. After the drop swelled on his skin, he quickly wiped it off with the cuff of his jacket. "What the hell!" he exclaimed. The perfume had wiped off but it left a stain – a little black spot on the skin. He scratched at the mark but it would not rub off. No longer interested in the Water of Abel, Isaac turned his attention to his brother's nest-egg. Dark burnished coins with golden serrated edges: the sole fortune of Helonius.

"This money could make Victoria very happy!"

Helonius had worked and saved many years for this money. He'd intended to build a house on the outskirts of town with it, as soon as he and Alissa were married. Isaac felt the weight of the money in his hands. "A tidy sum! Necessary indeed! Victoria is not the type of girl who will hike back to this village with me through fields and forests. We'll take a first-class rail back together." Such pleasure it gave Isaac to hold this heavy mound of coins in his hand. "So, if Helonius doesn't care enough about earthly pleasures to come meet his sweet little Alissa while she is waiting for him and crying in the village square, then he obviously doesn't care enough about earthly possessions to mind that a few, *or all*, of his coins are missing!"

With that, Isaac took from his own shelf his empty waist pouch made of cow hide and began filling the well-sewn purse with the lush fortune. "Still, I won't take *all* of his money. I will leave a couple coins behind for him. If he comes back while I'm on my voyage, he might want to buy something to eat in town; or he might want to buy some more of that flowery perfume if it doesn't cost too much."

All the while Isaac spoke, his brother's coins flitted into the leather purse, filling it to the brim. After the pouch was well filled, he took the oiled straps of suede and, holding them, securely fixed the pouch to his crotch, so that it pulled up firmly against his body. He then tied the straps around his back in two secure bows. Once completed, once the purse was well secure, Isaac grasped it where it hung tight in the middle of his crotch and felt the impressive, stately mound of thick coins bulging firmly through his pants.

CHAPTER XLVIII

"Isaac's Voyage"

Isaac left his house and skipped off with a glad heart. Strong was the chord and knot that bound his late brother's prosperous purse to his waist. Sweetly pressed in the deep of his jacket pocket was his fair girl's strip of lace. And that map to show the way, he'd rolled up and tied with a string and packed it in a satchel he wore slung on his back. As he ran, his hopeful breast ascented to the high clouds, and the dirt flew behind him. He took the eastern road where no man did, nor did any beast, give witness to his departure.

Bold-browed Isaac did not slow his pace until the houses of the village were behind him; not until he'd entered the far-flung fields. The golden fields were spotted with black spindly trees twisting upwards towards the hot sky. So black were those trees! So gold were those fields! One would say dead spiders with brittle legs were lodged on their backs in viscous puddles of yellow honey.

The clever adventurer traveled through the territory where, unbeknownst to him, his brother's body lay rotting. The remains had been picked apart and carried off by birds, as well as by black-gummed dogs. Stopping for a time to take breath, Isaac found between the strands of leaves and shoots of dry grass a human toenail. "Good luck!" he smiled, holding it up to the light of the sun. He put the toenail in his pocket and continued on his way. Adventurous of spirit, his way proved steadfast, his feet flit lightly over the ground. One would say his shoes were two dusty gyrfalcons gliding swift over plains to snatch prey from well-worn trails. The needle of his compass darted like an arrow. His strides were long and he covered much ground. All the pleasant sights given to a wandering man were his. In the day and the evening-time there was the earth: its canyons and passing shades among the trees and the hills; and in the night there was sky, plenty of dark milky sky, and more and more stars.

It came upon a night, that time in the sun's circle that wearies wayfarers, that Isaac found upon his glad path a little hut built beside a violet-tinted stream that ran like a string beneath the moon. Yearning sleep, he approached the crude dwelling and crouched to listen for sounds. All seemed abandoned. Letting the swift moonlight enter through the door, Isaac looked around the tiny hut. There was a bed dressed with coal-black blankets. The matted quilts were pressed into the creases of the stick frame. In the other corner of the hut, lay a small infant's cradle. It too was dressed but disheveled, as if freshly a child had slept there. The edges of the frayed quilts were pressed into the cracks in the straw. Brave Isaac yawned and made an aloof stride towards the bed for to sleep. He crawled into the mound of black blankets and pressed his tired cheek to the cushion. The bed smelled very strange – like the skin a very young infant, newly born. Isaac held his nose in repugnance and wished for dreamless sleep to fall upon his eyes but could not rest with the overwhelming odor of baby skin. Being too big for the cradle, he spied the ground for a place to rest. The earthen floor looked cold and hard, but the stench of the bed was strong, and so Isaac gathered the black blankets and crawled off to the corner of the hut to sleep. His rest did not come, however, for the odor swam in every fiber in that blanket he held for warmth.

The late hours of night had approached and the hut let pass a chilly draft. Isaac cast the blanket aside and made for the baby cradle. From it, he took the dark quilts with frayed hems and carried them to his earthen corner to try sleep again. No avail, these cradle blankets smelled too, like mice or other rodents. In disgust, Isaac tossed all blankets aside and vowed to sleep without any. The weary traveler shivered out the night.

CHAPTER XLIX

When the white-gowned sun bleached the sky with its hot rails of light, sleep left the lids of clever-minded Isaac; and the strong-willed traveler left his temporary lair to continue on his way. He bathed his head in the violet stream beside a spring, and took from his satchel his pipe and pouch of tobacco and smoked some tender leaves.

"Glorious morning!" he exalted aloud, "If not for a terrible night's sleep!" He felt again for the sweet strip of lace given to him in the days of boyhood by the foreign girl he was now traveling to find. He studied his map and rolled it up again. He felt his crotch so as to be sure his brother's money was securely in place. His groin bulged firmly with the heavy pouch of dark, thick-rimmed coins, and he was glad.

"A fortune of metals and fine long road. Oh, fair Victoria, I'm coming!"

In the evening, a showering of sparks brought a wet tumult of rain from the sky as a lightning storm began. Isaac paced through the dark plains of grass, rainwater streaming down his face, his wet clothes sucked like leaches to his skin, cold tongues lapping his marrow. Far off he saw a shack. It appeared a faint light was burning in the window. After a bolt of lightning passed, he tramped towards the shack. 'If there is someone,' thought Isaac, 'he will offer me dryness and respite. If there is no one, I will offer it to myself.'

A close inspection of the shack revealed two windows: one black, the other transfusing a small light like that of a single candle. Isaac stood before the front door and rapped on it; soon as he did so, the light in the window blew out. 'The wind or a man's breath,' he thought. Just then, the door opened and an immense figure rose to the top of the doorframe. A faint silhouette showed a man with beard, frayed like a goat's. 'A hermit,' thought Isaac. "May I come in?"

The black figure silently ushered Isaac into a small, dark room. Isaac felt around with his eyes in the darkness but could not discern the terrain of the room. The figure lit a candle on the table by the stove and the light swept over his face, revealing puffed features and cracked, leathery skin. The man told Isaac to sit at the table.

"It's pouring such rain!"

The host didn't respond but silently brought bowls and set them on the table. He brought a dark bottle of some liquor or other drink with a burnished label. He set that in the center.

"I didn't think I could make it to the next village," Isaac continued, "Let me dry a little, then I will go find my way in the night."

"I am not such a host as you may find in the village," the man replied, "Perhaps if you had come upon a frail widow, she would have nursed you with sweet milk!" And here the large bearded man interrupted his speech with hearty laughter, "Nay!" he roared, "You will never find a widow here! Not here!" Isaac looked around the dark room with unease. He noticed a wooden club perched in the corner dripping with water. The wooden chair he was seated on creaked as the sound of rain pounding on the roof continued. He reminded himself of the reason for his voyage, wondered about the path he would take and what it would be like to reach the Minor City. He thought of his miserable father back home and his absent brother. "Go to that chair and put a dry shirt on." The man pointed to a rocking chair in the corner of the room. Isaac did as asked and changed into the man's dry shirt. Meanwhile, the man settled back at the table and poured a drink of whatever was in the bottle.

It appeared to be brandy.

"There," said the man, "You are dry now. We will eat."

It was a tepid grey stew that was served. As the host ladled the thick broth into the bowls, the meat of whatever had been at the bottom of the bowls rose to the top. "Goat," said the man, as he heaped spoonfuls of stew into his mouth. Isaac looked at the bowl. The meat was grey and had hair pushing through it. The broth was no longer hot and as it thickened around the edges, it left a hard rind in a dark ring. Isaac heard the stirring of thunder far off, and the drops of rain on the tin roof. He looked over at the window and watched the drops creasing down the pane. 'The way those drops slide down the window glass,' thought Isaac, 'Murky drops stained with worry. One would say they are worms squirming in the sod, slithering to . . . Aye! What am I speaking of? Worms? Nonsense! They are not worms but drops of rain! I am thinking like a madman!'

While Isaac ate his stew, he heard the sound of a feminine cough coming from a room behind a closed door.

"Don't worry," said the man, "It's my wife. I'll be right back."

The host stood and went into the other room. Isaac glanced at the wooden club in the corner.

"She is ill," said the man with a grim face as he returned to the table, "One of must keep watch on her through the night."

Isaac stole another glance at the dark window and the rain sliding down it. It appeared to be unflinching rain. He thought it best to wait it out. 'One would say they are drowning worms.'

"Come with me!" the host suddenly exclaimed. He was now standing by the closed door holding the wooden club that had been in the corner. "You have eaten my food. You are wearing my dry linen. Now honor my hospitality and help me care for my wife."

Isaac followed his host into the small bedroom where a sickly, frail woman was lying beneath a old blanket.

"She stops breathing every now and again," he said mournfully, resting the club against his shoulder, looking down at his sleeping wife.

"Only in the night it happens. She stops breathing in the middle of her sleep. And she would die if someone didn't give her these drops." He motioned to a vial with a dropper on the nightstand. "...Then she wakes back up and everything's fine. But if one didn't watch her to see when she stops breathing, she would die altogether."

'Apnea,' thought Isaac.

"...So, you have eaten and you are dry and it is storming outside. So, you will watch my wife through the night and give her these drops, just like this . . . you see how I give the drops?"

"The entire night? I am to remain awake?"

"Somebody must!" the host roared, dragging another wooden chair into the room. He placed the second chair by the door and sat in it. All the while, he held his barbed wooden club. "Take this chair! Somebody must watch my wife while she sleeps or she will die. Somebody must give her drops when she stops breathing. I must rest. I am no longer a youth. You are a youth. Are not all the young immortal?' At this, the man laughed sardonically. "Well?" he roared, "Are not all youths immortal?!"

"Immortal, yes," said Isaac to his host, "yet still it is hard to stay awake an entire night!"

"They are insomuch as the same thing!" the man boomed with greater laughter, "How can one stay alive forever if one cannot even stay awake an entire night? Do your eyelids rule your immortal soul? Then even you will age! Even you will fall and die! You will see!"

Isaac looked with great unease and his formidable host. He looked at the barbed club and the man's glinting eyes. He was far from the next village, he knew. A dark and wet field ridden with storms separated him from it. In the shack, beneath the shadow of his strange host, Isaac turned back to the woman in the bed and listened amongst the sounds of rain for the even sounds of her breath.

Midway through the night, attentive Isaac caught a lapse in the woman's breath. Her chest ceased to rise and she lay stiff like a rafter. Isaac cocked her head back and fed her drops. He remarked the dryness of her chin, the thin grating feel of her skin and her wrinkled upper-lip. Her throat received the drops and she choked and her breathing resumed. She then went back to sleeping normally and Isaac continued his watch of her.

With the approach of dawn, Isaac felt his weary eyes closing. Turning his stiff neck, he spied his host seated in the chair by the door. The man was sleeping sound, his beard brushing on his chest like a broom sweeping on the floor, his club resting on his lap. Isaac looked from him, back to his sleeping wife, then sat up straight and tried to stay his eyes which were fluttering shut. As he fought off the pelt of sleep that was crawling over him like a shadow passes over a chair in a dimming room, he imagined he saw the bearded man's fierce eyes glaring at him, and his body too – now hovering over him, now hovering by the nightstand. How could the man be so roused and alert now? He was just a moment ago sleeping in his chair soundly, the club draped over his lap. Confusing! Isaac was so confused and he ached as well . . . Oh, how he ached! The ground beneath his body had loose iron nails that were scratching his skin. A bulbous flush of heat was rising up from the wood to the top of his head. Isaac opened his eyes slowly and felt the top of his head where a painful bump had appeared. He was no longer in the chair, but was now lying outstretched on the floor in the middle of the room. The dry shirt he had been given to wear had been removed from his body. He was bare-chested and his head throbbed and there was a hard lump on his shoulder where he'd been apparently beaten as well. He looked to the corner of the room that was lightening with the rising sun. Beneath the window he saw a wad of cloth stuffed in the corner and recognized it as the shirt he'd been given to wear. The chair by the door was empty. 'Where is my host?' Isaac held his throbbing head and tried to sit up.

"You fell asleep!" echoed an angry voice. The bearded host was now seated in the chair by the bed where his wife was lying asleep. He held his club, and now seeing Isaac had awoken, he turned to him angrily and spit words... "You were sleeping! In the chair you were sleeping! While my wife could have stopped breathing and died? You ate of my food and dressed yourself in my linen, and then you go and let my wife promenade alone with Death?! . . . Ungrateful youth! If I beat you again with my club, maybe you will be grateful!" Isaac, still numb from sleeping, looked slowly around the room. He noticed the door to the other room was open wide. "I should castrate you!" growled the bearded man, "I should chop off your testicles! . . . One such as you should be castrated with a kitchen knife, your testicles I'll throw to the jackals!" . . . "There, there..." he turned back to his wife, adjusting her sleeping head on the pillow. Isaac's presence in the room seemed to no longer concern the bearded man. The man let his club slide from his lap as he smoothed the dry strands of hair on his wife's head thrown upon the pillow. Isaac lay motionless on the floor for many moments, expecting the man to grow upset enough to hit him again with the club, but nothing came. It seemed the man had forgotten about Isaac. He cracked his eyelids open and saw the man still smoothing the brittle strands of his wife's hair. He decided to leave, and slowly crept out of the room.

It appeared the rain outside had stopped. The crisp white light of the sun illuminated the dirty panes of glass of the shack window. On the rocking chair by the table, Isaac found his wet shirt and took it, tucking it under his armpit. Right then, he had a frightening thought. He reached down and stroked his crotch. Fortunately, he could feel that heavy pouch of dark coins bulging firmly in place. Good that the host didn't find the pouch when he'd clubbed his guest!

Pulling down his trousers a little, Isaac made sure the chord of his purse was well-tied. Beneath the table, his satchel and wet jacket lay haphazardly. He picked them up and started on the silent balls of his feet to march to the door. On his way, he looked in his satchel. The map was there, the tobacco too.

Outside, the rain had indeed stopped. Isaac paused a moment to fill his pipe. Fortunately, his tobacco was dry. In his jacket pocket, he found the damp strip of lace. The bearded man had taken nothing. Isaac watched the shack with a careful eye as he walked slowly away and started to imagine the door was any moment to fly open. So much was sure, the dangerous host would charge the runaway Isaac down and strike him with his club and steal the money on his groin — yet nothing of the sort happened. The shack sat quietly in the middle of the field while

Isaac hurried away from it, laughing with triumph. He headed straight for the horizon where the signs of a little village could be seen not far off.

CHAPTER L

"Isaac finds Immortality
(or at least a priest's robe)"

Isaac staid his path and staid his appetite for the whole of a day. Being only a little the worse for the wet clothes on his back and the beating he'd taken by a wooden club, he walked with heroic determination, always his eyes on the eastward path. The map he'd bought back from Osiah the cartographer in his native, forgotten village proved to be a good one; and his eyesight too proved sure, and so by early evening, when the sun cast its last resplendent rays, Isaac came upon the first village.

It seemed a place the size of his own native town. From the edge of the village, he spotted the belfry of the cathedral on the skyline. Surely, he knew, a village square was near that cathedral. Surely there would be a hotel in that square.

The traveler sauntered along, puffing his pipe with a groin full of money and a weary wish for sleep. When he came to the cathedral, he found sure enough there was a village square. He spotted a wooden sign over one of the houses near the square that read: VILLAGE INN.

The keeper of the inn was a voluptuous hag. She told Isaac that the inn only had one bed to let and it was taken. "A prophet of sorts," she told Isaac, "He's been traveling a long way. Paid a handsome sum of money! . . . No, I'm sorry. I simply can't turn him away. I don't know what you can do. You might have to sleep in the square. There aren't any hotels or other inns in our village. It's a small village, you see. You can ask the priest. He'll be at the church. He might let you sleep on a pew…"

Inside the church, Isaac took a sip of the holy water, as he was thirsty. He then went to go nap on a pew. The bench was hard and he fought for sleep. At one point, while his eyes were fluttering, his lashes prancing about, he looked to alter at the center of the church and saw a smooth-faced young boy in a white satin robe standing very still and holding a large wooden cross. Dreams swirled with dreams. It seemed early evening still. Fragments of light were pouring through the stained glass windows. Isaac awoke in the silent church and looked again at the colored windows to sense the time. It seemed very late now. And why not sleep through the night? If it were at all possible. Isaac rose from the pew and looked again at the alter. Sure enough, next to the alter he saw standing a creamy-faced boy in a white robe, holding a cross that seemed twice his own size. So it hadn't been a dream! The boy was standing motionless, looking straight ahead with a blank and steady look, planted at the right hand of the alter. Isaac climbed off the pew, secured his mound of currency between his hearty thighs, and walked over to the boy.

"What are you doing, boy?"

"Practicing holding the cross." The boy spoke without moving, except for his lips. His voice was high-pitched, like that of any prepubescent boy.

"How long have you been here, holding that cross?"

"Hopefully more than an hour, but I can't tell you for sure."

"Why are you doing this?"

"Oh!" the boy exclaimed, and here his brow moved and knitted itself with a look of defeat. He turned his head to face his interrogator, "There is a wedding tomorrow. I am going to be the cross-bearer. I have to stand like this holding this giant cross for one hour. All through the ceremony. I've never been a cross-bearer. Have you? It's hard work, I think. I'm practicing. I have to make sure I can do it."

"All very interesting," said Isaac, rubbing his eyes and yawning, "How long will you be here, boy?"

"Oh, as long as I can. I have to prove to myself that I can hold this cross for hours and hours. A wedding is an important thing, don't you think? They're counting on me to hold this cross during the ceremony."

"I'm going back to sleep on the pew," said Isaac, and started heading off to the place he had been sleeping.

"But Mister!" the cross-clutching boy called to Isaac, "Why are you sleeping on a pew?"

"Because your town doesn't have a hotel. It has an inn, but the bed is taken. And I'm tired so I'm sleeping. Keep holding your cross until you get it right."

The boy looked sheepishly at Isaac. "I would say you could sleep at my house, but my brother and my mother are sick and we can't have visitors."

"Don't lose your cross," Isaac warned the boy.

"Oh, I'm not. I just wanted to set it aside for a minute. I'm tired of holding it. I'll try to think of a solution for you."

"Solution for what?"

"I know! You can sleep at the village priest's house! He opens his door to anyone, and I know no one is sick there. He has a big house with a lot of room. His wife is a good cook, too!"

"Sleep at the priests…" Isaac began to say, but before he could finish, the boy had disappeared – ran out of the church. His cross, he had left propped against the alter any old way. Isaac settled back on his pew with his hands beneath his neck and tried to fall back to sleep. "Priest with a wife," he mumbled, "Unholy priest."

A little while later, the boy came back and woke Isaac and told him he'd talked to the priest and the priest had said he was welcome at his house and that it smelled like food was cooking there so there would probably be a dinner waiting too; and Isaac thought of dinner and of how he hadn't eaten that day while the boy explained that the priest's wife was a good cook. Isaac contemplated the word 'wife' while he let the boy explain how to get to the priest's house... "Number eighteen in the passage, behind the rectory, a tall tree, etc., etc." and with that the boy was gone; and Isaac, having nothing better to do then to patronize a priest's wife, bed, and wife's cooking, went to look for the rectory.

The priest smiled naïvely at Isaac when the latter introduced himself. "Come in, come in! You are the traveler, I see. Well, our house is a hospice for wandering souls. I'll get my wife."

The wife had steel grey eyes that cast themselves with worry upon Isaac as he entered their home. She had been apparently in the kitchen arranging a bouquet of flowers. Petals were a-mess in her neatly-coiffed hair. Isaac studied her hips: a rump like a well-fed mare.

"Isaac, Madame . . . a traveler."

"Oh!"

"Yes, dear," the priest said to his wife, "Howlie's boy, dear, the cross-bearer for tomorrow. He told us about the traveler asleep in the church." Then to Isaac, "You'll sleep well, my young friend, we have a nice guest bed, Our home is a sanctuary for the Lord's wandering lambs."

"Mutton!" cried the wife, "I forgot to baste!" And with that she was off.

"There is an important wedding tomorrow so I'm finishing my sermon. I'll be in the study for a few. Go ahead and be seated at the dinner table." Saying this, the priest walked into the adjoining room.

Isaac looked around the dining room, mumbling to himself, "Cheap antiques, an old clock, the smell of strange food."

The priest's wife turned from her stove when she saw Isaac entering the kitchen. He looked at her as a wild animal looks upon trapped prey. She backed away from the meat she was pouring broth over. A pot fell on the floor and made a crashing sound. Isaac turned and peered through the dining room into the far study. Isaac had a full view of the priest standing before a long mirror, watching his reflection as he read aloud his sermon.

As the guest, Isaac sat at the head of the table at dinner. The priest sat on his right and the woman sat on his left. "I'll just have potatoes," said Isaac.

"No mutton?"

"Just potatoes." Isaac felt under the table until he managed to find the knee closest to his belonging to the priest's wife. He put his hand on the rough fabric of her skirt and she jerked at first. Her thigh trembled slightly; then after a minute, it continued to tremble slightly; all the while her eyes grew wide and Isaac watched her face as she tried to conceal her alarm. While her legs trembled, she passed the bowl of firm peas to her husband. Isaac smiled goodheartedly and continued rubbing her thigh.

"Lord bless the food," said the gentle priest, heaping more onto his plate. He turned to his guest, unaware that his guest was fondling his wife, and asked, "So where are you from, happy pilgrim?"

"From the West."

"God be with you. Why are you traveling?"

Isaac answered heedlessly, paying his attention to the tender vibrations of wife's leg beneath the table. The priest rattled off questions and mumbled blessings about the food and the travelers of the world and the children of God. He said again and again that a man should always offer shelter to another. That while a pair of shoes may belong to one man, his roof belongs to all; and that the priest would share his dinner table even with a leper, should one be traveling through and be in need of a bed and a meal. All the while, Isaac knew that if he could only get his hand up a little farther, he would find great moistness between the legs of the priest's wife. Suddenly, she gasped and dropped her fork onto her plate and it made a clang. Sweat beaded on her forehead as she made a second little gasp.

"Are you feeling alright, dear?" the priest asked his wife.

"Yes!" she gasped.

"Perhaps go to bed a little early tonight, dear. We have that big wedding tomorrow. The whole village will be there..." He then turned to Isaac, "You must attend the wedding tomorrow in our village, as a guest of the priest. You are more than welcome. The handsomest young couple in the village are to be married. Miss Wendy and Jeremiah. Everyone is so excited to see such beautiful people form a union..." Isaac found such talk about unions to be vulgar, yet continued listening, "...That Wendy is such a lovely girl, isn't she, dear? They will have beautiful children, etc., etc."

Meanwhile, Isaac found the wet spot he was looking for.

"So why are you traveling?" the priest asked.

"I'm looking for a goat," Isaac replied, "Our goat ran away. A wedding you say? What time?" At this, the priest's wife jerked her leg fully away from Isaac's hand and coughed ferociously. She pressed her napkin to her mouth and called, "Gobo!" to her husband.

"Yes, Honey?"

"Nothing... I..."

"I have to use the bathroom," said Isaac, tossing his own napkin down on his plate.

"Of course," said the priest, "Just down the hall."

"Please come into the bedroom a moment," the woman asked her husband once Isaac was away, "I need to talk to you." At this same moment, Isaac was relieving himself in a bathroom that smelled heavily of cheap vanilla soap. In the study, the wife took her husband aside...

"Do you know what's going on?" she asked.

"No dear, what is it? Why are you sweating?"

"Gobo, tomorrow is the wedding of Miss Wendy! The village has been waiting years for this!"

"Yes," the priest smiled his gay smile, "Won't it be a lovely thing?

I'm going to practice my sermon again after dinner. And you get some sleep because you're looking…"

"No!" his wife interrupted, "Don't you see! Tomorrow is Wendy's wedding and this Isaac character, this… this… traveler, whom you've opened our home to. We don't know anything about him and he's looking for a lost goat!"

"Well? What's wrong with looking for a goat?"

"What's wrong with that?! Don't you remember the tragedy of Samuel and Sarah?! We can't let that happen again!"

"Oh, I see." The priest bowed his head and rested his brow in the palm of his hand, as if considering the situation. He did remember the tragedy of Samuel and Sarah. It was the last major catastrophe the village had experienced. A few years back, another lovely couple was about to be married. Sarah was a blonde beauty with great blue eyes, and her fiancé, Samuel, was an industrious young man. The whole village was looking forward to the event just as they were now looking forward to the wedding of Miss Wendy and Jeremiah. Well, the night before the wedding, just as the village priest was practicing his sermon in front of the same mirror as he was on this night, just as his wife was cooking dinner and arranging bouquets for the service, just as on this night, years later, a stranger entered the village. He was an unknown traveler and he came and knocked on the priest's door after the innkeeper suggested he go there to find a bed. Just like Isaac, this traveler too was given a friendly welcome at the priest's house. He too ate with the priest and his wife. And the next morning, upon the gracious invitation of the village priest, he came to attend the wedding of Samuel and Sarah – only, before the ceremony began, the traveling stranger went around behind the cathedral to where the bride was preparing herself for her march down the aisle, and he stole her. The stranger kidnapped the bride and left town. Poor Samuel was so sad and confused and looked so pathetic standing alone at the alter in front of that crowd of people, in that fresh suit with no bride to marry him. And now, the priest was considering the possibility of a reoccurrence of that shameful event now that his wife had reminded him that the stranger who had stolen Sarah years back had also told the priest and his wife that he was traveling because he was looking for a lost animal. Of course, that traveler had lost a weasel and not a goat like Isaac; but they were insomuch as the same thing. Now, years later, the priest and his wife were seriously worried that perhaps Isaac would steal Wendy the next day.

During this time that the priest and his wife were hashing over matters in the study, Isaac was sneaking around the house. He had finished his business in the bathroom and came back to the table to find the priest and his wife were no longer seated nor were even in the room and the door to the study had been closed. He promptly decided to have a look around for curiosity's sake. He took his satchel and jacket from by the door and found a staircase and started up it.

On the upstairs floor of the house, Isaac found the master bedroom. "So this is where they sleep," he observed, eyeing the bed. A night breeze blew through the open window, lifting the flower-print curtain in gusts. Isaac walked over to the dresser by the bed and opened the drawers one by one, stopping a moment in between to touch between his legs to make sure his money was firmly in place. "I would have thought they would be smaller in the rear," Isaac muttered, holding up a pair of the priest's wife's panties to inspect them. He felt the ivory-colored fabric in his fingers and then brought the undergarment to his nose to smell. "Ech!" he scrunched his nose with distaste and threw the panties back in the drawer and continued rifling through it. It was while he was digging through piles of panties and stockings that he found something that pleased him very much…

"What do we have here? A priest's robe!" Isaac smiled savagely as he thrust his find into his satchel. He thought to return again downstairs immediately, then thought the better of it. Going to the window, he looked out at the night. It was no far drop to the garden below. The window sat right above a nice platform that sheltered the front step. He could climb out on that platform and descend by the nearby tree limbs if he wanted. And thus he did, smiling all the while, mischievously to himself. He had his jacket and his tobacco and pipe, his strip of lace belonging to the fair Victoria, his purse of money too; and now he had too a black satin priest's robe. As he leapt from the last limb on the tree to the walkway facing out to the street, he whistled the beginning of a snatch he would continue in mighty song walking hurriedly through the darkness away from the village towards the eastern road…

"Night in my eyes! Heroic night! A feast lies in my belly; in my satchel lies the robe of a priest. I'll sleep on a dampened lawn tonight, or on a hardened crag; now that I am armed, with this immortal rag!"

CHAPTER LI

"The Tiller's House"

Al records of the second village Isaac visited have been lost. It is, however, known that he did indeed stop and take respite in this second village away from his own. Sources say he spent at least one afternoon there, kissing amorous girls...

Isaac could still taste the sweet lips of those girls on his own lips as he wandered eastward through the fields, continuing on his journey. Head bowed in thought, he savored the tastes of their mouths – flavors that faded which each league he passed. The sunlit eastward path stretched before him, as the sun dropped behind him, throwing light over his shoulder. He thought of how now that sweetness on his lips would soon fade completely and be only a memory. Then, the memory itself would fade and no longer be; and those kisses would cease to exist altogether. "Oh, tragedy, this life!" For a few rare moments, Isaac began to feel sad.

It was then he came to a place in the road that no longer looked like the western fields where he had been raised. Off to the left there was a lake that appeared as a lush salty sea, the simmering sun behind him cast flakes of light like the silt of gold on ever-turning waves. Before the lake was a house, built upon a rough and rocky butte that jutted out over the lake. It was a house unlike the village dwellings he'd known in the western fields. It was a house of stone with mosaic tiles and a flat roof. A place fit for an island in the Aegean Sea. Isaac peered to the top of the house and saw a man was up there tilling the roof. Isaac watched the figure of the man as he went along his way. After he had passed the house, he turned around to have a better look at the man; but by now, the man was obscured by the sun setting behind him and Isaac could only see his dark silhouette. No longer was Isaac thinking about those girls from the village and their sweet scents that were wandering away from his lips with each moment that overtook the last. Now he was thinking about this tilling man and his strange lakeside surroundings, and the road he was walking on – was it still his road? All of this newness did nothing, though, to quell his abjection. He called to the tilling man, placing his hand over his eyes to shield the sun. He called to the tilling man to ask about the road. The tilling man answered thus...

"It is the right road, young man, but stop a moment and answer me... Why do you look so abject?"

Isaac bowed his head again and recalled those sweet unsuspecting girls from the last village and how gay of a time it had been. Now he was on some dusty barren road next to a rocky butte, and a lush salty lake. Now he was next to a strange house, upon which stood a stranger, tilling and tilling, and Isaac couldn't help but to feel abject.

"I just wish moments weren't so fleeting!" he called to the man on the roof, "They pass so quickly!"

"Fleeting?!" responded the tilling man, "Moments? They pass quickly?! . . . Why, once a man is finished growing, he still has twenty years of youth. After that, he has twenty years of middle age. Then, unless misfortune strikes, nature gives him twenty thoughtful years of old age. Why do you call that quickly?" And with that, the tilling man wiped his sweaty brow and continued tilling; and the dejected Isaac continued wandering.

"Stupid fool!" Isaac muttered quietly to himself as soon as he was far enough away not to be heard.

CHAPTER LII

"The Third Village – Dusk"

Dusk had fallen when the priest was called in to bless the dying man...

When Isaac arrived in the third village on his journey, it was the tail-end of the afternoon. Securing his money between his legs, he hid himself behind a house and dressed in the robe he had stolen from the priest. Now a holy man, Isaac went around to the front of the house with the intentions of asking for a meal and a bed.

It was a crude house with a roof of densely packed straw. Inside lived an old man, gaunt with grey hair and a younger wife who herself was old, and thin, with very long teeth that were spotted brown and brittle. Before Isaac could open his mouth to explain to the grey-haired man that he was a holy priest traveling for the sake of God, and thus needed a tender meal and a well-made bed, the man nodded to him and beckoned him to come inside.

He shut the door behind Isaac and led him to a small table where he sat down next to his long-toothed wife. Discreet Isaac held his mouth and waited for them to speak, for he could see these villagers had something in mind.

"I knew it was better to call a priest than a doctor," the man whispered to the woman. She appeared sad, broken down. She held a clay cup of boiled herbs and drank slowly from the tepid broth. Isaac watched on carefully.

"You have the wrong house," he turned then to Isaac, adding, "…Excuse me, Holy Father, I meant . . . well, please come with me. It is in the house of my wife's cousin where the priest is needed."

Isaac followed the villager and his wife out the back through a rustic courtyard where some hens were scattering seed. Though the afternoon seemed to be lingering, the sun was swelling, leaking milky dye, and Isaac knew it would soon set.

Through the courtyard, the three solemn figures walked and entered through the back of a stone country house. There, a black-haired man with gloomy eyes and burly shoulders opened the inner door and ushered the newcomers into a large room where there was a basin and stove, a cooking table, and table for dining, and many chairs. Wine and bread were on the table and the woman of the house was busy preparing food — always quiet, always head hung at her task — though her hands kept busily making foodstuffs to eat. Isaac felt great hunger in his belly. Beneath his black priest's robe, he felt a pinch in his navel.

The woman kissed her cousin meekly hello and sat her sad body down in one of the chairs. The burly-shouldered cousin rubbed his hand in his black hair and beard, and then sat and stood again. All the while, he wrung his hands in nervousness.

"I'll be right back," he then said to his cousin in-law, as he headed into the adjoining room to check on his brother. He explained that his wife was cooking and would soon have dinner for all. "There is some wine and bread on the table, but don't eat of it yet. We will wait until… We will wait, for there are ample foods to come." Then, nodding at his wife, he walked into the adjacent room and shut the door.

With her husband gone, the wife who was cooking turned to the wife of the grey-haired man and asked her where the priest had been called in from. Uncertain of the answer, the wife of the grey-haired man mumbled a few unclear words and then turned to Isaac questioningly.

But before she could ask anything, Isaac addressed the crowd in high and holy words...

"I came from a neighboring village."

The women nodded, and one said, "Well, Father, after you bless my cousin, we will eat here. Then you may come over to our house to sleep." Saying this, she sadly bowed her head. Isaac silently walked over and put his holy hand on her shoulder to console her. Meanwhile, the black-haired cousin was returning from the sickroom.

"He will not last much longer," he said to the family. Then turning to Isaac, "Father, will you please..."

Isaac nodded to all present and blessed them with two fingers drawn through the air. He then turned and walked into the adjacent room and closed the door behind him.

The room was dim. Isaac saw out the window that dusk had fallen. The dying man lay beneath a thin sheet on a small bed. The room was otherwise bare, except for a dimming candle on a wooden nightstand and a wooden bedside chair.

Isaac stood over the feeble man and made the sign of the cross. Forthwith, he seated himself at the bedside chair. In the dim light, the sick man trembled. He was as frail as his brother was strong. The dew of death beaded on his forehead and in fever he shook. As he gasped his breaths, Isaac could hear distinctly a rattling noise coming from his throat.

"Father, Son and Holy Ghost," muttered Isaac, turning his gaze from the man to the dusk outside the window. He felt again his belly pinch with hunger. He heard the dying man's throat again rattle. "Have you any last words?" Isaac asked, tapping his fingers distractedly on his satin robe as he watched his subject.

"The fall of spring and a darkening cloud."

"Come again?"

"The fall of spring and a darkening cloud..." the man muttered twice in feeble gasps, "...I carried that line with me for ages..."

Then he died.

'Why that line?' Isaac wondered to himself, '*The fall of spring and a darkening cloud* . . . Why, that line? It's of no great worth!'

Isaac then closed the dead man's mouth and eyes and went off to see if dinner was ready.

CHAPTER LIII

"The Fourth Village – Dusk Again"

Some said a prophet was entering the village. Some said it was a blind bard who carried a well-worn lute. Others said it was an enchanted fortuneteller who could predict the future with the deck of sly cards he kept stuffed in his groin. Most, however, believed it was a simple religious novice, a young honest priest who was traveling east to preach in the Minor City. Whatever the account, news had spread of Isaac's journey before he reached the entrance of the fourth village.

It was a town on a hill with houses of lime rock and tiled roofs constructed in the eastern fashion. A village smaller than Isaac's own, it had no public square and only two shops and a single schoolhouse, which instructed all youths from their days of suckling to their hour of marrying. Wanton Isaac, dressed in civilian clothes now – dusty jacket and wrinkled shirt, sweet pipe filled with the tobacco shrub's tender leaves, and his hard metallic mound pressed firm to strong and youthful thighs – entered the village on the hill.

Six little shoes clicked on the cobblestones as three pretty schoolgirls walked along. They were laughing and gossiping, as is proper for schoolgirls. One, the darker and prettier of the three, waved her hands as she told a wild story. The girls carried leather school bags that swung at their sides brushing pleated skirts. Two were fair of hair and one was dark, all had creamy pale white skin, sweet little necks, tiny alabaster legs with short schoolgirl socks. They giggled about something or other and then, entering the yard of their house, they hushed each other and started inside.

Isaac, who had been watching these girls from behind a fence, seized his happy chance and ducked behind the gate where he promptly changed into his holy robe. Now a benevolent priest, he started up the steps to the door of the house.

No answer. He knocked again. Had he not just seen three pretty girls enter here? Now someone was coming…

A middle-aged man with a paunchy stomach stood smiling at Isaac… "Dear Father!" he cried, clasping a hand to his chest. He then backed in the house and shut the door on Isaac. Isaac could hear him rustling about inside. Isaac stood on the front porch tapping impatiently on the side of the house with his knuckles. He could hear the man's voice gibbering through the door…

"Girls! The holy priest has come! It is a priest!"

The door opened again and the girls' father stood before Isaac with an imbecilic look, like that of a rustic come to see the celebrated curiosity that is touring the countryside in a circus master's cage. "Oh priest!" he exclaimed, dribbling saliva on his lower lip. "You are a priest!"

'This man is an utter fool,' thought Isaac as he waited for his invitation inside.

"I am called Alsabide," said the man, "I have three daughters…"

Alsabide urged Isaac to come in and sat him at the dinner table.

"You are not married, my son?" Isaac asked Alsabide in a voice feigning priestly authority.

"Oh yes, good father. My wife is visiting her mother on their farm. Please meet my girls."

The girls arranged themselves by the table for Isaac's inspection.

273

They had changed out of their pleated skirts, but they still had their hair in schoolgirl braids, just as they had when Isaac saw them walking down the street. Soft alabaster faces, lips like the seeds of pomegranates, small tender breasts yearning to spill out of little shirts, petite noses like upturned autumn leaves. Two with light-colored eyebrows and innocent grey eyes. The smallest with pretty burnished eyes, dark brown eyebrows, high blooming cheekbones and a cleverly sensual face.

"Good father will eat with us, won't he?" Alsabide asked, clanging flimsy table-wear, setting a place for Isaac at the head of the table; he brought cold slices of cheese and pickled vegetables, a brick of creamery butter and warm eggs. The girls came to sit and ate candy and giggled over private jokes.

"They say you are bringing luck and fortune to all the villages with your holy prayers. My wife is hoping to get a new job. She's at her mother's trying to learn shorthand. Can you pray for her shorthand? Can you stay with us tonight? A priest in our home for the night will bring much luck. Look, girls! A holy priest!"

"Dad!" interrupted one of his daughters, "I'm getting a cat."

"A cat!" cried Alsabide, "Great heavens!" Then turning to Isaac, "Will you read to us from the bible after dinner?"

"So it shall be," said holy Isaac. He looked across the table at the darkest of the girls, the small one. She looked back at him with piercing eyes and smiled a clever smile. Isaac smiled back.

"Anna will be seventeen next week," said Alsabide, signaling to the older of the two fair-haired girls. She blushed timidly and turned away. The dark sister giggled.

"Where's your bible?" asked Isaac, wiping off the crumbs of bread that had gathered in the lap of his holy robe. With a swift swipe of his hand he felt the crotch to ensure that his purse was well garnished.

All five gathered in the living room. Alsabide furnished Isaac with a healthy chair and a bible and he himself sat on the edge of his wooden seat, anxious to hear sacred words from holy lips. The girls gathered smiling in their little gallery, the dark beauty in the middle.

Isaac opened to the Song of Songs and began to read. The girls giggled as Isaac read and his eyes gleamed like the enamel of a wolf's teeth.

When all were tired and sleep begged to pull on tender eyelids, the girls went to wash for bed. Alsabide showed Isaac to his bed and thanked him for the bible reading. He then asked Isaac for a favor…

"My good father, will you please tuck my daughters in and pray for them? Your reading really inspired me. I was thinking, listening to those beautiful words, if this holy man should tuck my treasured daughters in to sleep, blessed will be their dreams and holiness shall shepherd them on the waves of midnight visions."

"Very poetic," replied Isaac, "I will indeed do you this favor. Point me to their rooms."

The first room Isaac visited was Anna's, the older of the two fair ones. In the dark bedroom he wished her a good night and kissed her mouth and touched her breasts and she was breathless by the time he left.

The second room was the younger of the two fair ones. He made the sign of the cross and said she was pretty and young and had nice small hips and he stroked them with his hand and kissed the lobe of her ear until she trembled from the heat of his lips and she turned her face towards his and pressed hard her young lips against his and the two embraced for a long time and he felt her warm chest heave against his, turning sweaty; and the two were breathless and wet by the time he left.

The last blessings of the night were for the dark-haired beauty with the clever eyes, alabaster breasts, and blooming cheekbones. She waited silently in bed while Isaac entered. He made the cross over her, told her she was a sweet girl who deserved that the glory of God rain down upon her; and with that, he brought his lips down upon her. The clever girl, however, stopped him. She turned away and asked Isaac not to touch her.

"I am not a fool," she said to Isaac, "My father is a fool. And whenever I think of him, I am reminded of how much of a fool he is."

CHAPTER LIV

"Afternoon in the Fifth Village"

"My map says there are only five villages between my village and the Minor City. And this is the fifth village I am coming upon, so this shall be the last village before: Victoria! . . . La, la, la . . . Victoria!"

Happy to be singing her name, brave Isaac entered the stone gates of the fifth village. Happy to be so near to the future, he strolled along with a glad heart.

'What is this church? No, it is nothing. Some kind of clock tower. I'll just go back here and...' change into the priest's robe, Isaac was thinking. And thus he did. Now disguised as the priest, he walked the quiet village streets in search of a house to call on for a bed, food and adventure.

After circling the village, he found a house that pleased him. In the fenced yard were lush flowers and fragrant herbs. The house itself was of trim stone. It looked like a place that houses fresh young women: those ready to cook, drink and play merry games. Isaac approached the front door and knocked.

It was an old, withered blue-skinned woman who answered. She had a head full of moles and quick little eyes. A ragged old woman, with a fine neck like goose-skin – one would expect such a creature to wear a woolen shawl, but the priestly Isaac was surprised, as he clasped his pious hands and bowed before her, to see that her little withered body was clothed in a bright green ballet tutu.

"Oh, blessed father! How may I be of service to you?"

"I am Father Helonius," said Isaac, bowing to the withered dame, "I am a priest on exodus to retrieve a stolen child. I will be needing a bed for the night, and a well-prepared meal."

"Of course!" the dame clasped her hands, "Come in!" She ushered Isaac into a dusty little sitting room and asked him to sit on her sofa while she fluttered into the kitchen to prepare a tray of tea and dainties.

Moments later she returned with the tray and sat herself beside her guest on a velveteen couch. Tea cups rattled with her fritteling hands. She offered Isaac something called 'ginger yarn.' He was yearning for food and chewed some up with gladness.

"Thank you, my child," Isaac said to the old woman, taking a china cup of tea. The tea was steaming hot and bright blue.

"Father Helonius sure is a handsome priest!"

"Why is the tea so blue?"

"It is a special herb from our region," said the old woman, "Blue-ring, it's called. I has a mighty taste and grows nowhere else in the world. You are traveling, you say? I can tell by your accent that you are from the West. Handsome, you are! Do you like the tea? You do? Why do you put your finger in it like that? Oh, it's nothing, that... Here, come closer, let's relax." Isaac could see the old woman's lips were getting more and more fleshy as she spoke. They glistened and her body seemed to heave with her breaths, now frail and skeletal, now puffy and plump. She smoothed her green tutu with her wrinkled hands. "Do you like it?" she said this and that and therefore, and spoke of many things, while Isaac's belly filled up on strings of ginger yarn. At one point, the old woman asked what Father Helonius kept under his robe. When he didn't answer, preferring the bitter tea to words, she asked him if he wouldn't share his holiness with her right then and there. 'I had better leave,' he thought to himself, 'After all, I have this priest's robe. I can stay wherever I want. Perhaps a house without lush, untamed leaves out front. Rather something tidier, and perhaps prim girls on the inside. I can have what I please, why sit beside a wrinkled grape in a tutu?' Thus, when the old woman went back to the kitchen to prepare some more blue-ring tea, Isaac slipped out the front door and ran down the street towards the clock tower.

"Why do I feel so flushed with heat?" Isaac asked himself as he walked along the cobbled road. The clock in the tower was chiming, "...and damp, too! I feel damp!" With the hem of his robe, he wiped the sweat from his forehead. "Why is it so hot? What month is it? But there is no heat. It is autumn isn't it? Or summer, perhaps. Say it is autumn, and this village seems to be ending before I even come to it; and if it isn't autumn, why am I so cold all of a sudden? Look at the horizon! Look at that blustery summer horizon!"

It was true the horizon could be seen. It appeared through a gap in the village where some garden fields were sewn with crops. Not blustery, but calm; not sun-baked, but damp; an eerie horizon coated in heavy mist. Over yonder fields sank the sun, that fiery yoke of a vessel, thick and bulbous. It floated stagnantly at the base of the mist, just about to fall over the earth. Long-traveled Isaac trod the heavy sod, looking down at the garden fields. There in the soil he saw a thriving crop: a million red radishes were sitting upon the earth. Bright red were they in contrast to the dark, muddy soil and the mist of silver sky that cached the setting sun. Full splendor took a hold of Isaac at this moment and he began to run about the field of radishes, scattering them with his feet.

It was while he was busy at his rampant task that he saw a girl squatting down in the middle of the dark field. She was crying. When she looked up, Isaac saw how extremely pretty she was. More pretty even than little blonde Alissa back home. Perhaps even as pretty as the fair Victoria who hailed from the Minor City... What tender eyes! Isaac stopped scattering radishes and ran up to the crying girl and asked her what her name was.

"Hermia," she replied, speaking between a million tears that toppled out of her eyes with little thought for where they fell. Isaac bent down and scooped up some radishes in his hands and offered them to her, but this only made her cry more heavily. Isaac then dove into her lap and she began to stroke his head. She stroked his head and stopped crying so as to kiss him. Her sweet clover-colored lips pressed themselves against his own and he rejoiced in this as she told him, "Now we will forget this nonsense, won't we? You and I, we will forget this nonsense. You will be my leader, my master, my lover. Maybe my father, too. And we will travel wherever you want and I will love you and worship your perfect body…"

The sweet young girl said these words over and again as she drenched Isaac with amorous kisses. She then invited him into her house…

It was a little brick dwelling with a smoking chimney, just next to the radish fields. She laid him next to her in her bed, and he felt her hot skin on his cheek. He felt her hot skin and he felt as it grew colder and colder. Icy cold now, Isaac woke up in a bed, a cake of ice wrapped in cloth was pressed to his head.

"Oh, holy visions," cried Isaac, "My head!"

A man came into the room with a look of concern on his face.

"Father," said the man, "How are you feeling?" The man looked to be a farmer. Dirty workpants, a weather-worn and simple face. A radish farmer? Apparently those fields had been his. Was this too his brick house? Isaac turned his head to the side and saw that the beautiful Hermia was gone from the bed.

"Father, you are roused. Do you realize what you have taken? We were worried for you!"

Isaac, trying to collect his mind and memory, peered past the farmer and saw in the doorway stood sweet Hermia, though now she seemed dressed differently, and was slightly less beautiful than she had been. The farmer noticed Isaac looking at her and turned to introduce

279

her. "This is Helena, my daughter. I'm sorry she hit your head with the broken shovel handle, but she had spent so long planting those radishes and to see you out there trying to rip them out of the ground... Well, it sent her in a bit of a rage! The ice is bringing the swelling down. It scared her too! She thought you were the Grim Reaper coming to punish us. You have to admit, Holy Father, to see a figure in a black robe out in the fields at dusk, running around pulling radishes up from the soil, throwing them any which way – well, one has to worry that the end has come! She was afraid you were Death, but mostly she was just angry and... Come on, Helena..."

Helena, who had been standing in the doorway, studying the patient in the bed while biting her lower-lip, now came to the bedside. The farmer continued rambling his story... "While she was angry, I thought you must be crazy. Either way, it seemed like a bad omen..." Isaac took the opportunity, while the farmer was speaking, to slide his hand down beneath the blanket spread over him and feel his crotch to see if the mound of money was still there safe in the purse. Upon his groin he felt that thankful pouch well-tied and safe from all snooping hands. So the devilish girl had beaten Isaac with a broken shovel handle. So that's what it was! Her father had apparently carried him inside and made a bed for him. Still, neither of them found the fortune of money between his legs.

"As I was saying," the farmer went on, "I thought you must be crazy . . . that is, until I saw the blue on your lips."

"What is wrong with my lips?" Isaac felt them, wondering.

"Oh!" said the farmer, "You had traces of the blue-ring herb on them. It is a very dangerous plant! It makes people go crazy and do things like pull radishes out of other people's fields at dusk. I saw the blue-ring on your lips and the wildness in your eyes and I was worried for you. Who gave it to you? Certainly no one ever took it on their own wanting. Usually fondlers give it to people they want to fondle. It makes their memory go like that! Whoosh! Then, they say, you act like a cat that wants to be scratched until you run away looking for mischief. I see it's passed now. Who gave it to you?"

Isaac didn't tell him about the old woman with the blue tea.

"Father," said the farmer, "please excuse me for a minute. I'm going to bring you some more water. You should drink as much as possible to get the poison out of your system."

With the farmer gone, Isaac was left alone with Helena who stood beside his bed.

"But was it you I saw crouched in the field crying?" he asked the young girl.

"Yes," said Helena, "I was crying because you were pulling out my radishes."

"And did you not say, 'We will forget all this nonsense and run away together and you will be my lover and I will worship your perfect body?'"

With this, innocent Helena turned her pretty mouth into an ironic expression and she laughed loudly at the priest. "I said nothing of the sort!" Then she added quietly, "Well, I did say, 'let us forget this nonsense,' but that was because I wanted you to leave my radishes alone. But I never said we'd run away together! After I said 'let's forget this nonsense,' you started forcing kisses on me; and so it was then my father hit you with the shovel handle. You don't remember, do you?"

"No," Isaac responded; and then, "I thought your father said *you* hit me with the shovel."

"I did first. But it didn't work. Then when you started kissing me, my dad came and hit you with the shovel handle. That time it worked."

"Oh," said Isaac. And with that the matter ceased to be anything and the farmer returned with a pitcher of water and made the guest drink. Isaac slept the night in that spare bed and ate oats with the farmer and his daughter in the morning, and he never did reveal to them that he wasn't a priest. He even blessed the oats and offered to clean up the radish fields he'd torn apart – knowing full well that he would not be obliged to do this, because it would be rude, perhaps unholy even, for a farmer to ask a priest to clean up his radishes. And anyway, Helena, who took great pride in her flock of radishes, had already cleaned up the fields while Isaac was sleeping that night; and so there was no work left to be done. Of all this, Isaac knew full well. And so, after the humble breakfast, Isaac took leave of the farm. And with the village and all its outlying farms far behind him, he headed off towards the early morning sun, down the eastward road.

CHAPTER LV

Long-traveled Isaac kept on that eastward road, ever more hopeful as traces of saltwater smells came carried in the west blowing wind. "Soon the sea," he mumbled to himself. His good map said there were no other villages between his own and the Minor City. Dreams of the winged Victoria fluttered in his bountiful breast. He was free of cares and glad at heart.

Long up the road there appeared to be a small settlement. A couple houses was all. Evening had come, casting shadows in the hills. The road was firm and the sun brushed it in places where the trees allowed the rays to pass through brittle limbs and paper-thin leaves. Isaac in his swift steps, walked along until he came to a wounded animal.

The beast appeared to have been run over by a cart. Its leg was macerated and bleeding. Isaac untied the strap of his satchel to search for his priest's robe. "Okay, lamb, I'll wrap you in my robe. You'll be a holy dying lamb afterwards." As he pulled the robe from the satchel, the animal whimpered. Isaac's sturdy pipe and pleasurable tobacco fell from the satchel to the packed earth on the side of the road where lay the dying beast. Isaac, however, did not witness this unhappy loss. He thought of the robe that had brought him moments of joy and moments of woe.

Thus, bidding grateful adieu to his immortality, Isaac unwadded the robe and wrapped the lamb in it. He tied it and the lamb shivered. He then grabbed the snout of the animal wrapped in priestly wear, and turned his face towards his own to have a look at the sacred animal.

"Sacred animal, you! Sacred shivering… shivering… beast! Christ, you are no lamb!"

It wasn't a lamb at all, just a white dog. Isaac finished tying the priest's robe around the shivering dog and left it on the road to die. He then headed up to the settlement at the crest of the hill hoping to have shelter for the night.

CHAPTER LVI

At the top of the evening hill, long-traveled Isaac peered through a grove of stately eucalyptus trees to where he thought he saw a harbor far below in the distance. Drafts of brine came subtle in the dry breeze, while the evening passerines perched on their limbs of song. Isaac fastened his clever eyes on the two squatty houses built on the stretch of land. The road leading to the houses was crowned with a wooden sign. It read: FANDERASSE. Isaac swung his satchel, ever so light, and left the wilderness in swift steps to call on the housekeepers for nourishment and a bed.

The first house was of weary wood, dark and rotting. It sat on several patches growing beans and leafy meal. Around it too were olive-colored pasturages for grazing ewes and horned things. The house beyond that was of cleaner wood, stood taller, and hosted no pasturages or fields of beans. Isaac chose the grander of the two, and walked beyond the grazing lands to the clean wooden house.

"I wonder what men or girls live in this house," he asked aloud as he mounted the steps to knock on the door. He made a cursory caress of his sturdy groin once upon the stair, lest his mound of fortune be loosely tied and want to fall and spill before the eyes of the house's recluse inhabitants.

"Will they be wise and hospitable, generous in their gifts to this wayfaring stranger? Or will they be hostile and pose as a threat? For now Isaac, there is little earth between you and the beautiful Victoria. The same salt that comes faintly to your nose in these heights of wilderness, is blown across the surface of her tender skin, through the strands of her perfect hair, down in that unknown and unseen city. The city sits where tomorrow's sun rises and not another sun will set before I see her, before we are reunited; now I must rest. Is nobody home?"

"A visitor?" came a voice to answer Isaac's patient knock. When the door opened, a man of immense height rose to hover over cleverminded Isaac. He was lanky and black-haired, with deep-set eyes, well-knit brows and lupine shoulders; this lord of the house resembled a wild dog leaping from great trembling stilts of wood. The stilts, though they were legs, shook as the house-dweller stood in the doorway, as if he'd been sitting for a stretch and this trip to the door was the first time he'd stood up all day. "Who are you?" he asked Isaac.

Isaac thought to tell the false tale and say he was a priest, but then he realized he no longer had his robe, so he said he was a simple traveler.

"Traveling from where? From the west, you say?"

Isaac nodded and pointed past the man to a jar that was inside his house on the table, in which some things were floating in water.

"What is that?"

"No matter," said the giant house-dweller, leading Isaac into a room of wood with books and a desk. "You see I've been writing."

No, Isaac had not seen that.

"Do you need a map?" he asked, fishing with his pale hands through the mighty bookshelves.

"A map?" Isaac questioned.

It was a strange room the man lived in.

"Where are you going?"

"To the Minor City." Isaac reached into the shallow portion of his satchel to take from it his map of the way. He spread the map out on a place that the man cleared for him on the writing desk. "What is 'Fanderasse?' I saw a sign…"

"It's where you are," said the man.

"I've been here, and here, and here…" Isaac pointed on the map, from his village in the western fields, to the towns along the way where he'd stopped for respite, "…and I want to go here," he ended with his finger on a dot bleeding its ink in the harbor near the sea, "…to the Minor City."

"That's not far from here."

"Where is *here*?" Isaac let his finger drift across the map's uncolored terra incognita where he believed himself now to be standing.

"Here is Fanderasse."

"What is Fanderasse?"

"It is my town."

"It is a town?"

"It is *my* town. I own it. It isn't on your map, I see. Thoughtless map! One day it will be. Where are you going? To the Minor City you say? Oh-ho! Look behind you!"

Isaac whipped around quickly, fearing at first what he would see. He remembered in a flash the man who had clubbed him, back when he'd first begun his journey. He almost worried that this second man might try a similar thing. but Isaac was not afraid. Fear was beneath him now. He saw the house-dweller was merely pointing at the dusty windowpane that looked out into the yard. He saw the sun was setting and was doing so oddly. It seemed to be tearing the membrane of the sky in a way that was staining the whole horizon with a strange milky purple light. No, not milky, but watery. The light floated like cold steam. Isaac then turned back to his host who had his own eyes fixed on the windowpane. What a gloomy face he had! After a moment, the lord of the house looked back at Isaac as if expecting words, but his guest said nothing. Isaac kept his gaze on the strange evening sky beyond the window. He then turned back to his host who was now speaking…

"So, you are going to the Minor City," said the man, "I myself am from the Minor City. I came out her to start this town. I am now the mayor of this town I call Fanderasse, yet I hail from the Minor City. The city is not far off. Just east down through the hills. You can smell the salt air of the harbor from here. Your feet will take you fine through the hills. Then, at the bottom, there is a small port where a light-rail will run along the sea. It ends at the Minor Station. Come sit on one of my many chairs and I will tell you about it. Come sit and I will tell you all about it…"

Isaac was offered place in a wooden seat near the cluttered bookshelves and the cluttered writing desk. He was offered black bread with cold cabbage and diluted wine. His host worked to clear off his writing desk so Isaac could set his plate and cup. The desk was cleared of the staunch tallow of the candlestick, of the books and parchments . . . the inkwell . . . the writing paper . . . everything.

"I'm writing the new Book of Revelation," said the man, "The old one is inaccurate."

"Of course it is," agreed Isaac. He observed his host's shadowy movements; then looked around the room to see what kind of stout tools there were lying about, what kinds of weapons; but he saw none, only books and writing tablets. It was the home of a scholar, perhaps an astronomer. Looking up at the ceiling, Isaac notice a trapdoor in the roof. The builder had fashioned a rustic skylight. The firmament above was darkening into night, and little stars began to come into sight through the hole in the sky above. Isaac turned a second time and discovered a wooden ladder had been propped against the trapdoor. He was sure the ladder hadn't been there before. He turned to look again at his host whose face was darkening as was the sky; and, as the candlestick wasn't lit – now it was lit! . . . The candle tallow hosted a leaping flame. On the table that had been clear before, now lay a heavy book, open to a middle page. A closer look at the book revealed text that was written out by hand, a neat script in black ink. The inkwell was stained and smelled of food. Or else it was the food on the plate nearby that smelled of food.

"What is your name?" the host asked Isaac.

"Helonius," Isaac lied.

The host offered Isaac a map of the Minor City. "To help you get around when you arrive," he muttered over his shoulder as he dug around in his bookcases looking for the map. "I have an old one somewhere, tucked in one of my books. You can camp up on my roof tonight. I have a bit of straw."

Isaac listened to the man's long and drawing voice. With his fingers, he coursed the calfskin spines of the books on the wooden shelf beside him. He then brought his attention to the nest of stars in the sky. He heard his host pulling paper from the shelves.

"Did you find it?" Isaac called down to the room through the trapdoor from the roof where he had been sent to wait while the man searched the shelves for the map. He had been waiting there a long time and his jacket he'd left down in the room on the chair, and he was beginning to shiver.

"Come down . . . I have it!"

Isaac and the man sat by the writing desk, facing each other, each on wooden stools. Upon the desk that was cleared anew, the host spread the parchment map. "It is an old one, as I told you. And look, it is torn. Most of the city is missing."

"Is there a public square in the city where one can go to find one who lives there? One in particular, I mean?"

The host smiled at his guest's naïve question. "There are many squares. Many ornate and vast, many cached and hidden. You will come to see the Minor City is no mere village. But go ahead and make your rounds. You will find what or whom you are looking for."

In the dimness of the room, Isaac leaned over the parchment map of the Minor City. It showed only the Minor Station where the trains come in, the district called Otchajanie, a few bridges leading to the Peninsula, the Otchajanie Bridge, part of the Shipyard District and parts of Fishmongers' Row. The rest had been torn off. It was an old map indeed.

"I used to live right here," said the man, pointing to an area on the map. Isaac leaned in to look and brought the burning candlestick closer to see. The paper was of fibers the color of coffee and the buildings and streets were drawn and dyed by hand. "I used to live in an attic apartment. I was young and handsome. I knew greatness would befall me and I knew it would come in a flash and all would end for every one of us. It was then I began writing my apocalypse. I wrote it while I was studying at the university. After I quit the university, I continued writing the apocalypse. I had three hundred pages. All written in black ink. All handwritten in a black leather-bound book like this. I told you I lived in an attic apartment? Well, I had a trapdoor in the roof. Just like this one over your head. One night, it was late. I was thirty years old. It was late and the moon was full and I was up with sleepless fury writing the end of my apocalypse – putting the very crown on it. I was almost finished when I was struck by a strange quality of light shining down through my trapdoor. The moon. I looked up and do you know what I saw? . . . You think I'm going to tell you that the moon had turned blue or something. But it wasn't at all that. It wasn't what you'd think. It wasn't that the moon had changed colors. Rather, the moon was gone. I looked up and saw the sky was crystal blue and the sun was tossing across it like a white disc. One would say a flashing disc of metal was soaring in the sky. It's half past midnight and the sun is shining overhead? Can you imagine? No, you can't!

"...I had a ladder going up to the roof then, just like now, and I climbed it to see why the sun was shining in the middle of the night; but when I reached the roof, the moon was back and it was night again. I heard foghorns blowing from the ships in the harbor in even blasts. The air was spicy and odorous. I propped myself up on the roof and mused about the sun. I was given to wondering where it went, when I saw next to me a piece of torn cloth sitting on the roof tiles. I picked up the cloth and inspected it. It was silk, the cloth of the panties belonging to a girl. It was a girl I had taken up on the roof a week before..."

...Here, Isaac's host smiled and gave a quick roar of laughter. His eyes branched out like train tracks, flourishing wrinkles. Isaac, who was listening to the man's story with great attention, stopped a moment to pass his hand discreetly into the pocket of his jacket to make sure his own torn piece of cloth was still there. The strip of old lace belonging to Victoria, which he'd brought all the way from his village in the western fields. He felt it well, pressed into the bottom of the jacket pocket. He sighed with reassurance and went on listening. His host continued...

"I had taken her up there a week before. She was a harlot and lived down in the Otchajanie District. 'Good silk,' I thought when I felt the fabric, '…damp and torn.' Then I figured it all out!

"Immediately I forgot about the sun shining in the middle of the night; I took the girl's panties and put on my topcoat – it had been raining slightly – and I left my attic room and headed down to Otchajanie. I went to the place the girl usually was. She often sat in a window next to a bowl of prunes. She was there on this night. I merely wanted to return her torn panties to her and ask one question. She, however, wasn't there. Another girl, an older woman, worn and heavily rouged, was sitting in the window in her place. I asked after her to the woman… 'She's gone,' said the woman, 'left town for the season. Had a job somewhere in the country. Taking care of children, I think. The country air will be good for her, etc., etc.…'

"As the woman told me all of this, she munched the rind of a prune and fixed the torn strap on her sandal. I noticed how worn-out her shoes were – those thrifty sandals. I even insisted on the discovery. Then I remembered why I had come. Quickly I turned away from the worn woman, stuffed the panties back in my pocket, and headed back to my room near Fishmongers' Row. I ran up the squalid stairs to my attic room and when I got inside I saw the most horrible thing…

"Entering into my room, I saw there on my work table: a pile of ashes!

"…Can you imagine my horror? Three hundred pages, three years work, all mysteriously burned to a pile of ashes! Nothing else burned, not the table it was on, just my manuscript of the apocalypse. I gasped! My neck immediately tightened with the realization. I wanted to cry out but couldn't utter a sound. I looked then to the trapdoor on my roof and noticed the door was shut and locked from the inside. How, can I ask, could the door be locked from the inside? There was nobody in my room at the time! My manuscript was burned and the door was shut and I knew it was all over!

"…'It will never be known!' I cried, sifting through the ashes on my worktable. 'I'll never find greatness in this city, genius though I am!' I sifted and sifted. 'The end will come and no one will know why!' Fortunately, I had the main principals of my apocalypse memorized…

"…Still, I knew I needed to leave the Minor City. I was then a young man seeking greatness. I was seeking, – I digress here, Helonius, – you see, it was important that the world, or at least my society, knew that I was a genius. And the Minor City is a sprawling place. You haven't been there yet, but you will see. It is a sprawling and unforgiving place and the people are deaf – deaf or else stupid. You can be a genius – the greatest genius that has ever lived – and you can climb up through the trapdoor of the roof in your attic room and shout out over all of the rooftops of the city that you are a genius, but the next day you'll walk through the town and ask around after yourself and no one will even know your name. That's how quickly they forget! So, I decided to come out here and start my own city. And apt time it was for me to leave that place; you see, for when I left, at least three or four young women were pregnant with children I'd sired…"

Isaac's host winked.

"I told you I was a handsome man!" he roared with laughter. Laughter and lament.

"…So alone I came here to this wilderness and founded Fanderasse. It was then just me. I built the little house across the way, had some bean fields and starting rewriting my apocalypse. What you see here is the manuscript. Years later, a wandering man stumbled upon my settlement. Horace, an old hunchback of sorts. He comes from far south, from the Acropolis. He's the relative of a powerful official there, second cousin or something. He was fleeing into exile. Wasn't sure whether or not to stay in the Minor City or travel west to places less obscure. Yes, if there's one thing the Minor City is, it's obscure! . . . I offered that he join my town and sold him my house. I then built this new one here with the trapdoor in the roof just like my attic room had back in the city. Now Fanderasse is a city of two households. I have a milk cow and serve as mayor. Old Horace has a pea patch and swine, and grows all of the lentils for our city, as well as leafy plants and chicken eggs. His is a busy job. But I have this apocalypse to write. I am not being hasty in my writing, for I am no longer young. And besides, I know how it all will end. Here, Helonius . . . Take this map. Pretty much all is gone but it shows the station and the Otchajanie District. Here's a little bit of the Peninsula, but it's just hanging on by some thin fibers... Oh, I'm sorry! Did you burn your hand? No? Oh! I thought the candle burned you, but I'm glad it didn't. Anyhow, yes . . . time sure withers a map! Anyway, there's nothing on that Peninsula, it's just a residential district. Here you'll come to the station. The light-rail goes from that port I told you about. Arrives here at the Minor Station..."

Isaac tried to study the map along with his host but the candle was dying down and his eyes were failing him. "What's over here on the other side of the station?"

"What? Oh, nothing. As you can see the map is torn. There is nothing over there. Anyway, take this map and run up to the roof to sleep. I'll tell you more in the morning. But essentially when you get to the Minor City, you want to head down here to Otchajanie. Go see the way the moon comes up over the hillside on the harbor when you stand on the Otchajanie Bridge. If you only see one thing in your life, it should be that. Why, may I ask, are you traveling to the Minor City? Indeed, indeed. To bring back a bride, you say? A bride and a stolen child? Well, Helonius, come back this way afterwards with your bride and rescued child. We will feast together. I'll want to hear what it's like in the city these days. It's been so long since I've been there. You'll be a hero, I assume, coming back with a bride and a rescued child. A beauty, you say she is? Well, if you don't make it back this way, I will remember you and I'll sing your name from every rooftop. Oh, it is true, there are but two rooftops in the whole of my town, but I will sing your name from them both. Come, find your place up the ladder; it's getting late and it's not my habit to stay awake too late. Be careful on the roof. Don't roll off like Elpenor. Do you see those shades in the trees through the windowpanes? If the wind is too strong, there are some bristly blankets beneath the floorboards here – and more in the cupboards . . . sleep well!" And with that, Isaac's host crawled off to his bed by the stove.

Isaac climbed the ladder and spread out some straw and fixed his jacket for a pillow. He lay beneath the bristly blankets beneath the swollen moon and thought for awhile. The sky was bright enough and he saw shades in the trees. He felt his good money in place. He listened when the wind died down but heard only the calm of night. Some animals began to stir in the wilderness. He wanted to smoke, and so felt into his satchel to retrieve his pipe and goodly tobacco. What bitter regret to find it wasn't there! Had it dropped down in the room where his host was sleeping? All he wanted was to calmly smoke his pipe and watch the night before sleeping, but his pipe was gone. He guessed it had either dropped out in his host's house, or else it had fallen out when he'd used the robe to wrap up the wounded dog. He could easily roll off the roof, climb down and go search for his pipe in the darkness. He didn't want, however, bright as it was with the moon, to be searching at night for a pipe by digging through the fur and surrounding leaves of the corpse of a freshly dead dog.

Better just to breathe and to sleep, he decided. The air was thick and mineral-rich. As he inhaled, it brought him renewed strength for all that was too come. As soldiers eat brave meals from hearty plates, abundant of sauce with ample bread, so as to put courage and strength in their hearts on the eve before going into battle, so did long-traveled Isaac drink now the wind, its richness and strength; and never did he once think not to go on, but rather to go back and change his fate. Never did he consider the life he could have had, if he were to return to from where he came; if he were to go back alone, in the clothes of an aimless wanderer. He could still build a little house on the outskirts of his native village, away from everyone, like his brother had planned; and there live a long and uneventful life. Yet, it never crossed his mind to go back or anywhere but forward as he had always done, as he would continue to do.

Isaac awoke early before it was light and saw a bat was perched near the trapdoor in the roof. He inspected the bat and saw that it was clutching a cricket it'd caught. He noticed then the bat was dead as well as the cricket. The bat's legs were fused to a little spring trap.

That morning brought rain.

CHAPTER LVII

"Isaac's Arrival in the Minor City"

Brave-minded Isaac wandered the unfamiliar lanes and foreign passageways of Otchajanie. So small in stature was he compared to the giant inhabitants who fluttered around like noisy night-birds in the bustling streets.

When the misty evening fell with all its darkness, Isaac found himself alone in quiet places. He clutched his torn map, which had led him from the Minor Station to the Otchajanie Bridge. On the bridge, a wind whipped across the desolate railings made for crossing on foot. Heavy clouds covered the moon and he saw not one shard of its silver light pass through to light upon the bridge. Only a heavy, long-flowing mist, humid and rich in eastern salts, hung along the pilings, slowly creeping upward. Long-traveled Isaac knew not where to go to find what he sought, nor where to pass the night; and so he walked up and down the bridge, looking again over the faint lights from the city on the harbor, trying to penetrate the haze.

He soon came upon a girl sitting alone, perched on the edge of the bridge. She was crying, or else was just staring out at the dark waters: one would say an abyss so far down that the night sky above was closer than the water below and easier to reach. Isaac passed her from behind and glanced back at the slender form of her silhouette where she sat. Her light raincoat flapped against her, its hood clung to the top of her head and wild hair flung across her cheek, so that Isaac could not see until a gust of wind brushed it back revealing the arc of a nose, so familiar, and the gentle pout of well-remembered lips. This image caused a host of memories to play before his eyes. The notion that he had found her surged with conviction in his mind...

'Victoria,' he cried in silence, 'Be it she!'

Isaac stepped forward until a fear clenched his ribs, seizing his stomach. He did not have the courage to approach her. This was the one, he was certain, for whom he'd traveled long and far, and dreamed away youthful years. Of this he had no doubt. With heavy feet, he tromped back to entrance of the bridge to where stairs led down to the dark district of Otchajanie.

His steps took him hastily through an alley. His thoughts flashed around his determination to go back and approach her at any cost. He feverishly turned around again and again on the bricks of Otchajanie, focusing on the nearby stairs that led back to the bridge.

In only a few moments, he knew, he would be back on that bridge and would come upon her and speak to her and reveal himself to her... "It's me," he would say, "long-ago Isaac." He would take her chin in the palm of his hand, "Here we are now!" they would cry, revealing themselves to each other in all of their glory. Fever burned hot with anticipation!

And so, while Isaac was walking briskly through that dark sinister alley, narrow and built of old bricks, harrowed with darkened doorways, he was stopped by a figure who emerged from the shadows. Either it was a slender beggar, or else a tall thief armed with a steel blade – his visions deceived him.

Isaac turned quickly from the passageway, fearing nothing any longer, having only a few steps to make before coming clear of the alley and being once again on that great expanse of a bridge where his girl, Victoria – he was sure it was her! – was sitting on her misty perch, no doubt waiting for the moon to penetrate the clouds; and he could even see her now from the darkness of his final alley. His last glance of her gave quick instruction to his feet to make haste. Yet the thief, no beggar it was, overtook him in the shadows; and, drawing a steel blade, slender knife, he pushed it deep into the soft stomach of adventurous Isaac, and the latter fell to his knees.

Wide-eyed Isaac looked desperately upward at the tall figure, searching for some resemblance of eyes in the dim face, as if to entreat him to give back that which was his, but the thief's face was too dark and shadowed, his eyes were covered and could not be seen, and Isaac shrieked aloud in gruesome pain.

"Quiet your mouth!" issued forth the thief. He pressed a filthy hand to his victim's lips to silence him. Now Isaac merely groaned. A pool of viscous yellow fluid seeped into the whites of Isaac's eyes and a charge of blood came to his lips. He fell back from his knees onto his spine with the knife in his stomach; and like a fleshy wood-eating worm split by a kindling axe, he began to squirm.

The thief bent down and searched through his victim's jacket pockets. Isaac groaned again and fought for life, flipping like a snake in a fire, but now the thief paid no more attention. He paid no notice as he rummaged through his victim's pockets as if the victim were already dead and could not react. Meanwhile the knife came clear from the wound and clacked on the bricks of the street next to where Isaac's hand lay pale and outstretched. It sat there and reeked of blood, shone but did not gleam, for there was lightlessness.

The nimble thief tore from Isaac's shoulder his satchel. Empty of all, but a torn and withered map. He threw it aside and pulled from his subject's pocket the strip of ivory-colored lace, once had scent, once clean and fresh, detached from the hem of a young girl's dress and given to a boy in a sunny village far from the sea, in the western fields; now it sat hopeless and filthy in the wretched hand of a miserable cutpurse. One final jab of the thief's foot, and the air flew from Isaac's mouth. He groaned now louder, and the blood rippled in his throat like midnight waves lapping on a harbor shore. Drops of red tinged his lips like clothing dye. And the black-eyed thief let a smile of delight as he found a treasure on his subject's groin.

With a swift tug, the thief made fly the chord and that holy pouch of tender fortune slipped into his grateful hand. Now, in cradling hands, the thief gripped his welcome income, grandly made, and gave a last look at the dying traveler, long-tried feeble Isaac. The thief tore open the pouch and inspected the contents.

A look of defeat crept over his face.

"What the hell am I supposed to do with this!" he cursed, looking around in anger. His eyes darted from the lace in his one hand, taken from the otherwise empty pocket of his fallen foe, to the money pouch in his other. Then, with swift dispatch, he let fly the mound of heavy coins and they scattered in the cracks of the alley bricks.

"A few foreign coppers!" he spat, "And this!" to the piece of sentimental lace, "Useless rubbish!" He tossed it on the body of Isaac that was rising and coming back down with its long but sure, final breath – a weak and insignificant breath stolen from the eternal night air – and as it did so, the thief scampered off into the darkness.

Isaac spewed out a loud resonant final groan.

His chest then fell to infinite depths, collapsing in a lifeless heap. The strip of lace sunk upon his chest, crumpled in the darkened alley.

Meanwhile, the thief made his way quickly through the shadows until he reached the Otchajanie Bridge. After he climbed the stairs, in stealth, he darted along the rail.

On this night, the bridge appeared empty, all save for the mist and the fog. All seemed quiet, save for the bellowing foghorns cutting in even blasts through the damp and heavy night; quiet save for the remnants of the last, loud groan of death traveling to the bridge from the cached alley where Isaac died.

On the bridge, the thief saw a girl approaching. He stepped away from the rail and slithered down off the footbridge and hid himself in the shadows to let her pass and go unseen. The girl had a desperate look on her face. She ran passed the thief without noticing him. She was clutching her light grey raincoat tightly around herself. The hood of her jacket covered her face. Water dripped off her skin, coursing in streams from her hair, off her naked wrists and hands. She looked startled and confused as she made her way from the bridge towards the alley, quickly, hurriedly, with searching eyes, as though she'd heard a strange noise or was looking for someone.